DREAM WALKER

THE BAILEY SPADE SERIES: BOOK 1

DIMA ZALES

♠ MOZAIKA PUBLICATIONS ♠

Published by Mozaika Publications, an imprint of Mozaika LLC.
www.mozaikallc.com

Cover by Orina Kafe
www.orinakafe.design

e-ISBN: 978-1-63142-553-0
Print ISBN: 978-1-63142-554-7

CHAPTER ONE

I SWALLOW a droplet of diluted vampire blood.

"Alarm and surveillance disabled," Felix whispers in my earpiece. "Breaking and entering may commence."

Before I can reply, the blood kicks in, lifting the weight off my eyelids as my sleep deprivation retreats. Except the droplet must've been too big, or I drank it too soon after the last dose. I feel an unwelcome side effect—orgasmic pleasure—coming on.

Tightening my grip on the lockpick until it hurts, I stab myself in the forearm.

"What the hell?" Felix exclaims. "What'd you do *that* for?"

The camera on my lapel didn't catch my stealthy sip, so I can see why this looks odd on his end. "Never mind that."

The pain quickly annuls my euphoria, and I thank my lucky stars I took the time to sterilize my equipment, or else this would end with gangrene.

When I pull the lockpick out of my arm, the wound heals instantly—and best of all, no sign of the orgasmic pleasure remains.

There we go. I didn't enjoy that vampire blood one bit, other than the boost of alertness that was my goal —and my libido skyrocketing to the levels of a teenage boy in a strip club.

"I thought your weirdness was limited to cleansing rituals." Felix sounds bizarrely sexy in the vamp blood afterglow.

I don't reply. Instead, I take a quick internal scan to make sure no part of me is still feeling the pull of the highly addictive substance. With all my current problems, becoming a vampire blood addict would be like jumping off a cliff after drowning myself in cyanide.

All good so far. I grasp the doorknob. "I'm going in."

"What you're about to do is illegal on this world," Felix reminds me, as if I didn't already know.

"What about hacking all those banks?" I whisper back. "You wouldn't like it if I lectured you about that."

A Cognizant like me, albeit one permanently residing on Earth, Felix calls himself a technomancer. He can make silicon-based technology do his bidding, a power he wastes on feats that any human with in-depth computer knowledge could pull off.

"Dreamwalking won't help you escape human prison," he replies. "Or survive it, for that matter."

"That's arguable." I decide against telling him about the time I gleaned one of his wet dreams, specifically the one where he fancied himself a guard getting attacked by suspiciously attractive female convicts. "But if you've done your job properly, I won't end up in prison."

"I can only take care of the smart alarm. If this Bernard guy is paranoid enough, he might have the older, dumb alarm set up as well, and it'll blare as soon as you get inside. Or he might have a dog. Or he might even be awake."

I sneak a guilty peek at my wrist, where most people would see a furry bracelet. But he's actually a creature called a *looft.* Normally, his kind live on cow-like *moofts*, but Pom, as he calls himself, has adopted me as his host. Right now, he's sleeping, as usual, but the pitch-black shade of his fur reflects my inner turmoil. If I die, Pomsie dies with me; that's how our relationship works.

So I'll have to not die. Simple.

Turning my attention back to the heavy wooden door, I stroke Pom to calm myself down. When my hands have steadied and his fur has turned a more neutral shade of blue, I pick the lock.

"Seriously, Bailey," Felix says as I touch the doorknob, "there've got to be better ways to make money. With your—"

I mute the earpiece. Obviously, there are more legit ways to earn what I need, but those ways don't pay nearly as well as my current employer. I'm already a month behind on Mom's medical bills, and if I don't come up with two million cc—Gomorran cryptocash—in the next two weeks, they'll turn off her life support. No honest jobs would let me make that kind of cash in the little time I have left. As is, I've had to forgo sleep in order to make ends meet. In fact, I haven't slept more than a couple of hours at a stretch since Mom's accident four months ago, staying up naturally at first, then using pharmacological stimulants, and eventually resorting to vampire blood.

I reach into my pocket for one of my last two sleep grenades and twist the doorknob.

No alarm blares.

No dog barks.

No one shoots me dead with a gun.

I press the button on the grenade and toss it into the apartment.

Sleeping gas hisses as it spreads throughout the place.

"That gas goes inert in two minutes," I whisper for Felix's benefit. "If there's a dog in there, or if Bernard was awake, they're asleep *now*."

I unmute in time to hear Felix grumbling something about a *decent plan*. What he doesn't realize is that the most dangerous part of this job is coming up.

I tiptoe inside the penthouse. Valerian, the guy who hired me to do this, must pay Bernard well. This place is spacious, especially for New York, where real estate is nearly as pricey as on my home world of Gomorrah.

I locate the bedroom and squint through the

darkness at the bed. Whew—Bernard is curled up in a fetal position, covered by a heavy blanket.

I creep toward the bed.

"Doesn't he look like Mario?" Felix whispers.

Comparing a man to a digital plumber isn't as crazy as it sounds. When I first met Felix, we bonded over our love of video games.

I examine the pudgy man's mustachioed face. "More like Wario, Mario's archrival."

"Neither of them has a scar like that."

He's right. The scar on Bernard's forehead belongs on the face of an interdimensional warrior, not an engineering executive at a VR company on Earth.

"So what now?" Felix asks.

"I have to touch him."

Felix chuckles.

I roll my eyes. "Not in a dirty way."

I peer at my victim's eyelids for rapid eye movement. Nothing. Crap. I pull off my gloves and do my best to prepare for the unpleasantness that is to come—specifically, the least risky but most disgusting aspect of what I'm about to attempt.

Skin-to-skin contact.

The bead of sweat wobbling along the edge of the scar on Bernard's forehead doesn't help, nor does his mooft-dung breath.

"What are you waiting for?" Felix asks. "Is it your OCD again?"

"Caring about hygiene doesn't mean I have OCD." I touch the bottle of hand sanitizer in my pocket, my lifesaver here on Earth. "Besides, he's not in REM sleep."

"Which means you'll have to do that dangerous subdream battle thing when you enter him?"

"You make it sound way too rapey. I'm not going to 'enter him.' I'm just visiting his dreams. But yes, if the subdream battle thing kills dream-me, real-me will go insane."

Actually, that's an understatement. Not long before her accident, as a way of discouraging me from using my powers, Mom showed me footage of what happened to a dreamwalker who'd died in the dream world. He went on a killing rampage like a rabid puck and cannibalized his victims. I checked on this, and even years later, he's still being kept in restraints in a padded cell.

"So you're going to wait until he goes into REM sleep?" Felix asks.

"Ideally."

"How long's that going to take?"

I sigh and consult my Earth phone. "Ninety minutes, if it was my gas that knocked him out."

I hear Felix clicking away on his keyboard. Then he says, "I see that he takes Ambien. I doubt it was your gas that put him under."

"Dammit." I resist the urge to kick the leg of the bed. "That drug suppresses REM sleep. I might have to come back later or—"

"Bailey." His tone sharpens. "You're about to have company."

6

I spin around to the door, my heart rate spiking as Pom's fur darkens on my wrist.

"Vampires," Felix rattles out. "Enforcers. They have every exit covered. Running would be pointless."

Pucking puck. Why couldn't it be any other type of Cognizant? Vampires only sleep if they want to, so my remaining grenade won't knock them out—and I don't have anything else at my disposal.

My gaze falls on the walk-in closet in the corner of the bedroom. "Can I hide?"

"They probably have your DNA. How else could they have zeroed in on you with such precision?"

He's right. Even *I* didn't know I'd be here until I'd read my encrypted email an hour ago. This is bad. Armed with my DNA, a vampire could find me anywhere in the Cogniverse.

I stroke Pom, trying not to panic. "What do they want?"

"No idea," Felix says, "but I doubt they care about your breaking and entering."

"Arguable." I whirl back toward Bernard. "Sounds like I have no choice. If I want to keep Mom's life support running, I have to go in, REM sleep or not."

"And I'll do my best to stall the Enforcers. I think I can make the elevator run slower, maybe even—"

"Thanks." Ignoring the shaking of my hands, I pull out the hand sanitizer and slather it on Bernard's hairy forearm. "Here goes nothing." I reach for the (hopefully) decontaminated patch of skin.

In a way, there are silver linings to this clusterpuck.

If the subdream kills me and I go homicidally crazy in the real world, at least the vampires will put me down before I can cannibalize anyone. Plus, all this adrenaline is short-circuiting my usual fears of picking up *Staphylococcus aureus* and other cooties from my target.

My fingers touch the man's skin, and my muscles stiffen for a moment as I catch a faint whiff of ozone and experience the sensation of falling. Then the room darkens around me, and the world of wakefulness goes away.

CHAPTER TWO

I'M STANDING on top of black water, with a sky like magma above. Barreling toward me are a dozen creatures, each more hideous than the next.

The first looks as if twenty sets of ant mandibles had mushroomed to the size of a truck and had sprouted antennae and legs. Another resembles a massive spiral worm, or maybe a syphilis bacterium, with centipede-like legs ending in knife-sharp talons. The least horrific of the creatures reminds me of a tardigrade, a microscopic animal that lives in water and has no discernable eyes or nose, a hole for a mouth, and eight limbs that end in claws attached to the body of a sea cow—except there's nothing microscopic about this tardigrade. It's ten feet tall.

The mandible creature is in the lead, leaping toward me as it shrieks through each of its mandibles. If I decided to chew up some diamonds, that's probably what it would sound like. Magnified a thousandfold. I get the creepy feeling that the thing is trying to say something, but on a frequency more likely to make my ears bleed than to pass on any information.

A furry appendage snakes from my wrist and elongates into a whip as the shrieking beast leaps at me, mandibles clacking in unison.

I crack the whip. A sonic boom ripples the black water around me. My whip slices the mandible creature into even halves that plop at my feet, spraying me with sticky green goop. I'm paralyzed with disgust —which is when the syphilis creature's talon pierces my left shoulder.

The pain is nauseating and sharp, and I feel lucky that my whip is attached to my body, else I would've dropped it. Disgust now a distant memory, I crack my weapon again. With a second sonic boom, I cleave the syphilis thing in half and dodge the bloody stream that spurts out.

Seeing what happened to their brethren, the remaining monsters attack with a lot less enthusiasm, which is good because I'm losing blood from my shoulder by the bucketful. Before they realize that I'm weakening, I go on the offensive, cracking the whip.

Boom. Boom. Boom.

Only the tardigrade is left standing, and it turns to flee with a speed one wouldn't expect from such humongous bulk.

I leap after it, whip ready. "Oh, no, you're not going

anywhere." A sonic boom later, the tardigrade rains down in pieces.

As soon as it does, the world around me changes.

CHAPTER THREE

MY SHOULDER THROBS as I whip my head around to take in forty-foot squared-dome ceilings, yellowish blue marble floors, reddish green walls, and a floating collection of glowing geometrical shapes that are impossible in the waking world, such as the overlapping-on-itself Penrose triangle. I inhale deeply, dragging in the sweet-savory aroma of *manna*, my favorite Gomorran food.

Of course. I'm in the main lobby of my palace. Meaning this is the dream world, and the monsters I just defeated were part of what I call the subdream. Puck. Once again, I didn't realize what was happening, despite such unrealistic bits as walking on water and Pom's turning into a whip.

A stab of pain brings me back to the moment. This shoulder injury is behaving all too realistically, which means I'm just a few liters of blood loss short of dying in the dream world and thus going insane.

Oh, well. Now that I know where I am, I can change things as I see fit.

I float out of my dream body as if I were having a near-death experience. The pain instantly disappears. I study the body beneath me and mentally cringe. That shoulder is *bad.* The rest of me, though, looks pretty boring for a dream.

With barely any effort, I heal my shoulder. Then, because I can, I make my body taller and thinner and exchange my utilitarian cargo pants and camo shirt for a cool leather jacket, tight black jeans, and knee-high boots. A good start. I replace my frizzy black curls with the look I prefer—fierce flames of fire that make my head look as though a firebird has made a nest on it. Since I'm in a rush, this will have to suffice.

I jump back into my body. As soon as I do, Pom appears in front of me—something he does whenever I'm dreamwalking and he's in REM sleep, which is almost always.

Here in the dream world, he's not a fluffy wristband. Like me, he takes on a dream form.

The size of a large owl, with ginormous lavender eyes, highly mobile triangular ears, and fluffy fur that changes colors to match his emotions, Pom is pure weaponized cuteness. Allegedly cute beings like otters, pandas, and koalas are downright fugly in comparison.

"You left your face the same," he says in his singsong falsetto. "How come?"

"You don't like my face?" I muss his fur until he turns blue, and head toward my tower of sleepers.

He floats up and flies behind me like a selfie drone. "Your face is tolerable. At least Earth humans seem to like it."

"If you're referring to the staring, I think they're just trying to figure out my race and ethnicity."

He zooms in front of me. "What's that?"

"It's like when we're trying to figure out what type of Cognizant someone is on Gomorrah. Earth humans use those labels in similar ways, with some groups not liking other groups—like necromancers and vampires."

"Oh, but that's an easy guessing game." His ears waggle in excitement. "Orcs are green, elves are thin and willowy, dwarves have beards, giants are—"

"Right." I speed up as I get to the staircase. Though time moves faster in the dream world, or feels like it does, there's still good reason to make haste. What the heck—I take flight instead of bothering with each step. "But it's not always that simple," I continue as Pom catches up to me. "Werewolves look no different from me, unless they turn."

His furry face takes on a sage look. "So what do most humans guess for your lace and felicity?"

"It's *race* and *ethnicity*. And their guesses are all over the place: Latin America, Africa, the Middle East... Some think I'm just a tanned person of European descent with a perm—I guess it's the tiny nose and gray eyes."

"I like your eyes." Pom flits in front of me again, his gaze unblinking. This lack of common-sense social skills is why I usually ask him to be invisible when I work with my clients.

He must pick up on my thought because the tips of his ears turn red.

"Thanks for the compliment," I say to appease him. On a whim, I change my eyes to flame red to match my hair.

Pom's ears go back to blue. "Humans are stupid. You're obviously not from any of those places."

"Right." I take a shortcut by making a portion of the wall evaporate in front of me. "The good news is that my looks give me an advantage. We Cognizant tend to settle in those parts of human-occupied worlds where we most resemble the native population—which means if I ever decide to permanently move to Earth, I could have my pick of much of the planet."

Pom's fur darkens. "Why would we ever want to live in such a backward place?"

He has a point. The sanitation system on Earth is still water-based, the VR technology is in its infancy, and the cars don't yet drive themselves.

"Gomorrah is better in every way." He's clearly picking up on my thoughts again.

"I need to be around humans to keep my powers," I remind him for the umpteenth time. "Plus, thanks to my amazing reputation among Earth Cognizant, I can get high-paying jobs here."

"As in illegal, high-risk jobs," he grumbles.

I suppress a surge of worry about the Enforcers in the waking world. Why stress Pom about something he can't help with? Instead, I put on a burst of speed and reach the tower of sleepers.

The tower is a cylindrical glass structure made up of several levels of glass-walled nooks, each with a single piece of furniture: a bed. Once I've successfully created a dream connection with someone, when they dream, they show up in one of those beds. Thanks to this tower, I only have to go through the unpleasantness of touching people in the real world once.

Bernard, the newest sleeper in my collection, has taken the place that freed up when I cured my most recent legit patient of his bedwetting problem and severed our link.

As we get closer to Bernard's nook, the rest of Pom turns black, and I curse under my breath.

Miniature dark clouds are flying above Bernard's head.

"That figures," I mumble. "Why'd I think I'd finally get a break?"

Those clouds indicate a trauma loop—a type of dream that's based on traumatic events in Bernard's life. Trauma loops plague sleepers on a regular basis, and they're so powerful that I find it easier to just witness them without changing anything. The good news for the sleeper in question is that my mere presence during these special dreams usually breaks their repeat cycle, which helps the sleeper feel better in the waking world.

This might be Bernard's lucky day. Not so much mine, though. I'm in a rush.

Pom flies up to the clouds and gives them a sniff, which is when a miniature lightning bolt hits his nose. "Ouch! That's a bad one."

I erase his pain and encase the clouds in a protective glass bubble. "Probably deep trauma."

"I won't join you, then." Pom's fur looks like coal. "The last time we worked with someone like this, it disturbed my sleep."

To highlight his point, he zooms behind me, as if Bernard might reach out and snatch him from the air, forcing him to see the nightmare.

"Something disturbed *your* sleep?" I turn to grin at him. "Did you sleep twenty-three hours and forty-four minutes, instead of the full twenty-three hours and forty-*five* minutes?"

He sniffs. "At least I'm not on vampire blood, like some."

"Well, technically, given our symbiotic relationship, you are on it. It just doesn't work on you, but—"

"Whatever. I'm not going in, no matter how much you beg." Pom lifts his chin and disappears like a Cheshire cat. Instead of his smile, it's his furry chin that hovers in the air until he's completely gone.

"I don't need you there, anyway," I say to the empty air. "I'm in a rush, and this will go faster without your yammering."

He doesn't take the bait.

I'm almost to Bernard when I smack myself on the forehead. Almost forgot to make myself invisible again.

Pointedly turning myself undetectable by sight, sound, or smell, I touch Bernard on the forearm the way I did in the waking world—except without any worry of contamination.

And then, unlike in reality, where I'm standing in a sleep-like trance, in the dream world I disappear from the palace and reappear inside Bernard's trauma loop.

CHAPTER FOUR

I FIND MYSELF ON A PLAYGROUND, one of Earth's most primitive anachronisms where children physically play. On Gomorrah, fully immersive virtual spaces replaced these long ago, which means no dirt, no germs, and a lot more entertainment options for the little ones.

This particular playground is creepy. Spiders and maggots crawl inside the sandbox, and the empty swing sways as though ridden by ghosts. Even the monkey bars look warped, and the trees remind me of an evil forest from a dark fairy tale.

I bet the original playground wasn't like this. Bernard's emotions are twisting the surroundings.

The man himself is strolling toward a see-saw, the hands of two cute children in his grip—a little girl who's a toddler and a slightly older boy.

Hmm. There'd been no sign of a family when I broke into his apartment.

"Daddy, I need to wee-wee." The girl is dancing from foot to foot.

"Me too," the boy says. "And I go first."

"No, me first." She gives her brother an imperious look. "Princesses first."

They bicker about it as Bernard herds them toward a park bathroom. *A public bathroom.* Gross. Private water-based plumbing is horrific enough.

I float a few feet behind them. Though this dream could easily be fiction—driven by, say, Bernard's subconscious regret over never starting a family—my powers allow me to know the truth without a shadow of a doubt: This dream is based on a memory. All trauma loops I've encountered have been memories—though, in theory, one day I might come across a dream that twists the memory too much. Should that happen, I'd use my powers to pull out the truth and, hopefully, break the loop that way.

So it's a memory—but from when? The scar on Bernard's forehead is missing, so it's safe to say this must've been a while ago.

"I can't hold it anymore," the boy says when they reach the bathroom.

The girl starts crying.

"You're such a baby," the boy says.

The girl stomps her foot and cries louder.

"Let's go." Bernard drags them into the men's room.

Oh, the smell... the sights... the *germs.* Pom was right to disappear; this could traumatize someone for life.

The walls begin to close in.

Puck, I'm changing the dream without meaning to. That's not good. If Bernard notices my influence, he could wake up.

I close my eyes. This is just a dream, and one colored by Bernard's emotions at that. No germs can get me here. I should think of this as exposure therapy for myself—a bit like what I do with my clients who have phobias.

Yeah, that's it.

The bathroom walls get back to normal, but just in case, I disable my sense of smell.

The siblings are still fighting. Visibly frustrated, Bernard helps the boy start his business at a low urinal and then drags the crying toddler into a stall. My nebulous presence follows them in, as this is Bernard's dream/memory and I can only experience what he does.

Through the crying, I hear someone new enter the bathroom.

The boy yelps.

Bernard freezes for a moment, then kicks open the stall door—just in time to see the back of a man rushing out of the bathroom.

The boy is gone.

This time, the walls are closing in because of Bernard. He grabs the hysterical toddler like a sack and rushes out of the bathroom, looking frantically around the playground. He spots the man at the park entrance.

"Stop," he yells. "Give him back!"

The kidnapper dives for a car parked by a hydrant, tosses the boy into the back seat, and jumps behind the wheel.

Bernard sprints after him, but the tires are already burning rubber. "What was that license plate?" Bernard shouts at the toddler in his grip.

The girl cries hysterically.

The agony on Bernard's sheet-white face is painful to look at.

"Bailey," a familiar voice says in my ear. "They're there."

Puck, I'm not done yet. There's more to this, I can tell. But there's a pressure on my arm that has nothing to do with the dream, and my cheek stings as if someone has slapped it.

Like a balloon popping, my dreamwalking trance breaks, and I open my eyes in the waking world.

A pale, weaselly man slaps my other cheek so hard that I stagger back, nearly falling on the slumbering Bernard.

Hearing the commotion—or more likely, waking from his nightmare—Bernard opens his eyes and sees the same thing I'm looking at.

A room full of vampires.

CHAPTER FIVE

THE EYES of the vampire who slapped me turn into mirrors as he catches Bernard's gaze.

"You will go into the kitchen and sit for ten minutes," he says in a honey-laced voice with a slight Scottish accent. "Afterward, you'll forget we were ever here. Understood?"

"Yes," Bernard says in the robotic tone people tend to take on under glamour. "I'll go."

"And forget," the vamp says.

"And forget." Shamelessly flashing us his hairy body, Bernard lumbers to his destination.

I do my best to get my racing pulse under control. "What's this about?" Taking out my hand sanitizer, I apply a generous amount to my slapped cheeks and touched arm. Who knows where that vampire's hands have been? "I was in the middle of something."

"We're here on behalf of the Council," says the tallest of the bunch, an unusually unattractive specimen of his kind. His hooked nose sits above a thin, downturned mouth, and his brown hair is limp and greasy-looking. However, his pale eyes hold an intense sort of intelligence.

"It's probably true," Felix whispers. "That's Kain, the new leader of the Enforcers. I remember him because of the *Legacy of Kain*. He even looks a little like the guy in that game series."

I'd tell Felix to shut it, but I don't want to give away his presence. No reason for him to go down as my accomplice.

"Why does the Council wish to see me?" I ask in a tone so calm it surprises even me.

"You will only speak when spoken to," growls the vampire who slapped me earlier.

"No need to be rude, Firth," Kain says to his lackey. He shifts his pale gaze to me. "I'm afraid you'll have to appear in front of the Council to learn more."

I count at least a dozen vampires around me. Not good. "Do I have to?"

"If you want to live," Kain says without emotion.

"Okay, then. I guess I'm dying to go."

He tips his head. "Put the contents of your pockets on the bed."

For a fleeting moment, I consider fighting my way out. Why else did I learn all those martial arts in the dreams of renowned masters? The problem is that vampires are much stronger and faster, not to mention I'm completely outnumbered.

Not looking at Pom, lest they realize he's

contraband from another world, I take out the sleeping grenade, my Earth smartphone, my Gomorran comms, and the vial of diluted vampire blood. I gingerly place it all on the wrinkled sheets, which are still warm from Bernard.

"I should check her," Firth says—overeagerly, in my opinion.

"Don't," Kain says imperiously. He strides over to poke in my stuff. Right away, he homes in on my Gomorran comms. "This is Otherland technology. It's forbidden to bring it to Earth."

"Oops." I grimace. "I didn't show it to any locals, I swear."

Kain nods at Firth, and the thin vamp crushes the device in his fist and pockets the broken pieces. What an ass. I'm glad I didn't bring my pricey hygieia wand from home. Earth hand sanitizers are infinitely worse at germ-killing, but at least they shouldn't be confiscated.

I'm about to snap at Kain for destroying my property—comms aren't exactly cheap, either—but Felix whispers into my earpiece, "He just did you a huge favor. If the Council caught you with that, you'd be in major trouble—well, more trouble than whatever you've gotten yourself into already."

Fine. Maybe he's right. Being an Earth native, Felix knows all the dumb rules here much better than I do.

Kain examines my phone before homing in on the grenade.

"That's to help with my work," I say quickly. "It puts people to sleep."

He puts down the grenade and picks up the vial. Uncorking it, he takes a sniff and looks at me with a raised eyebrow.

I feel my blood rush to my face. "It's not what you think it's for."

His eyebrow lifts higher.

"I only use that to suppress the need to sleep."

His eyebrow goes back down. "I thought even dreamwalkers needed sleep to survive."

I shrug, resisting the urge to point out the irony of a vampire lecturing me about blood consumption.

"You can have those back." Kain gestures at the bed.

I sanitize the phone, the vial, and the grenade before stuffing them back into my pockets. At this rate, I might need another bottle of sanitizer, unless they kill me soon and render that point moot. And since I'm already on this morbid train of thought, I hope they sterilize the sword or ax they plan to behead me with, a bit like humans do with needles for their lethal injections. One thing's for sure: There's no way these vampires are going to be willing to stop by a pharmacy for more hand sanitizer, even if it's on the way.

Firth catches my gaze with his beady eyes and mouths something that looks suspiciously like *blood whore*—a derogatory term for a vampire addict, which I'm not. Hopefully.

Either way, it's official: From here on out, Firth is

Filth, though perhaps I'll only call him that behind his back, for safety reasons.

"What was in that vial?" Felix whispers.

Glad the diluted solution looks more like water than blood, I ignore his question. It's not like I'm in a position to answer him, anyway.

The vampires escort me out to a limo, and we drive down the night streets of Manhattan at race car speeds.

"I hacked into the limo's GPS," Felix informs me. "They're going to the Council castle, just as they claimed."

Good to know. Now if only I knew whether that's good news or bad news.

Since Felix doesn't say more, I stare out the car window to stay sane. We're passing Times Square, one of the busiest parts of this city. It can't compare to even the quietest street back on Gomorrah, but the hustle and bustle makes me feel at home. Except there are no humans on Gomorrah—which is what all these people are.

It's mind-boggling. The Cognizant make up less than one percent of Earth's population, but from what I know about this world's homo sapiens, if they learned of beings with powers like ours, they'd see us as a threat and act accordingly. I don't know if they'd catch us for vivisection or simply wipe us out, but I'm sure the outcome wouldn't be fun. This is why we keep our existence under strict secrecy, going as far as enforcing the silence with a barbaric practice called the Mandate, which decrees death to anyone dumb enough to blab about the Cognizant on advanced human-dominated worlds like Earth.

Maybe that's what the vamps want. Have I been on this world long enough to need the stupid Mandate Rite? I thought you were supposed to request it—and plan to settle on Earth, to boot. I doubt you'd get escorted to the ceremony like a VIP.

Felix yawns into my earpiece. I could strangle him right now. The last thing I need is for my sleep deprivation symptoms to resurface.

He yawns again.

That does it. I sneak my hand into my pocket, pull out my phone, and stealthily text, *Take a nap.*

"What?" Felix says. "I'm not going to—"

Please, I text. I hide my phone before Filth sees me and breaks it like he did with the Gomorran comms.

"You sure?" my friend mumbles.

Turning so the vampires can't see, I show my lapel camera a thumbs-up and clasp my hands as if in prayer.

"Okay, fine," he whispers. "If they're really taking you to see the Council, there's not much I can do for you, anyway."

Great. I'm so much calmer now.

When we get outside the city, I decide Bernard has had enough time to go back to bed. That means I can return to his dreams, finish my job, and email Valerian with the account number of Mom's hospital on Gomorrah. Hopefully he'll still pay if I'm dead. I'm hoping I'll live, though. The money from this gig will only cover the outstanding bills, not her future stay.

But that's enough worrying.

It's dreamwalking time.

There are many ways to get into dreams. The classic method is to fall asleep myself, which could be tough thanks to the vampire blood I've ingested and all this existential dread. The strategy I've used more often lately is to touch a dreamer—like my legit therapy clients, illegal job targets à la Bernard, and most often, Pom, the looft on my wrist.

I stealthily slide one hand toward Pom. The last thing I want is to draw attention to his existence. As a looft, Pom spends ninety-nine percent of his life in REM sleep, providing me with a gateway into the dream world that's always at my fingertips. Well, almost always—he is, on a super-rare occasion, awake. Though you wouldn't be able to tell by looking at him in the waking world. Here, he's a fur bracelet regardless.

Stroking him to soothe myself, I concentrate on my intent to go into his dream.

Just like when I touch any other sleeper, my muscles tense and relax, I smell ozone, and I experience the sensation of falling as the limo around me darkens and the world of wakefulness goes bye-bye.

CHAPTER SIX

I FIND myself in my dream palace once more. Awesome. The vamps will be none the wiser—there's a reason I put up with what's essentially a parasite living on my wrist.

"What?" Pom appears in front of me in the angriest shade of red I've seen. "I can't believe you used the P-word."

I make my hair and eyes extra fiery. "How many times do I have to ask you not to snoop on my thoughts? You're only allowed to be upset when I say something mean with my mouth."

"But a *parasite*?" The tips of his ears go from red to blue. "I'm a symbiont."

"Sure." I fly up and head for the tower of sleepers. "Whatever you say."

"You have to mean that." He zooms in front of me, his ears going back to red.

"If you insist on having this discussion, let me ask you something: Am I or am I not your food source?"

"In a manner of speaking. I get my nutrients from your bloodstream."

"And where do your metabolic byproducts go?" Even as I ask the question, I shudder at the images it generates.

Pom turns a shade paler. "You mean like farts and poop? I don't think I do those things, but if I did, I guess it would go into your bloodstream. But your liver—"

"Is not there to save me from looft poo, I'm sure. In any case, what do you call a creature that lives off someone like this?"

He zips around me. "If it was useless, like a tick, you'd rightfully call it a parasite. But if the noble being provides the host with benefits, it's a symbiont."

"Benefits?" I fly over the staircase. "What are they? Besides blasting my eyeballs with extreme cuteness and helping me get into the dream world—both things I could hypothetically use a koala bear for. Did you know koalas sleep up to twenty-two hours a day? That's only an hour and fifty-five minutes less than you."

He huffs. "You can't bring a koala from world to world. And I do more for you than you think. I help you stay thin when you consume too many calories and—"

"Wait." I slow down to look into his big, guileless eyes. "Are you saying I pig out?"

"Well... I also help you regulate your appetite."

Huh. That may explain why I haven't been as hungry lately. "I didn't know that."

He puffs up. "There's a lot you don't know about loofts."

"You win," I say, mostly because we've reached the tower and I need to focus on Bernard. "You're a symbiont." Under my breath, I add, "Like gut bacteria."

"I heard that," Pom grumbles as I float over to Bernard's nook. "But guess what? All you Cognizant are parasites when it comes to humans. You wouldn't have powers if it weren't for their belief in you. You wouldn't—" He stops, seeing my crestfallen expression. "I'm sorry. That was mean."

I wave dismissively. "No, you can call me a parasite if you want. I was just hoping to finish the job." I eye Bernard's empty bed in disappointment.

"Oh, yeah, he's no longer sleeping," Pom says. "Check back in a few hours. I'm sure he'll be back later."

I do my best to suppress a thought along the lines of *assuming I have a later.* No need to worry the little guy.

Pom cocks his head at me. Did he catch that worry, after all?

Before he can question me and because I need to soothe myself, I take to the air, heading to an adjacent part of the palace.

Pom's fur brightens to golden as he realizes where I'm going. "Which memory will you relive this time?" he eagerly asks, flitting around me.

32

"Not sure yet."

My memory gallery serves a purpose similar to photo albums on Earth and VR videos on Gomorrah, making it easier to put myself into a dream that's based on a treasured recollection. Each plasma-framed painting hanging in the cavernous, museum-like space depicts an important snapshot of my life.

I float along the walls, scanning the various images until I settle on one.

"This?" Pom asks when I stop next to my choice.

"It's my earliest memory."

The tips of his ears turn light orange. "How old were you when that happened?"

"Seven, I think."

"And that's your earliest memory?" His ears are now a hodgepodge of colors. "Don't most people recall events before that age?"

I try not to show how much his innocent question bothers me. "I think it varies for everyone. I've always felt like there were parts of my childhood I couldn't recall—and Mom wasn't helpful when I asked her to fill in the blanks."

An understatement. Most fights between us over the years boiled down to her snapping at me for asking something about the past, like "who was my father?" or "where is he?"

Pom clasps his little paws together. "Well, then, do what you came here to do."

"Be back soon," I say and jump into the painting.

CHAPTER SEVEN

I'M SHORTER THAN USUAL. My body is that of my seven-year-old self, as are my emotions—unless I stop the replay and reflect as my adult self, which I rarely do.

Mommy's in the bathroom, and I'm bored. Spying an interesting object on Mommy's dresser, I climb onto a chair and rise on tiptoes to reach it.

It's coarse to the touch, unlike any other material I've ever handled. Is it clay? I don't know where I know that word from, but I'm pretty sure the object—a vase —is made of that.

Even more interesting are the handprints on it. There are four of them, and they belong to two smaller children. Or one child who put their prints onto the vase twice.

I strain my memory to figure out if they're mine.

Nothing.

"What are you doing?"

Mommy's voice startles me, and I drop the vase.

It hits the floor and shatters, clay bits flying everywhere as her eyes widen in horror.

I climb off the chair, head hanging low.

Mommy drops to her knees, pawing through the pieces as her face turns red and blotchy and her eyes fill with moisture.

I don't want her to cry. "Mommy, I'm so sorry. It was an accident."

Blinking rapidly, she envelops me in a hug. "It's okay, darling—it was just a material object. We can get another." But her voice is strained, and a wet drop falls on my forehead.

I begin to sob.

"No, no, darling, hush." She rocks me back and forth. "We can always make another vase."

I pull back, my mood lifting. "Can I put my handprints on it?"

She smiles, though her eyes continue to glisten wetly. "Of course."

The memory-dream ends, and I'm back outside the painting, my emotions in turmoil.

Maybe I shouldn't have chosen that specific memory. When I relived it before, prior to Mom's accident, it'd made me feel comforted, soothed, like Mom's arms were still around me. But today, it only intensified the hollow ache in my chest. I miss Mom so much it hurts. For all our fights, she's my only family, the only person in the world who loves me unconditionally. I'd give anything to turn back the clock and—

"Did you end up making another vase?" Pom bops around me, the happy purple of his fur proving that he's staying out of my head, as promised.

I shove away the gloomy thoughts, just in case, and paste on a smile. Now's not the time to dwell on my family or lack thereof. "Sort of," I reply as I take flight, heading back to the tower of sleepers. "The next day, Mom got me a VR headset so I could make hundreds of vases—and those never broke."

Pom speeds up to hover in front of me. "Whose handprints were those on the vase?"

I raise my hands and picture them tiny. "Mine, maybe. Could also be Mom's when she was small. She said she didn't remember." That was her response to most of my questions, in fact—a response I hated because it made no sense.

Why get so upset over a broken vase if you don't remember anything about it?

Pom must've gleaned that last thought. "She didn't yell at you for breaking it," he points out helpfully.

"No, she didn't." I sigh as the hollow ache returns. "She never yelled at me—unless I asked about the past."

Thinking about all this generates an overwhelming desire to check on Mom at the hospital. If I get lucky, there might be a way—but I need to deal with Bernard first.

Only Bernard is still not in his bed when Pom and I reach the tower.

Sounds like I have time to check on Mom, after all.

I fly over to another nook. *Score*. The dreamer I need is there. I'm lucky today—being taken to my possible death aside.

"Who's that?" Pom lands on the bed and examines the gargoyle female from wingtip to pointy tail.

"She's a nurse I found sleeping on the job when Mom was first admitted to the hospital. I made a sneaky connection to her, in case I wanted to check on Mom via dreams."

"Ah." Pom leaps onto my shoulder. "I want to go with you."

I scratch behind his ear, make both of us invisible, and enter the nurse's dreams.

———

THE GARGOYLE IS DREAMING of the hospital— another bit of luck. She's doing data entry at the nursing station, her head down.

Catching a moment when her attention is on the screen, I change the surroundings to match Mom's room.

It's a room I've grown to loathe. There, machines do everything Mom's brain refuses to, from breathing to nourishment.

Pom's feet reassuringly squeeze my shoulder.

When the nurse looks up from the screen, her subconscious mind fills in the details of the dream— using her memories, which is a boon for me.

"Hi, Lidia," the nurse says, approaching Mom's bed.

Mom doesn't reply. With her lack of brain activity, it's a philosophical question whether she actually heard what the nurse said.

The nurse lifts Mom's leg. "How about we do a little exercise?" She proceeds to move Mom like a doll.

Of course. Being in bed for so long, Mom's muscles are atrophying, or would if it weren't for what the nurse is doing. My chest squeezes tight. This is why I need the money, why I need to survive.

This is also why I should, at the very least, finish Valerian's job.

Exiting the nurse's dream, I check on Bernard.

He's still not back.

I return to the gallery and play a memory to banish the hospital room from my mind's eye. It's a memory of me blowing out the candles on a cake for my ninth birthday, and unlike the vase incident, it doesn't make me feel worse when it's done.

When I return to check on Bernard, he's still missing.

Pom's visibility returns in that Cheshire cat manner. "Isn't that Felix?"

I glance at a nearby nook. So it is. My friend fell asleep, after all.

Though I told Felix to do this very thing, a part of me thought he'd have trouble snoozing while I was in danger. Then again, it must be four in the morning, and unlike me, he hasn't imbibed vampire blood.

I float over to the nook where he's audibly snoring,

his dark hair in even greater disarray than usual. Like me, Felix must stump anyone on Earth who tries to pinpoint his ethnicity—though unlike me, he comes from a long line of Earth Cognizant and does, in fact, resemble the humans from his home country of Uzbekistan. If I had to describe him to a fellow Gomorran, I'd say he looks like a tanned, skinny elf, only extra hairy and without the pointy ears.

"You might want to sit this one out," I tell Pom. "He's been through some ordeals."

Pom promptly goes away to do whatever he does when he's not pestering me. Good. I actually want him out of the picture so Felix and I can talk freely about the danger I'm about to face.

Making sure I'm still invisible, I reach out with one finger to touch Felix right above his unibrow. Connection established, I leap into his dream.

CHAPTER EIGHT

I'M in an abandoned warehouse with windows facing the Empire State Building. Huh. Do they even have warehouses in this part of NYC? Somewhere off to my right, a girl is screaming so loudly I'm glad my eardrums aren't real.

I turn to see what's going on. A foaming-at-the-mouth puck is clutching Felix's petite girlfriend in his furry paws as a dozen or so other pucks try to rip her out of his clutches. Poor girl. With hairy bodies, horns, and hoofed feet, pucks look a lot like the depictions of satyrs and demons on this world—only with shark-like teeth. On Gomorrah, pucks have the worst reputation of any creature, in part due to negative portrayal in the media, but mostly because they like to rape, kill, and eat their victims—and not always in that order.

Put another way, Felix's girlfriend is pucked.

"Help me, Neo Golem!" she cries out in a voice

that's surprisingly intact, given all that screaming. "You're my only hope."

Seriously?

As if in reply to her plea, the warehouse door bursts into tiny pieces and a huge figure lumbers in.

Ah, right. When Felix got embroiled in saving the world, he and our gnome friend created a robotic power suit for him. Having obviously read too many Earth comic books, particularly *Iron Man*, Felix made this design—and even chose a superhero name for himself: Neo Golem.

The robot lunges at the nearest puck with a speed something this big shouldn't be capable of. Grabbing the puck by the left horn, he tosses him out the window, where the creature smashes into the Empire State Building.

The pucks let the girl go and circle Felix.

He slams a robotic arm into the stomach of the puck who'd held his girlfriend, causing the creature to fly at the wall and slide down in a broken heap.

A bigger puck gores Felix's shoulder with a diamond-hard horn, shredding metal like tinfoil. But when he rips the horn out, there's no blood. He must've missed Felix's flesh. That's good. From what I recall, my friend faints at the sight of blood, especially his own.

As I watch, Felix retaliates with a kick, hurling the attacking puck at his brethren. They tumble like bowling pins.

"Yeah!" Felix shouts. "You don't mess with Neo Golem."

The robot's chest opens up. In the place where Felix's nipples would be, two giant guns show up—and fire at the remaining pucks.

One spectacular explosion later, Felix is left alone with his sobbing girlfriend.

Wow. I can tell that the last part of the attack was based on a real memory of some fight Felix was in. I'm tempted to check it out, but I'm here for a different reason.

Felix sheds his robot suit and strides over to the girl.

Now this part is clearly pure fiction; his naked body looks way more muscular than his figure would imply in the waking world.

They kiss. Oh, boy. If I don't interfere now, I'm pretty sure I'll find out the X-rated way this damsel intends to reward her knight in shining armor.

Making myself visible, I clear my throat.

Felix's head snaps toward me. As he takes in my face and fiery hair, his eyes grow to the size of saucers, literally so—which is only possible in a dream.

I hastily return my hair to normal and clothe Felix in jeans and a T-shirt with a wave of my hand. "It's me, Bailey. I asked you to take a nap so we can speak, remember?"

Felix looks between me and his girlfriend. To make sure she doesn't distract him, I make her disappear.

Felix rubs his eyes. "What the hell is going on?"

"This is a dream," I say patiently.

He doesn't look like he believes me, so I change our environment to the place where I usually perform talking therapy—a pillowy cloud floating above a soothing ocean.

"A dream?" Felix plops onto the plush white couch my patients like to sit on.

"An unrealistic one, at that." I perch on a cushy, fleece-covered chair that appears conveniently under my butt. "Think about it. The warehouse was in Manhattan, as in Earth, but there are no pucks on Earth. Also, the pucks could've—and would've—killed the girl first, then attacked you. And that *You're my only hope* bit… Would anyone really say that, outside of *Star Wars*?"

I can see the dawning comprehension in his eyes.

"Don't feel bad. Dreams are my thing, after all."

He swivels his head from side to side, taking in our surroundings. "Unreal. I was totally clueless."

"It's hard to question dream reality." I let my hair go fiery again.

He looks awed. "It's like being in *The Matrix*."

Oh, crap, his favorite. If I don't change the subject, I'll get an earful. "I wanted to ask you about this Council that kidnapped me. I have a vague idea of how they work, but I could use more details."

"Hold on." He sits straighter. "How'd you get into my dreams? You're in that limo with the vampires."

I'd hoped he wouldn't question this part. "I had a connection with you already."

"Since when?"

I sigh. "Remember how you fell asleep during that video game design course we took together?"

"Nooo…"

"Well, you did." I change the environment around us to match that classroom, so he can see what I saw that day: his head on the desk, some drool in the corner of his mouth. "See how your eyes are twitching? That's REM sleep. Too good an opportunity to pass up." I pantomime touching his forehead. Of course, when I'd really done it, there was hand sanitizer involved.

"So you snuck into my dream without my permission?" His voice rises, and I worry he might try to wrestle control of his dream world from me— something I can fight but prefer not to, especially with a friend.

"This was right after you hacked my laptop and made fun of my project," I remind him.

"That's different. This is a much bigger invasion of privacy."

"You started it."

He pinches the bridge of his nose. "Fine. What was it that you wanted to know about the Council?"

"Anything you can tell me. Pretend I know nothing."

"Right," he says in a professorial tone. "In that case, the Councils are a form of government. Their main objective is to make sure the Cognizant remain hidden from humans."

"Okay, maybe not so basic." I stand up to pace along our cloud.

"Then I don't know what to tell you."

"How about something that can help me?"

He considers it for a moment. "Councils are made up of the most powerful Cognizant in the region they cover. The New York Council is among the most powerful Councils on Earth."

I roll my eyes. This is going nowhere fast. "So?"

"So don't piss them off."

"That's a huge help, thanks. Any other pearls of wisdom you wish to impart?"

His unibrow furrows. "Well, yeah. Think about it: The very fact that the Enforcers took you to see the Council is good news."

"Oh?"

"Without the Mandate, your standing in our community is shaky at best. They could've just killed you on the spot, and no one would've said boo."

I halt my pacing. "Some government."

"Before going to sleep, I tried using my powers to figure out what they want. Unfortunately, their computers aren't connected to the human internet."

He tried to hack them? Is he nuts? "Don't do anything that'll make them come for you next."

"Nothing I *can* do, anyway." He studies me. "Do you seriously have no idea what they might want?"

"No clue. I only know a couple of people from this Council, and the most powerful of them isn't even on Earth at the moment." I run my fingers through my fiery hair, sending embers flying. "There's Kit—you know, the shapeshifter? We met at the rehab where I work. I think she likes me, and she's on the Council. Maybe she can help? I doubt she's behind whatever this is."

Felix nods. "Kit's good people."

I strain my memory for anyone else on the Council. "Hey, maybe it's—"

Before I can finish my sentence, Pom appears next to me, his fur light orange.

Felix's eyes widen improbably yet again. "What is *that?*"

"I told you about Pom." At Felix's blank stare, I clarify, "My looft."

"The fuzzy bracelet?" Felix eyes my currently naked wrist.

I grin. "In here, Pom looks like this."

Pom bends his short, chubby legs in a curtsy. "Nice to meet you, Felix. This dream isn't as bad as Bailey made it out to be."

Felix studies him warily. "Thanks… I think."

"I think it's best you wake up now," I tell him.

"But—"

"No reason to bore Pom with our problems," I say pointedly.

An actual lightbulb appears over Felix's head; I'm not sure he realizes he's inadvertently summoned it. "Got it. But before I go, can you show me some cool dream stuff?"

I smile and snap my fingers to take us to my palace.

Felix looks around, agog. "Cool… Reminds me of

Peach's castle from *Mario*, but with Escher and Salvador Dalí influences."

I snatch a Penrose-triangle clock from the air and let it melt into my hand. "You're not far off. I changed this place a bit after we took that course. Video game design made me a much better dreamwalker."

Felix looks up at the ceiling, a part of the palace so old I don't even recall making it. Consisting of multicolored glass, it's a mosaic depicting a mandala shaped like an archery target. He then stares at the walls and the floor. "What's with the crazy color scheme?"

I grin. "They're known as 'forbidden colors' because their light frequencies automatically cancel each other in our eyes. But we're not really seeing through our eyes here, hence red-green and blue-yellow, as I imagine those shades to be. I'm thinking of adding ultraviolet and infrared accents as well."

Eager to show off further, I take us to the memory gallery and explain how I use it.

Felix looks enviously at a painting of a surprise birthday party Mom threw for me when I turned twelve. "I'd pay a million dollars to revisit some of my childhood memories."

"I could make it happen for you," I say. "Just not today."

"Of course." He grins. "Thanks for showing me this."

"You should take him to the tower of sleepers," Pom suggests. "It's *my* favorite spot."

I grab Felix by the shoulder and fly him to the tower.

"Trippy," he breathes when he sees the nook with another version of him sleeping and another version of me standing over him with my finger on his forehead.

"That's you and me in Pom's dream, my gateway to the dream world in this case," I explain. "We're now in the same location, of sorts, but in your dream. Hence the extra bodies. When I exit your dream, I'll be in that body—and I'll get back to my *real* body in that limo after I'm done in Pom's dream."

"Like I said, trippy." He looks up and squints at a nook a floor up. "Wait, hold on… Is that Ariel?"

Crap. I forgot they're roommates. In hindsight, I shouldn't have taken him here. What if Ariel doesn't want him to know she's a patient of mine?

"You seriously need to wake up," I forcefully tell him. "Now."

He intuits my concern. "Oh, don't worry. She told me you're helping her."

I give him my best poker face. "I can neither confirm nor deny."

"Well, I want to thank you anyway. Ariel's been through a lot, and ever since she went to rehab and started your treatments, I noticed real progress with all her issues."

I wince internally. "Please, let's not talk about my hypothetical therapy sessions."

"Understood. Just keep doing what you do. I don't need to know what it is."

I sigh. "Anything else?"

"Sure." He looks around again. "How do I wake up?"

"Just wish to do so."

He closes his eyes, which I didn't tell him to do, and gets a constipated expression on his face—but clearly doesn't wake up. After a few seconds, I grow bored and push him from the dream world with a small jolt of my powers.

Both Felixes shimmer into nothingness. On my end, the version of me from Felix's dream disappears, and I find myself in the body next to the empty bed where Felix was a moment ago.

Pom flies up and lands on the pillow. "So. Are you going to help Ariel now?"

"Might as well." I head over to her nook.

"Good," Pom states. "I like Ariel."

Of course he likes Ariel. Pom's male, after all. Sort of. Maybe.

On Gomorrah, we call Ariel's kind of Cognizant *ubers*. That's not because they chauffeur everyone around—our cars drive themselves—but because they're uber strong and uber attractive. The term among Earth Cognizant is *strongmen*, which is dumb because female ubers are just as strong as males, and because the label doesn't begin to cover their extraordinary looks.

Reaching Ariel's bed, I look her over. With her glossy dark hair and lightly bronzed skin, she's striking even for an uber. Her face, with its strong nose and finely defined jaw, is so symmetrical you'd think a video game designer had toiled for years to craft such perfection, and her body is what humans on Earth label "an impossible standard of beauty."

I'm actually glad Felix noticed her here. This might be my last chance to provide therapy for anyone, and Ariel isn't just a patient anymore. She's become a friend.

"Stay invisible," I tell Pom.

He nods disappointedly.

I touch Ariel's melted-candy-smooth forehead and sink into her dreams.

CHAPTER NINE

DRESSED IN AN ARMY UNIFORM, Ariel is running effortlessly with a hundred-pound pack on her back. She looks stunning, as usual, despite being sweaty, barefaced, and covered in grime.

I've been in a version of this dream before. This is an echo of Ariel's Army training.

"Ariel," I call gently.

She stops short and pulls out her gun, panic in her dark brown eyes.

Just in case, I turn the bullets into cotton. "I'm Bailey. You know me."

"I do," she says, still obviously disoriented. "What are you doing here?"

"You're dreaming," I tell her.

She looks confused for another moment, then a grin slowly spreads across her face. "I'm at the rehab facility?"

"Not sure. I'm doing remote therapy right now, so I have no idea where your body is."

I take us to my therapy space in the clouds above the ocean, and before she asks me to do so, I change her clothes into her favorite little black dress.

Instead of sitting down on the couch, she shifts from foot to foot. "So... what did you want to do today?"

I give her a soothing smile. "That's a question for you. Did you want to experiment with memory or—"

"No!" She tenses like a cobra ready to strike. Then she deliberately relaxes and, in a calmer tone, asks, "Can we do some more of that exposure therapy? I feel like I'm almost ready to be around vampires without freaking out."

As I thought—Ariel has deep trauma she's not ready to deal with. A terrible thing happened to her during her service, an event I witnessed in a trauma loop when I first started working with her. She's blocked her waking memories of it. I've been coaxing her to go there again, but she's clearly not ready. At least she's up for *some* forms of dream therapy. Not like some other patients of mine... and definitely not like Mom.

I've always suspected that Mom has been through something traumatic, but I have no idea what it is, as she's never let me treat her in any capacity. Quite the opposite: The mere idea of my dreamwalking in her sends her into a fit. When I was a kid, she made me swear never to enter her dreams, and I've kept my oath to this day. I sometimes wonder if she came to

Gomorrah—a place without humans and their power-boosting beliefs—to lose her dreamwalking abilities completely. Maybe our powers are somehow tied to whatever traumatized her.

Familiar guilt floods me at the thought. The morning of Mom's accident, we argued about this very topic. I said things I regret and wish—

Ariel clears her throat.

"Sorry," I say, "what kind of exposure should we start with?"

"Blood," she says, her gaze downcast. "I feel brave today."

She doesn't need to say more. Vampire blood addiction is the reason she checked herself into rehab. She got hooked after she was healed by the substance and then started using it recreationally, probably as a form of self-medicating.

"Blood it is." I take us to a room I've used a few times, one modeled on a club in Gomorrah frequented by vampire blood aficionados. There are so many toys and instruments of sexy torture you'd think a BDSM dungeon threw up in here. Chained to a cross in the middle of it all is a vampire, who I make look like Filth —a small token of spite.

Ariel picks up a big knife and approaches Filth. I get out of her way and observe.

"You know you want it," Filth says in a tone much friendlier than I think the real version of him is capable of. "Drink from me."

With small, careful steps, Ariel draws near enough

to cut a deep gash on his forearm. I try to make sure the blood pours slowly and, for lack of a better word, temptingly.

Ariel stares at it, hypnotized. I do as well. I sometimes worry I'll become addicted myself, thanks to my use of vampire blood to banish sleep, but so far, I seem to be okay. Then again, even if I were a blood addict, I doubt I'd be tempted by Filth's blood.

Ariel's face shows her mental turmoil. I hold my breath. She's either going to lean in and greedily gulp from the wound, as she's done during most of our sessions, or she's going to turn away, as she's managed to do only a couple of times.

Sweat beading on her forehead, she turns away from the blood and walks toward me.

"Great job." I pat her shoulder and usher us back to the clouds.

Ariel still looks doubtful. "This is all well and good, but I don't know if I'd be able to resist such temptation in the real world."

She doesn't give herself enough credit. "I think you'd be able to. You're—"

The whole world quakes.

"Open your eyes, bitch," booms a voice that sounds like Filth's.

Ugh, not now.

A slap wrenches me from the dream world, and I find myself back in the limo, Filth looming over me.

"What?" I snap.

"You're not supposed to dream," he hisses.

"I wasn't. That was a meditative trance."

"Don't do that, either."

I slather hand sanitizer on my stinging cheek and glare at Kain accusingly.

The head of the Enforcers shrugs. "We know you can communicate with people in your sleep."

"So what? Even the police allow an arrested person a phone call."

"We don't." Filth settles back into his seat with a sneer. "Close your eyes again, and I'll cut your lids off."

"Don't talk back," Felix urges in my ear. He sounds on the verge of fainting. "He looks like he means that."

It's true. Filth looks eager to mutilate me.

What a puckwad.

"Firth," Kain says, "she's not to be harmed." He turns his glare on me. "Do stay awake until we arrive at our destination."

"Fine." I stare at Filth for a few miles straight, doing my best not to blink. The bastard doesn't seem to care, though. He just sits there with a smirk on his weasely face.

Deciding that the stare-off hurts me more than him, I look out the window instead. A full moon illuminates picturesque forests and distant mountain peaks as we drive into a fenced area past a sign that forbids trespassing. As we approach one large mountain, the dirt road turns into a nicely paved one, and a few minutes later, we reach a blockade manned by vampires who salute us—or rather, who salute Kain.

My hopes of escape evaporate.

Enforcer vampires are everywhere.

The limo crosses a moat and heads toward skyscraper-sized doors on the side of the mountain, thrown wide to reveal a medieval castle that puts even my dream palace to shame. The craziest part is that the entire castle is inside the mountain—a Cognizant with stone control must've helped with this project, because it's truly impressive.

The limo pulls into the mountain, where very unmedieval lighting illuminates gorgeous bastions and crenellated towers. I mentally file away the images in case I want to plagiarize them for my own dream architecture.

The limo comes to a stop.

"We're inside the bailey," Filth says libidinously.

I force out the most maniacal false laugh I can muster. "You're *so* clever."

He grabs my upper arm and drags me out of the car.

"Let go of her," Kain orders with a frown.

Filth releases me, and I massage my smarting arm as I apply more sanitizer to it. Pretty sure I'm going to have finger-shaped bruises there.

Inside the castle, we pass through cold stone corridors filled with hooded figures of monks. One of them hands a folded bundle to Kain without saying a word.

"Is that the Brotherhood?" I ask no one in particular.

"Speak only when spoken to," Filth barks.

"Yes, they are," Kain replies almost at the same time. "Don't you have them on Gomorrah?"

"I think so," I say, "but I've never met them myself."

The Brotherhood is a group of Cognizant without any powers, or at least any powers I'm aware of. They follow some strange religion, the details of which I don't know.

Eventually, we reach a large set of doors opening into a miniature indoor coliseum lit by candles floating in the air—a nice touch.

Filth points at the circular platform in the middle. "Stand there. Don't go to sleep."

"That will be all," Kain says to his minions.

As all the Enforcers leave, Filth included, Kain unfolds the bundle of fabric given to him by the monk. It turns out to be a black robe with a hood.

He puts it on. "Now we wait for the Council meeting. It's going to happen first thing in the morning."

"That's a long time away," I say. "Any chance you can tell me what this is about?"

"No. But what I can do is make the time pass faster while you wait."

"Sure, but how—"

As his eyes turn into mirrors, I realize my mistake.

He's about to glamour me.

I'm resistant to vampire glamour, at least from the run-of-the-mill vamps, but Kain is clearly powerful, and drinking vampire blood does make one more susceptible to their—

"You won't remember the next five hours," Kain says in a voice made of melted caramel.

The next thing I'm aware of is how stiff I feel standing in the same spot.

Only now I'm surrounded by the Council.

CHAPTER TEN

DRESSED in multicolored hooded robes similar to the one Kain put on, the New York Councilors look as though they took their fashion advice from some creepy secret society.

"Good morning," I say politely, and even contemplate curtsying. "I'm ready to learn why I've been detained."

"Finally," Felix says in my ear. "I thought you'd never snap out of it."

Kain stands up. "Please state your name for the record."

"Bailey Spade." I scan the room for allies, but it's hard to recognize anyone in these hooded getups.

"Thank you," Kain says. "I'll be the designated neutral party in these proceedings."

"I think that's good," Felix whispers. "He let your Gomorran tech slide. Maybe he's more than neutral."

In the third row, a slender figure in a magenta robe stands up and pulls her hood back.

I know her. This is Kit, the shapeshifter I met through my rehab job. She's currently in her favorite guise, that of a round-cheeked blonde straight out of a Japanese role-playing game or anime.

"I'm serving as the Defense for today's proceedings," she says in a high-pitched voice that matches her video game appearance.

Another woman in teal robes stands up and pushes back her hood, revealing high cheekbones in a familiar oval face. "And I'm Gertrude, the Plaintiff in today's proceedings."

Puck. I know her as well. I just hadn't realized she was on this Council.

Gertrude came to see me on Gomorrah, complaining of symptoms that sounded like REM Sleep Behavior Disorder. People with that condition physically act out their dreams, sometimes by speaking and sometimes by moving their arms and legs. I told Gertrude I couldn't help with that, or anything else physical, because my powers only work inside the dreams. Instead, I advised her about obvious safeguards she could take, like installing a padded floor, removing dangerous objects from reach, and sleeping alone. Something—probably the sleeping alone bit—really upset her, and now it seems like she's been holding a grudge this entire time. At least enough of a grudge to want to speak against me today.

Has she never heard of the whole "shooting the messenger" thing?

"Be careful. This Gertrude has a scary power," Felix whispers in my ear. "Her skin mortifies any tissue it comes into contact with."

That's just great. A gangrene-giver has a grievance with me. Can things get any worse?

"Why don't I explain the charge?" Gertrude offers. When no one argues, she says, "The Defendant has revealed her powers to humans."

I did *what*? When?

There are hushed whispers in the audience.

"Crap, that's like breaking the Mandate," Felix says in the earpiece. "Not good."

I wish he'd stop with the pessimistic commentary. I'd silence the earpiece, but if the Council realizes I have it, I could get Felix into trouble.

"I'm sure whatever happened was an honest mistake." Kit turns herself into a version of me, with an unnaturally innocent expression.

"What *did* you do?" Felix whispers.

I still have no clue. I certainly never revealed anything to any humans. Why would I?

"Why don't we all decide for ourselves?" Gertrude fiddles with a phone.

A moment later, Filth comes into the room rolling a cart holding a 75-inch TV.

"Thank you." Gertrude's smile shows too many teeth, and Filth bows to her before leaving.

Gertrude descends from her seat with feline strides.

At the first row, she pauses next to a hooded figure. "Hekima, do you mind helping with this?"

The hooded figure stands up and reveals his face. His frizzy gray hair and kind, deeply weathered features make him look how I've always pictured my grandfather—not that I know anything about my grandparents. Mom always refused to speak about them.

"That's Dr. Hekima," Felix says. "He's a good guy. I had him for Orientation—a sort of school for the young Cognizant here on Earth."

That makes sense. His grandfatherly looks fit a wise teacher to a T.

Hekima joins Gertrude next to the TV and addresses the crowd in a deep, melodic voice. "Please speak up if you don't want the illusion of immersion."

"Oh," Felix says, "forgot to mention. He's an illusionist."

Another illusionist? Valerian, the guy who hired me for the Bernard job, said he was this type of Cognizant. Illusionists can make you see what they want you to see, creating a sort of virtual reality without the need for any hardware.

A few Councilors raise their hands to indicate that they don't want their minds messed with, but most are okay with it. I keep mine at my side as that will let me see the evidence better—plus I'm not sure if I'm allowed to refuse.

As Gertrude turns the screen toward the people who won't be subjected to Hekima's power, Hekima dramatically raises his arms, as if planning to conduct an orchestra.

Before I can blink, pulsing red energy streams from Hekima's fingers into everyone's heads.

As if switching from one dream environment to another, the meeting hall vanishes, replaced by an art gallery. Only three people are there to enjoy the countless paintings: Kain, Gertrude, and a very familiar human—a painter from my past.

Puck. I'm beginning to have an inkling as to my crime.

Kain's eyes go into glamour mode, and he directs them at the human painter. "You will answer all questions honestly."

"I will," the painter says robotically.

Gertrude points at the wall opposite them. "Why did you paint that?"

"Crap," Felix says.

Crap, indeed. The painting is of me—the way I look in the dream world, with fiery hair.

"This is my dream muse," the painter says. "She appeared in my dream on the night I got the idea to explore a completely new medium. Ever since then—"

Hekima must do his thing, because the gallery is whisked away, replaced by a bedroom I recognize as belonging to the painter. The Enforcers scour the room like crime scene investigators until Filth snatches a single curly brown hair from the carpet and gives it a disgusting sniff.

"That's it for now," Gertrude says as the coliseum

reappears around us. "To clarify, the Enforcers used that to find the dreamwalker."

"Vampires can do that, use DNA to locate someone," Felix explains needlessly in my ear.

"Furthermore," Gertrude continues, "Kain and his team followed her for several weeks. They witnessed her breaking into the homes and apartments of various humans, no doubt revealing her powers to them as well. The Enforcers finally caught her red-handed and brought her here." She looks at Kain. "Isn't that correct?"

He shakes his head. "We have no evidence that she showed herself in the dreams of anyone but the painter. And some of the apartments she broke into belong to fellow Cognizant."

Kit loudly clears her throat. "How is any of this news? We've all heard Bailey's nickname of Freda Krueger." She morphs into the burn victim and horror movie villain that inspired the nickname I dislike. "And we all know of Bailey's reputation as a Cognizant private detective of sorts."

Kain gets an unreadable expression on his face.

"When we need secrets stolen," Kit continues, "we go to her. Obviously, she does her thing by dreamwalking. It's like accusing me of shape-shifting." She demonstrates by morphing into several random people and animals.

Gertrude gives Kit a nasty smile. "If anyone hired the accused to expose herself to humans, we should hold similar hearings for them."

Expose myself? She makes it sound like I was hired to work in a strip club.

I'm unsure of the proper protocol here, but this has gone on long enough. "Maybe I could explain?" Before anyone can say no, I rattle out, "Nobody hired me to show my dream form to that painter or anyone else. I was hired to encourage him to work for a VR company —that's all. Dreamwalking is usually performed while invisible, but I forgot to conceal myself that time. It was an honest mistake. It hasn't happened since, and it won't happen again."

Actually, it almost happened today with Bernard, but they don't need to know that. Everything else I said is absolutely true. Valerian, the illusionist who hired me for Bernard's job, wanted me to "inspire" the painter to create masterpieces in VR. I think Valerian owns a VR company, likely the one where Bernard works.

"We can verify this claim and question the other victims," Kain says.

Gertrude frowns. "It doesn't matter. There's physical evidence of her crime. If she were under the Mandate, it would've activated when she 'forgot' to hide herself in that human's dream—assuming she's telling the truth about that, which I doubt."

"I think we should vote," Kit says. "I'm sure Bailey will be exonerated."

"I agree," Kain says, "and there's something unrelated to this case I want everyone to bear in mind."

Gertrude's frown deepens, but the other Councilors regard Kain with curiosity.

"As you know, we have a very puzzling investigation on our hands," he says, causing hushed murmurs to start again. "And Bailey is a sleuth."

I'm as much a sleuth as I am a ballerina, but I see no need to counter what he's saying if it could help me.

"I don't think anyone should worry about matters unrelated to her crime," Gertrude snaps. "It's time to put this to a vote. If you think the dreamwalker should die, as consistent with our laws regarding the exposure of our powers to humans, please stand up."

Die? Is she kidding me?

My heartbeat skyrockets as the hooded figures rise to their feet one by one.

I'm so pucked.

CHAPTER ELEVEN

EXCEPT THEY DON'T all stand up.

Kit and Kain sit down, and as I scan the room, I realize only a minority of this Council wants me dead.

Whew.

"That settles the matter," Kain says. "Now I move that we vote to task Bailey with our investigation."

"You know," Felix whispers, "I'm getting a feeling that the whole exposure thing was a ruse to get you to comply with the next bit."

He might be right. After dodging execution, I do feel quite ready to do whatever they want. Besides, this might be an opportunity I can't pass up, for Mom's sake. The Council has resources that—

"All for, stand up," Kain says.

Most of the Councilors rise to their feet, including the ones who wanted me dead a second ago. Flip-flop much? Either way, it sounds like I just got some kind of a job thrust at me.

As people begin to leave their seats, I speak up. "Isn't there something you're forgetting?"

"What are you doing?" Felix shouts in my ear.

Everyone looks at me as if my hair has caught fire—something I can't do safely in the waking world.

I fold my arms across my chest and stare them down. "My payment. I don't work for free."

Kain gives a rare smile. "You don't know what we want you to do."

"Whatever it is, I need to get paid for it," I say. "My mother was in an accident. Machines keep her alive, and my jobs barely cover her life support bills. So as payment for this job, I want you to heal her. Not with vampire blood—that didn't work—with an actual healer. Do that, and I'll do whatever it is you want."

Kain doesn't look surprised in the least. He glances at a woman two rows from him, who pulls her hood back to reveal fine features surrounded by glossy black hair.

"That's Isis," Felix says. "She's a healer who recently got a Council seat."

"Solve the case, and I'll help your mother." Isis levels an arrogant look at me. "I hope you realize what such a payment is worth."

Oh, I realize, all right. It would take all the money I've seen in my life multiplied a thousandfold to hire a healer on Gomorrah.

"Let's talk details," Kain says and strides out of the coliseum.

I follow his silent form through the castle and up a

narrow staircase into what must be a tower. The rusty iron hinges screech as he pushes open the massive door, and we enter a circular room with stone walls.

"Hey, your camera just cut out," Felix says worriedly. "Did you—"

"So," I say to Kain, ignoring Felix's technical problems. "What is it you want me to figure out?"

"Before I explain, you should know that this is a delicate matter." Kain leans against the wall and folds his arms across his chest.

Great. Delicate matter, powerful people. What could go wrong? "I keep all my work confidential," I say, eyeing him warily.

"Good. But I still want to highlight how sensitive this situation is." He flashes his fangs, turning his already unattractive face practically ghoulish. "If news of this gets out, I will personally kill you. Slowly."

The threat is delivered in the casual tone I'd use when asking a coworker what time it is. Wow. I thought Kain was on my side, but it seems he only protected me from Filth because he needed me intact for this job.

I raise my chin. "If news of whatever this is gets out, it won't be because I blabbed."

"Fine." His fangs disappear. "Here's the deal. Four members of the Council have died under strange circumstances. At this point, everyone thinks it's murder and that a member of the Council must be responsible."

Felix whistles in my earpiece, reminding me that the secret is already out.

I swallow hard. Someone killed four of the most powerful Cognizant on this world? How the hell am I supposed to solve something like that? I can't even figure out which of my coworkers at the rehab facility keeps eating my leftovers—at least not without invading their dreams.

Oh. He can't mean *that*.

"I'll convince everyone to give you access to their dreams," Kain says, way ahead of me already. "You'll be able to see their memories and figure out the culprit, right?"

"Maybe." I try to keep my voice even. "It's not as straightforward as that. Sometimes I have to work on—"

"Don't worry about the details. Whatever it takes, you'll do it."

"Yes, of course I will," I say, more to hype myself up than to reassure him. "My mom's life depends on it."

"Indeed." His fangs show up again. "And in case that's not motivation enough, your own life depends on it, too." Leaning in, he whispers into my ear, the one without the earbud, "I didn't inform the Council about the full extent of your crimes. Bringing Gomorran technology to this world is forbidden, and as you can imagine, if forced to vote again, especially after your failure, the Council would not let you off so easily."

I back away, my heart rate uneven. Around my wrist, Pom has turned pitch black. "You don't need to threaten me," I say, amazed by how steady my voice is under the circumstances. "I'll do anything to heal my mother."

"All the better," he says. "I just wanted us to be on the same page."

I straighten my spine. "I need the details of the murders and access to everyone's dreams, as well as the authority to interview people and review any records I wish."

"You'll get all that. I'll make the arrangements. Wait here." He disappears from the room with vampiric speed.

Felix clears his throat. "An unsolved murder case must look bad for him, what with being the new head of the Enforcers and all."

I hadn't thought of that. Still, he didn't need to be so—

"Hello, Bailey," comes a smooth, deep male voice from my right. "Given the circumstances, I decided we need to talk."

CHAPTER TWELVE

"WHO'S THAT?" Felix asks in the earpiece.

Great question. I peer intently at the location the voice came from but see no one there.

Then a man materializes in front of me.

And what a man. Tall and broad-shouldered, he's wearing a bespoke suit that hugs his muscled body in all the right places. His face, framed by thick, silky-looking dark hair, is even more impressive. Ocean-blue eyes glint at me from beneath straight black slashes of eyebrows, and his high cheekbones appear to have been carved by a sculptor, along with his chiseled jaw and dimpled chin. Oh, and there's a hint of stubble on that gorgeous face, as if he hadn't shaved this morning.

It's official. He's hotter than Adonis, the most popular uber singer on Gomorrah. Wait—maybe he *is* a celeb. Something about his face does look familiar…

As I study each feature, I catch myself wanting to kiss those firm yet plush lips. Which is beyond insane.

We've just met, and I have huge problems with touching in general, let alone touching that leads to the exchange of bacteria-laden bodily fluids.

Puck. I'm still staring at him. How long is it socially acceptable to stare at someone? Worse yet, my furry wristband has just turned an embarrassing coral pink —the color of sexual arousal.

At least this guy doesn't know that my looft displays my emotions this way, or what each color means.

Hold on. All this time, he's been staring at me just as intently. I've got to say something. Anything.

What comes out is a lame "Hi."

A sensual smile touches those kissable lips. "Hi, Bailey." He extends his hand. "I'm Valerian."

On autopilot, I clasp his palm, noting with some small corner of my mind just how big and warm it is. He squeezes my hand gently, then releases it, his smile widening at my continued dumbstruck silence.

For four straight seconds, I don't reach for the sanitizer—a record of some kind.

Then my common sense kicks in, and I get the bottle out and sterilize my hand, finally processing his introduction.

Valerian. That's the guy who hired me for all those VR-related jobs.

This is what he looks like? Until now, we'd been communicating via encrypted email. If I'd known all the facts, our meetings would've been in person. Maybe even in some romantic, scenic locations, like the shore of that beautiful lake on—

With effort, I tamp down on the inappropriate fantasy forming in my mind and say in as even of a tone as I can manage, "Nice to meet you in person, Valerian. Are you on this Council?"

"I'm not." The way he says it, though, makes it sound like he omitted the word *yet*.

I blink up at him. "Then how did you manage to get into the castle? For that matter, how were you invisible?"

"He was invisible?" Felix asks. "How—"

"Same answer to both." Valerian's sensual lips curve again. "As you know, I'm an illusionist. While you talked to Kain, I gave both of you the illusion of being alone in the room. Same when I came to the castle. I made it so nobody could see me. Oh, and I carry a device that turns off any cameras around me."

My earpiece fills with grumbling. "So that's why I can't see anything. Let's hope the camera comes back on when he leaves."

Ignoring Felix, I process what Valerian has said. When Hekima did his illusionist thing, he shot those energy arcs at everyone's heads. Apparently, that's not the only way that power is used. The reality is much scarier: You may have no idea when an illusionist is working his mojo.

Then something very disappointing occurs to me. Given Valerian's powers, he might not actually look like a sex god. I bet no one looks like this, and certainly not this Valerian guy.

How sad.

The weird part is that he seems equally fascinated with me, his eyes scanning my face as if he plans to draw me later. "I know this will sound like a pickup line," he murmurs, stepping closer, "but I can't shake the feeling that you look familiar. Have we met?"

I catch a pleasant whiff of warm male skin and pine, and my mind fills with images of sunlit forest meadows and long, lazy kisses on a picnic blanket. I swallow to combat the sudden dryness in my throat. "I don't think so, but you look familiar to me, too. Have you ever visited Tranquility? The rehab facility on Gomorrah?" *Or did you make yourself look like a celebrity?* is what I don't ask.

His hypnotic eyes gleam with amusement. "Afraid not. I keep my vices under control."

I'm suddenly dying to know all about those vices, but I force myself to focus. "Based on the jobs you've given me, you're into VR. Maybe you took some video game design classes here on Earth? Or on Gomorrah?"

"I'm self-taught." He looks at his watch, then at the door. "We don't have much time, so I'd like to get to the point."

"Sure." I conceal my irrational disappointment. "What point is that?"

All hints of amusement disappear from his face. "The last job I gave you is very important."

Job, right. That's why he's talking to me. "You're paying a lot for it, so I figured as much," I say, matching his businesslike tone. "Unfortunately, as you can see, I'm in a bit of a predicament right now."

He nods, his gaze somber. "If said predicament interferes with your ability to complete my job, I'd be happy to use my powers to lead you out of this castle."

"Wow," Felix whispers. "He can actually save you."

"I can't leave," I say to them both. "The Council gave me an opportunity I can't pass up."

Valerian cocks his head. "What if I match whatever they offered you?"

"I doubt you can. Besides, they have my DNA, which means they can track me anywhere you take me. I don't really want to spend the rest of my life looking over my shoulder for vampires."

"I see." He frowns, and even that expression looks good on his chiseled face. "So you're saying you're giving up on Bernard?"

"No, I already did the heavy lifting with Bernard. I established a dream link. When night falls, I'll find time to slip inside his dream and finish what I started."

The frown is instantly gone, and I decide I like his face much more without it. "Thank you," he says. "Are you sure you don't want to escape? I'm going to Gomorrah for a couple of days, so I won't be reachable if you change your mind."

"I'm sure. Oh, and there is a way I can reach you, even on another world." I try to make my next question sound as casual as possible. "How do you feel about taking a nap right now?"

He grins, flashing even white teeth. "Nice try, but I don't think I'm ready to let you loose inside my subconscious. We've only just met."

I do my best to ignore the butterflies filling my stomach. "Your call. It could've been fun to be in a dream together." Especially for me. I almost lick my lips at the thought.

"Are you coming on to this guy?" Felix hisses.

Crap, I totally forgot we have a third wheel.

Valerian's grin turns wicked. "We don't need your powers to have fun," he says in a voice like heated molasses as the room around us shimmers and becomes a lush bedroom with an enormous bed swathed in silk sheets and scattered with rose petals.

My pulse spikes as the butterflies start a gunfight in my belly. Is this really happening? Am I about to—

"Alas, we can't today," Valerian says, and to my huge disappointment, both the bed and his gorgeous self disappear.

"Wait!" I look around the empty room. "Why do you even need me? For the Bernard job, I mean? As you just demonstrated, your powers are very similar to mine."

His disembodied voice comes from near the doorframe. "I'm under the Mandate. That heavily limits what I can and can't do with humans. Besides, your way is going to be much better. Dream inspiration is a classic, after all."

"Uh-huh. Are you sure you don't just want someone else to take the risk?"

He doesn't reply. Must've already left.

I sigh, feeling strangely deflated. The idea of "having fun" with Valerian was more than a little appealing, and not just because we'd be able to do it via his powers of illusion or my ability to dreamwalk—and therefore without any exchange of bodily fluids. No, it's him. Something about the guy almost makes me forget the dangers of viruses and bacteria.

Speaking of which—I slather my hands again with sanitizer. What's wrong with me? I talk to a hot guy for two minutes, and I'm ready to risk syphilis? He might not even look the way he appeared to me.

Must be my lack of a sex life catching up with me. I have a complex relationship with my libido. In other people's dreams, I've experienced thousands of orgasmic encounters, both from their memories and their fantasies. In my own dreams, too, I've done whatever I wanted with anyone who took my fancy. Sometimes with many of them at once. In the waking world, however, I've never actually been intimate with anyone.

Despite an entire harem of partners in the dream world, I'm a twenty-six-year-old virgin who's never even kissed a guy.

Hey, that gives me a crazy idea. What if the Brotherhood monks were behind my being snatched by the Enforcers? Maybe whatever deity they worship needs a virgin sacrifice.

Nah. Too convoluted a plan for something like that.

Felix crackles in my ear. "The camera just started working again."

Before I can so much as reply with a thumbs-up, Kain strides back into the room with a thick folder in his hand. "Let's go to your quarters so we can review all this." He waves the folder and turns on his heel.

I have quarters?

I follow, panting to keep up—though for a vampire, he's practically crawling.

We hustle across half the castle to what at one point must've been the dungeon where prisoners were kept before being tortured or worse.

"How dreary," Felix mutters.

That's putting it mildly.

Kain leads me down a corridor that even the rats must find too depressing to frequent. The place smells faintly like fermented sewage, and I have to fight my gag reflex. With a determined expression on his face, Kain makes a sharp right and stops next to a large cell with an iron ring welded to the wall—always a nice little touch. He makes a gentlemanly gesture, ushering me inside.

"You've got to be kidding me," I mutter as I step in.

These are my quarters? Instead of a solid door, there are iron bars, exactly like in a prison cell, and there isn't even a modern toilet. There's just a hole in the floor with murky muck a few feet down, which looks suspiciously like the liquid that was slushing in the moat around the castle. Major eww.

The only thing that makes this place feel like anything other than a prison cell is a new bed, table, and chair. And the fact that the door isn't locked with the rusty padlock that's hanging on the outside. Instead, it actually has a bolt on the inside.

Hekima appears in the corridor behind Kain and peers through the bars disapprovingly. "Are these the best accommodations we can provide? Bailey is our guest, after all."

Kain sets the folder on the table. "You may have a point. This is where we were going to put her if she was found guilty, but she wasn't. I'll see if we can scrounge up something better."

"Please do," Hekima says. "Meanwhile, do you mind if I change the scenery?"

Kain and I shrug.

Hekima shoots his showy arc of energy at our heads, and the cell becomes a fresh-smelling, sunlit meeting room. Only the furniture looks the same.

"Right, then." Kain opens the folder. "Let's get to the murders."

CHAPTER THIRTEEN

INSIDE THE FOLDER, on the top, is a photo of a striking woman.

"She looks like Lara Croft," Felix whispers. "Or looked. Past tense."

"That's Tatum," Kain says somberly. "The first victim."

He flips the page, and I see Tatum's body lying on the roof of one of the castle's towers, an arrow in her heart.

"Why don't I show you what we think happened?" Hekima offers.

More illusions. Why not?

I agree, and an arc of illusionist energy hits my head.

I find myself at the scene of the crime, standing in front of a living Tatum. She smells amazing, which gives me an inkling of her Cognizant type. She takes a joint from her pocket and is beginning to light up when—with a sharp *whoosh*—an arrow pierces her chest.

"Let me slow that last part down," Hekima says after she collapses.

This time, I can see the arrow's flight path. It seems to come from the ground below—an impossible shot.

"When was this?" I ask as the arrow crawls toward the chest of the poor woman.

"Six days ago," comes Kain's disembodied voice. "At four p.m."

"And what can you tell me about her?"

"She was a succubus. The most powerful I'd ever met."

Just as I thought. That yummy smell is unmistakable. "Do you have any idea who would want her dead?"

The arrow begins to penetrate Tatum's breast.

"No one," Hekima says. "Everyone loved her."

"A bit too literally," Kain says. "As you can imagine, she had many lovers."

Right. When one of her kind wants someone, they use their power to make themselves sexually irresistible. This is why I stay as far away from succubi and incubi as possible; they no doubt have countless germs from all those partners, plus they can drain energy from their lovers during intimacy—something that can even lead to death, if they wish it.

No, thanks. I'll take my dream lovers any day of the week.

I turn away before I can get splattered with illusory blood. "Could a lover have killed her? Murders are often committed by people close to the victim. Maybe someone got jealous."

The room becomes normal again—that is, it goes back to its guise as a meeting room.

"As I said, she had many lovers," Kain says. "The pool of suspects is too large."

I examine the photo of her corpse again. "That arrow. Are you sure your recreation of her death is accurate?"

"We consulted experts," Hekima says. "I'm sure."

"But who could make such a shot? There are no elves on this world, so—"

I stop as Kain and Hekima exchange a glance.

"Some elves get plastic surgery to make themselves look more human in order to settle here," Hekima says.

Huh. I didn't know that. "Is there such an elf on the Council?" I ask.

"There is, for sure," Felix whispers excitedly in my ear. "He helped us in a recent conflict."

I'm about to ask some questions, but Kain flips a few pages in his folder and shows me a picture of a thin man.

"Yeah, that's who I meant," Felix says. "Doesn't he look like Tingle from *Zelda*?"

Kain flips the page again to a photo of a broken body sprawled over some rocks—a body that had to be the same individual as in the previous image.

"Oh, crap," Felix whispers. "He's another victim."

"We found Ryan dead just a few hours after we found Tatum," Kain says. "And before you ask, he was the only elf on the Council, and he wasn't merely Tatum's lover. He was her husband."

I rub my temples. I'm only on the second murder victim, and my head already hurts. To focus on something this brain-intensive, I'd need a full night's worth of sleep, something I haven't had in four months. "Is it possible the elf killed the succubus out of jealousy and then killed himself in grief?" I ask. "Humans commit this sort of murder-suicide all the time, don't they?"

"That's what we thought," Kain says, "until the next murder."

"Right," I say, remembering that there were four. I picture the broken body on the rocks. "So you think someone pushed the elf?"

"It seems so," Hekima says.

"Except that makes no sense," Kain says. "Ryan was extremely paranoid. I don't think he'd let an enemy ambush him like that."

"So maybe it was a friend," I say. "Did he have many?"

"One," Kain replies with a scowl.

"Leal?" Hekima asks. "But he—"

"It's feasible he could've done the deed before," Kain says.

Hekima raises his arms. "Do you want me to play out that theory?"

"Please," I say, and Kain nods.

Hekima shoots us with his mojo again, and we find ourselves on top of a cliff with the elf's back to us. A man with wild gray hair dressed in a white lab coat approaches the elf from behind. The elf spins around and aims a drawn bow at the newcomer.

"Leal," he says with a hint of a smile. "You startled me, old friend." He lowers the bow and turns his back to the newcomer. "I come here when I feel unsettled. It's almost—"

The gray-haired dude pushes him over the cliff, and we're back in the meeting room before the elf strikes the rocks.

Kain looks thoughtful. "I don't know about this. Why would Leal kill his closest ally?"

Why indeed? "Maybe I could go into his dream to find out?"

Kain sighs and turns a few pages in his folder. There's a picture of a balding man in a white coat, a dove sitting on his shoulder as if he were a pirate and there were a parrot shortage.

"I don't mean to disrespect the dead," Felix says, "but he totally looks like Dr. Wily from the *Mega Man* games."

Or any mad scientist, for that matter.

"The next image is disturbing," Kain says. "Take a deep breath."

I do as he suggests, and he turns the page.

Puck. The slab of meat in the photo is barely recognizable as a man.

Felix makes a strange wheezing sound. Did he just faint?

I drag my gaze away from the horrible image. "What could do that?" I ask Kain.

"The doves," he says.

I blink at him uncomprehendingly.

"I think he means like in the Alfred Hitchcock movie," Felix says in a thin voice. I guess he didn't faint, after all. "You know, *The Birds?*"

Kain turns to Hekima. "Can you show her a simulation?"

Before I can say *thanks but no thanks*, I see an intact Leal standing in a lab filled with cages of white birds. Without warning, the doves become agitated. One manages to break through the cage, followed by another and another.

Leal looks at the freed birds with no fear. "What spooked you, dears?" he asks in a raspy voice.

This is when a dove dives and pecks him in the eye.

He screams, clutching his eye, but another bird is already diving for his face again. More doves leave their cages and join the attacking horde (or dule, as a group of doves is called). Some of them hurt themselves in the process, but that doesn't seem to stop them.

"Enough!" I snap. "I get it."

Instantly, the blood and gore are replaced by the meeting room.

"Sorry," Hekima says, "I didn't—"

"It's fine." I force a smile, ignoring the nausea

twisting my stomach. "I did need to know what happened."

Kain and Hekima wait as I even out my breathing. And hey, a benefit of not having eaten in a day is that I can't puke—one of my least favorite activities.

"Is there someone on the Council who can control animals?" I ask when my voice is steady enough. "On Gomorrah, we call people who can do that—"

"Gemma." Kain flips a page in the folder.

A long-haired beauty stares at me from the photo. She's dressed in all leather and stands on high heels.

"This one looks like Bayonetta," Felix says, his voice back to normal. "She's this kickass video game witch who—"

Kain flips to the next page, and Felix makes a gagging sound. My stomach roils too. Though arguably not as bad as the prior image, it's still pretty gruesome.

Someone or something literally ripped this woman in half.

"I don't want to see a recreation of this," I tell Hekima before he can do his thing. "It's self-explanatory. Someone very strong pulled her in two different directions."

"Indeed," Kain says. "Gemma's kind are fragile, so unfortunately, we have many Cognizant on the Council with enough strength to do that."

Well, this is going to be fun. "Do you have any idea how any of this ties together?" I ask. Maybe if they—

Kain slams the folder shut. "That's what you're here to find out."

Right, okay. Lucky me. "Did the bird guy—"

"Leal," Kain corrects.

"Right. Did Leal have a grievance with the last lady—"

"Gemma," Kain provides.

"Yes, Gemma. Did Leal—"

"Leal only had one friend—Ryan, the elf," Hekima says, his grandfatherly features wreathed in pity. "Nobody on the Council liked him much, except maybe Kain and the other vampires."

"Oh?"

"I'd go as far as to say I considered Leal a friend," Kain says. "Or at least an ally."

"But why does everyone else not like the guy?" I resist the temptation to open the folder and look at the man in question.

"His powers," Kain says. With a sharp-edged smile, he adds, "He was a dreamwalker."

Another dreamwalker? I glare at Kain. "Why are you only telling me about that now?"

The vampire shrugs. "When was I supposed to tell you? Rumor has it, he had blackmail material on all the other members of the Council. They thought he'd gathered it in their dreams."

The ache in my temples intensifies. "So you're telling me he might've been killed for snooping around people's dreams?"

"It's feasible," Hekima says gently.

I take a deep breath and try not to look at Pom, who's rapidly turning black on my wrist. "But that's exactly what you're asking me to do. What's to stop them from wanting to kill *me*?"

Kain waves dismissively. "You should worry about the murderer. That's who'll really want to kill you—if you're any good."

"Thanks. That makes me feel so much better."

Kain smirks. "If I were you, I'd do my best *not* to find any compromising information inside the Councilors' heads."

I cup my hands over my eyes, the enormity of the task hitting me like a punch to the face.

"Why don't you do your thing with those Council members who have more reason to be under suspicion?" Hekima suggests. "Anyone strong."

I lower my hands. "Sure, I'll start with the ones who can rip me in half. I feel safer already."

"It's not a bad idea," Kain says. "Still, I want you to set up a dream link to everyone on the Council. Even me."

I take another breath, trying to think like the detective I'm not. "This Leal, did he leave any notes? As you said, he knew secrets about the Council. Maybe he wrote them down somewhere."

And maybe, just maybe, he also wrote something about the art of dreamwalking itself. I've never met any dreamwalkers besides Mom—we're pretty scarce on Gomorrah—and between her diligently avoiding the topic of our abilities and the fact that I never received any formal training in how to use my powers, there's a lot I don't know about my own kind.

"I'll take you to his lab," Kain says, his expression unreadable.

Hekima withdraws his illusion, and the dreary cell room comes back—as does the stench.

"Let me know if I can help any further," Hekima tells Kain. "And Bailey, if you need to know anything about the history of the Council or anything else, I'm here for you."

Felix chuckles. "Good old Hekima. He'll look for any excuse to run an Orientation."

I smile at the elderly illusionist. "Thank you. I'll find you if I need that."

Hekima's dark eyes twinkle. "I guess I'll see you tonight in my dreams."

"Not if I'm just setting up a connection," I say.

Hekima leaves, and Kain picks up the folder and strides out.

I sprint to keep up with him.

A few winding corridors later, we arrive at the lab I saw in Hekima's recreation of the grisly bird attack. Though someone has cleaned up, I can picture the bloody corpse all too easily. What's worse is that the doves are here now, roosting in the same cages they broke out of to murder their caretaker. And the smell emanating from those cages...

"Creepy," Felix remarks just as Kain says, "I'm going to leave you to it. Be back in an hour."

Hundreds of saffron-colored eyes stare at me hungrily from the cages. Before I can beg Kain not to leave me alone with the stinky killer birds, he disappears, closing the door behind him.

As if that's what they had been waiting for all along, the dule of murderous feathered beasts begins to coo menacingly.

CHAPTER FOURTEEN

THE COOING SWELLS to fill the room, mimicking the growing knot in my throat. But the birds don't attack me. They don't even try to escape from their cages. They just coo and eat grain from their feeders, and on occasion, I hear a wet splatter as one of them poops.

Serious eww.

Despite the stench choking my nostrils, the death-by-birds-inspired adrenaline begins to leave my system. And as it does, my eyes get gritty, my lids grow heavy, and a yawn escapes my mouth. Oh yeah, I'm starting to feel like someone who hasn't slept for four months.

I'd give a lot of money to take a nap right now. Then again, needing money is how I ended up so sleep deprived in the first place.

There's no time to sleep, though, no matter how I feel, and it's too soon to take another dose of my "medicine." So I do the next best thing, an exercise called *bellows breath*. I inhale deeply and rapidly for a short while, as if hyperventilating. Bellows breath can give a little burst of energy in a pinch, and I'm certainly in a pinch.

It helps a little. Instead of a ten out of ten on the horribleness scale, I only feel like a good, solid nine.

"You okay?" Felix asks softly.

I take out my phone and furtively text, *Never been better. Time to get back to my investigation.*

"You can just talk out loud," he says. "I doubt Leal's lab has any listening devices."

You sure? I text.

"Positive."

"All right," I say out loud. Even if someone *is* listening, they'll probably just think I'm crazy.

I look around, taking in the surreal paintings on the walls around me.

Stinky birds aside, this lab clearly belonged to a dreamwalker.

"Very cool," Felix says as I walk over to stand before a famous painting by Salvador Dalí—*Dream Caused by the Flight of a Bee around a Pomegranate a Second before Awakening.* "Makes me wonder what it would've been like to walk in the artist's dreams."

"Maybe Leal did just that," I say as I turn to see a painting depicting a staircase that loops in a circle instead of going up or down. Such structures can't exist in the real world, but they can exist in art and dreams. In fact, I have stairs similar to these in my own dream palace.

"That's M.C. Escher," Felix says needlessly. "That piece is called *Ascending and Descending*."

I force myself to ignore the cool art and search for anything relevant to the case. But there are no notes on the desk, no diary on the bookshelf, nothing else I can use. If the doves were parrots, I could ask them to repeat something, but as is, this is leading nowhere.

I study the way the art is laid out, using my dreamwalker's eye for detail.

Aha. Every painting is hung flush with the wall, except one. *Ascending and Descending* is not. I pull the heavy frame away from the wall and peer at the back. Score. There's a pocket here, and something inside it.

Fishing out the small device, I examine it carefully.

"Gomorran comms," Felix says, confirming my guess.

"Must be generations old." I turn the clunky little thing in my hands. "My unit was ancient, and it was way sleeker."

"Even an old comms device probably has a petabyte of data and more processing power than any supercomputer on this world," Felix says reverently. "Be careful with that."

"Otherland tech is totally forbidden," I say in my best imitation of Kain. In my normal voice, I add, "Unless you're on the Council, that is."

"They're hypocrites," Felix says. "At least the dreamwalker hid the device. Some of the other Councilors break their own rules a lot more openly."

Feeling a yawn coming on, I shake my head. "Back

to the investigation. Let's get into this thing." I bring the comms device closer to the camera. "This is your chance to show off your powers, in case that's not obvious."

He sighs. "I can't."

"What?" I tap the earpiece as if that's going to change his answer.

"I mean, I could, but it would have to be in person. The device is not connected to the internet and—"

"You can't be here in person." I twirl around to remind him where I am. "Maybe I can ask them to take me to you? But no, then they'd know about you."

"Yeah, I'd rather not be pulled into this. But there *is* a way I can get into the castle in person without much fuss. Ariel's cousin's best friend's daughter is having her Mandate ceremony there in a couple of days."

"Oh? What does that have to do with you?"

"Mandate ceremonies are a big deal. Everyone attends to show support, so it won't be suspicious if I tag along with Ariel."

"I hope I'm alive by then," I say dubiously.

"Well… maybe I can get some of the data from the cache right now. But we risk damaging the device."

"Do it then—but carefully." I don't think I have a couple of days to dick around.

"I'll do my best. Put the comms on top of your phone."

I set my Earth phone on the desk and place the comms device on top.

"Now be quiet," he says.

I watch the device for any sign of *something*. Just as I'm about to ask Felix what gives, a strange magenta energy snakes from the phone into the comms unit.

"Got something," he crows. "A few excerpts from some kind of diary. Emailing them to you now."

I pocket the device and open the first email from Felix on my phone.

Roger came back with the newest batch of the medicine today. The bird I tested it on fell asleep instantly, and stayed asleep for six hours, three hours longer than with the prior formulation. But just like before, it died instead of waking up. Still, at only $10 per dove, this provides unlimited access to the dream world. Next time, I'll have him—

The passage ends there.

"That's it?" I ask Felix. "Any chance to see what came before or after this excerpt?"

"No, but there's another piece when you're ready."

"In a second," I say and start searching the room again.

But no matter how hard I try, I find no sign of the strange drug described in the email.

"Why would he kill birds by making them dream?" Felix asks as I finish looking through a nearby desk.

"To enter the dream world without falling asleep." I look behind yet another painting—to no avail. "I use Pom for that. I guess this Leal guy found his own method."

"By killing the poor doves," Felix says disapprovingly.

"Right." I cast an uneasy glance at the cooing

creatures. "They got their revenge in the end, didn't they?"

"I guess. Sending you the other bit of text I found in the cache."

I check behind the last painting. Nothing. Oh, well.

I open my email.

Another werewolf, another failure. The inner wolf and the man attacked me together yet again, and I found them too hard to fight off. Lost my powers for the day as a result. Werewolves are proving to be the most difficult of all Cognizant to dreamwalk in. Eduardo isn't making it easy, either. He forbade his pack from allowing me to continue this research. The son of a bitch likes me powerless against him. I'll have to master the multibody technique if I'm to succeed. That way, one of my consciousnesses can attack the wolf while the other deals with the man. Alas, I fail at this too. Maybe if—

Crap, cut short again. I tap the earpiece. "Hey, I want to read the rest of that."

"Sorry, there's only one more tidbit left, and it's from a different part of the diary."

"Send it to me."

"One sec. I want to understand what he meant by what you just read."

"Isn't it obvious? Werewolves are a problem when it comes to dreamwalking. I've heard of this sort of thing with some other types of Cognizant. They say you can never sneak into the dreams of gnomes, for instance, not unless they let you in."

"Right, that part was more or less clear," Felix says.

"But I don't get the part about losing his powers and the multibody thing."

I reread the message. "I think he meant that he had to use his dreamwalking power so much inside the werewolf's dream that he ran out of juice. There's a limit to how much dreamwalking one can do in a day. He must've reached that limit."

"And the multibody bit?"

I read the text once more. "Sounds like he's talking about having two bodies in the dream world that can simultaneously think and feel. If so, that's very intriguing and not something I've ever tried to do. I can sort of leave my body and reenter it, but that's not the same. I'm going to have to give this a shot one day."

"How trippy," Felix says. "I can't imagine what it would be like to be in two places at once, even in a dream."

"Logic takes a vacation in the dream world, that's for sure. Now stop stalling and send me the next piece of this diary or whatever."

He types something so loudly I can hear it. "Done."

I pull up the email.

Any dream can be hidden behind the black window—my own, a dream of another subject, or the dream of the subject herself. The remarkable thing is that when a dream is a memory of the subject, the memory itself becomes deeply suppressed. She has no recollection of the events at all. More fascinating still is that the subject doesn't recover her memory when I reenter the black window. The breaking of the black window is the only way the subject gets to experience the events locked behind it. If it's her memory, she recovers them, but if it's an implanted dream, she dismisses it as a figment of her—

It cuts off.

Disappointed, I reread what is there. "You sure there was nothing more about this?"

"No, why?" Felix asks. "Does it make sense to you?"

"Vaguely." I greedily scan every sentence for clues. "Whatever this black window is, it seems to let you erase people's painful memories. I've never heard of that."

"That's *Eternal Sunshine of the Spotless Mind* kind of shit." Felix's voice is full of awe. "Makes sense, though —you do deal with the subconscious. Still, scary."

"Yeah." I pocket my phone. "And the bit about hiding his own or other people's dreams inside someone else's dreamscape—that's just as crazy. It would give dreamwalkers a way to hide information so that only another dreamwalker could find it."

"Not the best method," Felix says. "What if the person who has information hidden inside their dreams dies?"

We both fall silent. It's obvious he's thinking what I'm thinking: Could Leal have hidden something inside the dreams of the other victims, something that someone killed them to hide? But if so, who?

I head for the door. "I think I'd better get more information to work with." Another yawn threatens as I walk, and I instinctively pat the vial of vampire blood in my pocket.

Wait a second. It's too soon for another hit, so why am I even thinking about this? Is this a craving? The start of an addiction?

I'd better keep a close eye on this.

Performing the bellows breath technique to wake myself a little, I reach for the door knob.

What the hell? It's locked.

Did Kain do that?

That's just great. Now I need to do the opposite of bellows breath to fight my panic.

"He said he'd be back in an hour," Felix chimes in, as if reading my mind. "You don't have to wait long."

"Still." I eye the cooing doves. "These cannibals have a taste for dreamwalker flesh. We're probably delicious."

"Cannibal doves would eat other doves, not people."

"Thanks, Felix, that really puts my mind at ease." Before he can reply, I say, "In any case, the good thing about having Pom on my wrist is that I'm always ready to go into the dream world. Since I'm stuck here, I'm going to test out some of the things the dead dreamwalker was talking about."

Raising my hand so that Felix can see, I touch Pom's fur and slip into a trance.

CHAPTER FIFTEEN

THE YUMMY SCENT of manna fills my nostrils as I appear in the lobby of my dream palace.

Pom pops up next to me. "I've missed you."

I grin at him. "We're attached, you know. But yes, I've missed you too."

Pom turns purple, and his ears flap in a sort of happy dance.

I tell him an edited version of the events that have transpired so far, which boils down to getting "hired" to solve a case for the New York Council.

When I get to the part about Valerian, he says, "I can tell if he really looks the way you think. I can see through any illusion."

I look my furry friend up and down, which doesn't take long, given his small stature. "How?"

He floats up to my eye level. "I see through your eyes when I'm awake. Pretty sure the illusionist would have to target *me* with his powers to make us both see the same thing."

"See through my eyes, right. Perfectly normal behavior for a symbiont. Not something a parasite would do at all."

"Indeed," he says, oblivious to my sarcasm. "And it can be useful."

I snort. "Not really. You said you have to be awake. You're almost never awake."

His ears turn the color of carrots. "But you can wake me up."

"I can? How?"

"By mentally shouting for me." A lightbulb appears above his head. "Why don't you wake up and try it right now?"

Intrigued, I exit the dream world and open my eyes back at the lab.

Pom, I mentally shout. *Pom, wake up!*

Then I look at my wrist.

The way to tell if he's awake is that his fur will start to express his emotions instead of mine. Oh, and on a rare occasion, he'll deign to speak as a voice in my head.

The fur is light orange, which could be his curiosity or mine. There's not a peep from him in my mind.

Pom! Pom, wake up.

No reaction.

I touch his fur and draw myself back into the dream world.

"What happened?" he asks when I reappear in the palace. "You didn't do it."

"I shouted from the top of my brain like a lunatic." I shake my head. "I don't know, Pom. I don't think you can be roused."

He huffs. "With all that lack of sleep, your mind is just too muddy."

"Sure, blame it on me."

He gives me a furry frown. "It's a wonder you can function at all."

I just barely hold back an eye roll. "You know what? Let me tell you the rest of it." I proceed to explain about the bits of dreamwalker diary—my reason for coming here in the first place.

"Do you have a link to a werewolf to see this inner wolf business?" he asks when I'm done.

"Afraid not. I've never worked with their kind. I guess I'll find out what they're like when I have to deal with the werewolf on this Council."

The tips of his ears darken. "Remind me not to join you when you do. Sounds scary."

"Deal." I scratch the top of his furry head until his ears turn purple. "Now I'm going to attempt the whole 'double consciousness' thing."

"I'll watch." Flying up a few feet, he stares down at me intently—an act that makes him look borderline freakish, thanks to his tea-saucer-sized eyes.

I exit my body, becoming a dream ghost, and create an exact duplicate of that body. So far, so good. Next, I attempt to return to both bodies at the same time. I end up in only one—the original. The second body just stands there like a mannequin.

I exit my body again, give the two Baileys fiery hair, and will myself to enter both.

Nope. Still end up in just one.

Pom zooms down and pokes the second body with a toe. "Maybe you need to turn this into one of those dream characters you like to have sex with?"

"Pom!" I give him a menacing glare. "How many times do I have to tell you that's private?"

He turns beet red. "You didn't ask me not to spy on you every time. I assumed it was okay."

Great. First, I'd forgotten to make myself invisible when dreamwalking in humans, and now it turns out I'd also forgotten to ask Pom for privacy during my R & R. Must be the sleep deprivation.

"Let me try your idea," I say and replace the body in front of us with a dream character of me, something I've never tried before.

"Hello," the new me says sensually. "How can I be of service?"

Pom looks between me and my creation. "Do they all want to have sex?"

I shrug. "They're just like any person you meet in a dream."

"What we dream characters say and do is driven by the dreamer's subconscious," my other self says. "That's how I know she's often wondered about *this*." Leaping at me, she plants a wet kiss on my lips.

"Hey!" I push her away. "Not in front of Pom."

She smirks. "I'll stop if you admit it."

"Fine. Guilty as charged. I *have* thought about it. You. Doing things with myself. But I've never done it because it seems a bit narcissistic."

She strikes a centerfold pose. "Anyone you have sex with in this dream world is essentially me. I may pretend to be them, but we both know it's really you, or a part of you, pulling the strings."

This is not going as I'd anticipated. "Just stay still," I command her.

She freezes in a comical pose. I focus to see if my consciousness is in both of us.

Nope.

I float out of my body and attempt to land back in both bodies.

Another fail.

I dismiss the second me. "Looks like I'm not powerful enough to pull off the double consciousness."

"Or you might be too sleep deprived to use your power properly," Pom suggests helpfully, flitting over to sit on my shoulder. "It's like I told you. It's been more than four months since—"

"You're like a nagging husband." I grab his furry body and hold him in front of my face. "I can't raise enough money for Mom's bills if I waste time sleeping. Now I also need to solve this case ASAP."

His lavender eyes are unblinking. "So you're not avoiding sleep because you're afraid of bad dreams?"

Ugh. Who died and made Pom my therapist?

"Remember that privacy thing we talked about a minute ago?"

His shoulders slump.

"Yeah, you guessed it." I set him down. "Can I please get some for the next few minutes?"

"If you insist," he says glumly.

"I insist. And you must promise not to spy. I mean it."

"I pinky swear." He extends a three-fingered paw.

Since every digit is the same, I guess the rightmost to be the pinky and solemnly shake it to seal the deal. "Now scram."

He performs the slowest Cheshire Cat disappearance ever.

When I'm sure he's gone, I change my surroundings to my favorite bedroom in the palace and let my mind drift to Valerian. Even if his looks were to impress me, they *were* impressive. Visualizing him is easy; I guess his mouthwateringly hot face is burned into my imagination.

Without further ado, I make a dream version of Valerian appear in front of me, dressed in the same suit as in the real world.

"Hi, gorgeous," Dream Valerian drawls. "Miss me already?"

"Shut up." I try to keep my voice steady. "You know what I want."

He grins wickedly, and unbuttoning the top button of his shirt, he comes toward me. Even though I'm in the dream world and he's a simulation of what was likely an illusion, my body's response feels quite realistic—down to every detail.

This will be fun.

Even if the real Valerian doesn't look this way, I owe him for inspiring this dream design.

Moving with predatory grace, Dream Valerian closes the distance between us and kisses me. His sensual lips are as soft as I imagined. I melt in his arms, feeling his—

"Bailey," Felix's voice booms from all over. "The door."

Seriously? I had no idea Felix was such a cockblocker.

"The investigation, remember?" Felix shouts from the outside world. "Someone's here."

"Fine," I growl, and leaving a disappointed Dream Valerian, I return to the waking world.

The cooing of the cannibal birds is back, as is the stomach-turning smell of their cages.

I open my eyes. The door is already open, and Kit is standing much too close to me, a look of curiosity on her face.

I step back awkwardly. "Hi."

"I'm here to take over for Kain for a bit," she says, turning into him. "Did I come at a bad time?"

I plaster a smile on my face. "It's fine. I was waiting to get out of here."

"To do what?" she asks in Kain's voice.

"I want to interview the strongest members of the Council. Anyone able to rip a person in half."

"I see." Kit morphs back into her anime character self. "Who would you like to start with?"

I prepare to watch her reaction. "You."

Her face reveals nothing.

"With your power, you could turn into an orc and have its strength, right?"

She morphs into a giant green orc—a muscle-bound creature that Earthlings might confuse for the Hulk with tusks. "I'm a suspect?" she booms.

Being next to something this big activates primal fear in my amygdala, so all I can do is bob my head.

"Okay then," Orc Kit growls and smashes a fist into the door. The heavy wood shatters into tiny pieces, answering my question about her strength. The birds stop cooing and blink at the orc with panic in their cannibalistic eyes.

I know what they're thinking: *We're about to die.*

Then again, they might be thinking how delicious my remains will be.

"Now," Kit growls, taking a menacing step toward me. "Let's talk."

CHAPTER SIXTEEN

MY BREATHING SPEEDS UP.

Am I a victim of my own success? The first person I formally question turns out to be the culprit?

It could be. Kit could've turned into Leal, the dreamwalker, to get close enough to push Ryan, the elf, off the cliff. She could've turned into a bird, pecked Leal to death, and opened the cages to blame it on the doves. And she's just proven that she could've turned into an orc to rip Gemma, the animal controller, in half. The only part I'm not clear about is how she could've shot Tatum, the succubus, with an arrow from so far away—but perhaps she'd turned into an elf and got their perfect marksmanship?

But if Kit is the killer, why did she root for me at the trial? Reverse psychology, maybe?

One thing's for sure: If she kills me now, it will prove I'm right.

I back away. As much as I love to be right, this is too

high a price. Maybe I can still run? She's blocking the door, but—

Instead of lunging forward and ripping me to shreds, Kit transforms back into her tiny round-cheeked self. "I only get the physical qualities of whatever I turn into, not the powers."

Does this mean she isn't going to kill me? That's good. Now if only my racing heart would chillax.

"Is elven marksmanship a power?" I ask warily. "Or is that like orc strength, something you develop by having the right body?"

"That's a great question." She turns herself into a female elf. "Do you have a bow and arrow?"

I pantomime patting my pockets. "Let me just pull out the bow and arrow I carry on me at all times. It's right next to my sword and ax."

"Don't be mean." Elf Kit walks past me and sits on a chair, seductively crossing her legs. "As flattered as I am to be a suspect, why would I want to kill those four? Especially Tatum."

I take a seat across from her. "Why especially Tatum?"

"She was the best lover I'd ever had," Kit says wistfully and turns into Tatum, but without the signature succubus scent.

"Kit's a sex addict," Felix chimes in. "No surprise there."

I know that; it's the reason she was in rehab when we met. How does Felix know, though?

Hmm, maybe I don't want to know the details.

Kit shifts back into herself, and her expression turns unusually fierce. "Killing Tatum was an atrocity akin to destroying an irreplaceable work of art. When I find out who did it, I won't just kill them—I'll turn into a drekavac to do it."

I suppress an instinctive shudder. Drekavacs are horrifying creatures that are said to kill victims through unspeakable pain. They're even scarier than pucks.

"I don't think she's bluffing," Felix whispers. "She's killed someone that way before. Someone who deserved it, but still."

So Kit *can* torture-kill if she feels like it. She's looking more innocent by the second. *Not.*

"Can you please tell me where you were and what you were doing at the time of the murders?" I ask in as steady of a voice as I can manage. "Kain said Tatum died six days ago, at—"

"I know when every one of the victims died." Kit's face darkens further. "We all do. When Tatum died, I was having sex."

I blink.

"Not with Tatum, obviously." She turns into a blond bombshell. "I got embroiled with Lola two weeks ago and only wrenched myself away from her the other day."

"Lola's a nymph who's an enabler for her," Felix whispers.

I debate muting him again; he keeps telling me things I already know.

Refocusing on Kit, I ask, "What were you doing when the elf—"

"Lola. In every case." She flashes back to her normal self. "As you well know, when Lola and I get together, things can spiral a bit out of control."

A bit out of control? Sure, we'll call it that. I saw some of Kit's dreams featuring Lola when she was in rehab. To me, it seemed like Kit wasn't the one with the addiction—Lola was. That, or being insatiable is part of Lola's nature. The word *nymph* is the root of *nymphomaniac*, after all.

"Can you give me some details?" I ask as Felix uncomfortably clears his throat. "Was there anything memorable about those lovemaking sessions? What did the room look like?"

When Kit smiles at me in an overly friendly way, I also clear my throat, adding, "It's for dreamwalking."

She tells me about the rooms they used; then, with relish, she details the positions she and Lola got into, which toys went into which orifices, how many orgasms each of them had, and how often she changed shape into something or someone Lola felt like having sex with—as well as how many phalluses each of those forms had. Though Felix usually only faints at the sight of blood, he's so deathly silent in my earpiece that I wonder if Kit's details have knocked him clean out.

Pulling out my phone, I make a few notes to avoid forgetting anything, as unlikely as that seems. "I'll have to check all this in your dreams," I tell Kit when I'm done. "But if you were with Lola the way you say, you're not guilty."

"Great." She stands up. "Now who do you want to interview next?"

"Who else is strong enough?"

She turns into Kain, hooked nose and all. "An old vampire?"

"You suspect him?" I glance furtively at the door.

She turns back into herself. "I'm just telling you who's strong."

"But still, would Kain be working so hard to solve this case if he's the culprit?"

"Cute." She turns into me—a well-rested version, without bags under my eyes. "You're assuming that hiring you is the same as 'working hard to solve this case.'"

I narrow my eyes at her.

"Don't be mad." She turns back into her usual self. "You're an amazing therapist, don't get me wrong, and you can surely steal secrets when you try. But since when are you a detective?"

Up yours, lady. "You yourself called me a detective at the trial."

She shrugs. "I was trying to save your life. If Kain really wanted a detective, he could glamour a human one or find someone on—"

"But I can tell when people lie to me. I can go into dreams and compare stories with memories."

"There are more direct ways to figure out if

someone is lying," Kit says. "I'd say hiring you isn't that."

She's probably talking about the man I playfully call Bowser, a member of the Council who's currently on vacation. He simply *knows*, without a doubt, if someone is telling him the truth. If he were here, the case would be as simple as having him ask everyone, "Was it you?"

I wonder if that's why the killer chose to strike now, with Bowser away indefinitely. It's his or her only chance to get away with it.

"Let's see if Kain lets me dreamwalk in him," I say. "As a vampire, he doesn't need to sleep, so it would have to be voluntary."

"Good thinking." Kit turns into a giant, albeit a small one, and says in a voice deep enough to sing death metal, "Another strong person is obviously Colton."

"Who totally looks like the giants from the *Skyrim* game," Felix says conspiratorially.

"Who else?" I ask.

"There's Eduardo." Kit turns into a shaggy-haired man not much smaller than the giant, who then morphs into a huge wolf.

"I think Eduardo looks like Donkey Kong," Felix chimes in. "But never mention this to him, or I'm dead."

Sure, I was totally about to walk up to a werewolf and tell him he looks like a video game gorilla. I'm *that* suicidal. "Okay, who else?"

Kit transforms back into herself. "Does it have to be physical strength?"

"What do you mean?"

She turns into a striking black-haired woman with thick dark eyebrows, a small hoop in her right nostril, and silver studs in the upper and lower lips. "Nina isn't physically strong, per se," she says in a melodic voice that I assume belongs to Nina. "But her telekinesis is so strong she could use that to rip someone in half."

Oh, a telekinetic too. Fun. "I'd like to speak to her as well. Who else could rip someone apart?"

"No one I can think of," Kit says.

I stand up. "Then let's start with Kain, Colton, Eduardo, and Nina."

"Sure." Kit assumes her big-eyed, overly cute anime guise and dashes for the door.

I follow her through a couple of corridors. When we reach a massive door, her phone rings.

She pulls it out. "Hello?" She listens for a few seconds, but I can't hear the other side. "Sure, I'll get the usual. If they have sashimi-grade salmon, five pounds."

"Someone's hungry," Felix mutters. "Or, like me, has a cat with exquisite taste."

Kit listens for another second. "Yep, she's with me." She covers the phone. "Kain sent Firth shopping. Do you need anything?"

I ask for a case of bananas, six gallons of distilled water, a dozen bottles of hand sanitizer, and—just to mess with Filth—every feminine hygiene product I can think of, plus laxatives and adult diapers.

Kit doesn't blink an eye as she repeats my list to Filth. Sadly, I can't hear if he complains.

I sneak out my phone and text Felix:

See if you can hack into the store camera to record Firth buying all that stuff. Bonus points if the adult diapers don't scan, so the clerk has to look up the price manually.

He chokes with laughter. "I'll try."

Kit hangs up. "I think I know why you requested everything except the bananas." She turns into a monkey and scratches her head with her foot before transforming back into herself.

Felix groans. "I can't believe she just walked into *that* lecture. I'm going to put you on mute."

"If you must know," I tell Kit, "it's one of the very few things I feel safe eating on this world. You can carefully peel bananas without touching the inside. Even if the outside is crawling with salmonella, you can be safe."

Kit's eyes widen. "Really?"

I'm unable to resist the opening. "The food industry here on Earth is an abomination. Did you know there's human DNA in hotdogs? Or that the United States FDA allows maggots, rodent hair, cigarette butts, and mold in food? Did you realize that milk is allowed to have pus and blood in it, or that every meat you can think of has fecal—"

"Stop, please." Kit makes her ears disappear and reappear. "I don't want to end up eating bananas for the rest of my life."

"Sorry. Do you want to know what the sanitizer's for?"

She rolls her eyes. "That's pretty clear. I assume the other stuff is a prank on Firth?"

"That obvious?"

She assumes Filth's weasely visage. "You know how many jokes feature a vampire and a tampon?"

I grin. "You should tell me some. But only after I solve this case."

"Right." She becomes herself and knocks on the huge wooden door in front of us.

The giant—Colton—opens up. Unsurprisingly, he looks just like Kit's impersonation of him, except he's wearing an apron.

"I have a brisket in the oven," he booms. "Is this going to take long?"

Felix snorts. "Cue the banana rant."

I surreptitiously flick the earbud to hopefully deafen Felix. "Not long. But we can do this later."

"No, come in." The giant opens the door wider.

I step in but stay vigilant about touching anything that he could've contaminated during food prep. The aroma of fried animal flesh is unmistakable.

"Sit," he urges as we enter a surprisingly modern kitchen—well, modern for Earth. Given the medieval ambiance of the castle, I was half expecting to see some unfortunate pig's head on a spittle over a fire. Instead, there are white quartz countertops, stainless steel appliances, and a sleek table with backless chairs that appear to be sized for a giant. And, I guess, a brisket in the oven.

I clutch the sanitizer in my pocket for comfort. "I'll stand, thanks."

"Suit yourself." He plunks down in one of the chairs, making it creak under his weight. "What did you want to know?"

"It all boils down to one question," I say, eager to escape the unsanitary environment as quickly as possible. "What were you doing at the time Gemma was ripped apart?"

He frowns deeply. "You think I'd—"

"She has to ask everyone," Kit says. "Even me."

He lets out a resigned sigh. "I was herding the goats."

I shift my gaze from him to Kit, who turns into one of the puckish creatures and bleats.

Colton gives her a chiding look. "Goats keep the shrubs around the mountain at bay, give the monks a source of milk and cheese, and provide everyone with occasional mutton."

"Milk, cheese, mutton—another chance for the banana rant," Felix murmurs.

If I deigned to acknowledge his existence, I'd tell him that free-roaming goat products feel way safer to me than germ-infested industrial farm food, at least as far as *Salmonella* and *E. coli* go.

"What I really need are some details," I tell Colton. "Like what the sky was like or in what formation the goats stood—anything that made that afternoon memorable."

"Sure." He tells me that the day was foggy, and that a bunch of mushrooms had sprouted on the nearby hill. As he keeps going, I take notes on my phone.

"Thank you," I say when he's done. "That's all we needed."

"You sure you don't want to taste—"

"We shouldn't keep Nina waiting. Maybe some other time."

Kit looks at the oven longingly. I carefully elbow her. She turns into a monkey—no doubt a dig at my banana eating—and scampers out of the giant's lair with me literally on her tail. She leads me through more corridors to a door as big as the one that led to Colton's abode. Becoming herself again, she presses the doorbell.

A bloodcurdling wolf howl emanates from behind the door.

CHAPTER SEVENTEEN

"I KNOW," Kit says when she sees how white I've turned. "Eduardo's door chime takes getting used to."

"That was a chime?" Felix whispers. "It sounded like someone getting murdered."

The door opens on a tall, shaggy-haired man with intent lupine eyes. He also looks like Kit's impersonation of him—and like Donkey Kong, as Felix mentioned, only dressed in a bespoke suit.

"I was just on my way out," he growls. "What's this about?"

The guy is so intense I can't help but take a step back. "Do you have a minute? I'm interviewing everyone for the investigation."

He looks at his Jaeger-LeCoultre watch. "You have two minutes."

"Where were you when Gemma died?" I blurt. "Tell me in as much detail as you can."

His eyes narrow. "I was hunting with my pack. It

was foggy. We took down a buck with a broken antler. Is that detailed enough?"

"It is, thank—"

"Then get out of my way." He moves forward.

"Just one second," Kit says, staying put. "Where are you going in such a hurry?"

He stares at Kit the way The Big Bad Wolf must've looked at Little Red Riding Hood. I gulp. Werewolves on Gomorrah are notorious for their bad temper, and Eduardo doesn't strike me as a particularly zen member of his kind.

Without blinking an eye, Kit shifts into an orc.

"Pack business," he growls. "Now move."

"He's the alpha of said pack," Felix whispers more quietly than usual. "I'd obey."

I pointedly pull on Kit's sleeve. "Again, thanks. Kit, we have more people to interview."

"Have fun." Orc Kit turns back into herself and steps leisurely out of his way.

The next door Kit leads me to is no more than a large slab of rock. I see no handle or hinges. To the side on the wall is a doorbell with a camera, which Kit presses.

"Yes?" calls the melodic voice Kit simulated earlier. "What do you want?"

"Bailey is here to interview you," Kit says. "It's to help with the investigation. I'm sure you don't mind."

In reply, the giant stone slides up.

Nina looks just as Kit showed me earlier, only dressed in a black leather jacket and jeans. She's gesturing at the stone slab with her hand, a look of concentration on her striking face.

Of course—she opened the door using telekinesis.

"Come in." She waves us in with her free hand.

Kit waltzes in, but I hesitate as Pom turns black on my wrist. If Nina stops holding up that rock with her power, whoever is under it at the time will turn into a pancake.

Nina frowns. "Come on. I won't harm you."

Puck. If she didn't want to squish me before, she might after this perceived slight. "I didn't mean to imply you'd do it on purpose. It's just such a big stone, and—"

"If I wanted to kill you, I could make it fly *at* you." The stone rises another foot off the floor, then starts hovering in my direction.

"Fine." I hurry through the doorway. "Thanks for not dropping it."

Not dignifying that with a reply, Nina lowers the slab into place and leads us into her living room, where she gestures for us to sit on what looks like an IKEA futon. In general, her décor appears to be of minimalist persuasion, with a sort of New Age vibe.

"A drink?" A bottle of wine rises from the bar on its own and uncorks itself.

I shake my head. "Not on duty."

"Don't mind if I do," Kit says.

A glass flies up from the nearby table, the bottle pours wine into it in the air, and the glass glides into Kit's outstretched hand.

"Not just raw power but fine control," Felix mutters. "Impressive."

"How can I help?" Nina asks.

"Can you tell us what you were doing when Gemma was killed?" I ask. "It happened—"

"I know when," she says, her expression darkening. "Does this mean I'm a suspect?"

"Don't piss her off," Felix whispers. "She could go Darth Vader on your ass and choke you with her power."

"Everyone on the Council is a suspect," I say carefully, not loving the picture Felix paints. "I'm merely starting with whoever had the ability to easily commit the last crime, but—"

"She asked me the same thing." Kit's form flows into Colton, then Eduardo. "Others as well, and that's just so far."

Nina's face clears, and she peers at me curiously. "You're a dreamwalker, right? Just like Leal?"

"We have the same power, yes, though I'm not sure how I measure up to his abilities."

She pours herself a glass of wine in the air and sips it thoughtfully.

Could she be the culprit, after all? She's not answering my question, and overall looks like she's hiding something.

"So," I prompt cautiously, "when Gemma—"

"I was doing yoga," she says abruptly.

Huh. I suppose that goes with the New Age vibe. "Anything specific you recall about that session?"

"This is so you can verify in my dreams if I'm telling the truth, right?"

"Exactly. The more details, the easier my job."

"I was in this room." She makes a gesture that causes all the furniture to float up several feet, clearing the floor—as she presumably would do for yoga practice. "I started with child's pose, then flowed into downward-facing dog." She throws more yoga poses at me, and I note each one in my phone. "At the end, I always do a relaxing corpse pose. I'd never reflected on how macabre that sounds until saying it just now—as a murder suspect," she adds, fiddling with the hoop in her nostril.

"You won't be a suspect for long," I promise. "Now that I know what you were up to, I can easily clear you."

"Right. In my dreams." Her dark eyebrows pull together. "Talk to me once you have no doubt of my guilt." She glances at Kit. "Privately."

Okay, what is *that* about?

I throw out a wild guess. "If you know who the real killer is, I can ask Kit to leave so we can—"

"I don't." She lowers the furniture back to the floor. "But we should talk. Afterward. Now if that's all, you'd better go talk to the rest of your suspects."

Kit stands up and sets her glass on the nearby table. "Thanks for the drink."

Our exit beneath the giant rock comes with a lot less fear.

"Kain's next," Kit says over her shoulder. "Hopefully he's back."

Before I can ask her where he'd gone, I spot a familiar figure coming down the corridor.

It's Filth, and he's giving me the evil eye.

"If it isn't the blood whore," he sneers when I'm within earshot. "Do let me know when you're ready for an undiluted fix."

I give him a placid stare. "Did you have any trouble getting the tampons, errand boy?"

Felix chuckles. "I forgot to tell you, I did make the checkout process harder for him—and there *is* a video."

Filth's fangs emerge. "I'll rip your—"

"No, you won't." Kit has turned into Kain.

"Speaking of ripping…" I look over Filth's sickly body. "Are you strong enough to rip someone in half?"

Kain Kit gives me a glare. "Don't antagonize him further."

"I'm asking as part of my investigation," I say, stretching the truth only a little. "It's a compliment, in a way. You said only the oldest vampires can accomplish such a feat."

"I've never tried to rip something in half. I suspect I'd greatly enjoy it, though." Filth gives me a deliberate once-over.

"That's nice," I say. "So what were you doing when Gemma was killed?"

"I was on a job with Kain." His fangs go away. "Someone without a Mandate stepped out of line, so we put him down like a rabid dog—the way we should've done with you."

"Thank you," I say calmly. "Sounds like you and Kain are each other's alibis. I hope you don't take it personally when I verify your story with Kain and in the dream world."

"You keep doing your pretend work. I'll wait until you fail." He brushes past us.

Kit turns back into her usual self and heads down the corridor to a black metal door. She knocks on it, and just as I catch up, Kain opens the door.

"She's yours again," Kit says. She turns to me. "I have some business to attend to, but I guess I'll see you in my dreams?"

I smile. "Thanks for your help."

"How goes the investigation?" Kain asks, gesturing for me to come inside.

He leads me into a sleek kitchen that reminds me of Colton's, just with a normal-sized table and chairs, and sits me down on a stylish black bar stool as I bring him up to speed on everything except the alibi Filth provided a minute ago. It's unlikely their stories won't match, but if so, that would be a major breakthrough. And I can't dismiss what Kit said about Kain's potential culpability.

The vampire opens a bottle of distilled water and puts it in front of me like a bartender. "Tonight, you'll establish a dream link with everyone on the Council. You'll dreamwalk in everyone you've spoken with thus far, plus a few people I personally suspect."

I greedily gulp the water. "Actually, I might have to do one or the other. There's a limit to how much I can use my power in a day, and setting up links is draining. Why don't I just set up links and dreamwalk in the people I've spoken with so far?"

"I want everyone on the Council to feel as though their dreams can be invaded at any moment." He perches on a stool next to me. "Then, if you have enough power, we can dive deeper into the suspects."

"You don't think it was Eduardo, Colton, Kit, or Nina who killed Gemma?"

"Doesn't matter what I think. Just do as I say."

I swallow a less-than-polite retort. "Sure. By the way—and this is mere formality—can you tell me what *you* were doing when Gemma was killed?"

He doesn't blink. "No problem. Use your power to clear me of suspicion right away, so you can speak to me more openly about the case."

"I will—though it could mean I won't be able to set up links with everyone on the Council today."

"Fine, fine. Can always leave people with strong alibis for later." He gets up, takes a blood bag from the fridge, and tosses it into the microwave. "It'd been quite a day. An insane werewolf from one of the Otherlands arrived at the local airport and attacked the humans there. We had to kill him and glamour hundreds of victims to forget the incident."

"Wow," Felix whispers.

Indeed. I wouldn't want to be an Enforcer, that's for sure.

"JFK airport?" I ask as the microwave beeps.

"That's the one." He takes out his snack and returns to his seat next to me. Ripping open a corner of the bag, he takes a big gulp from it.

I suppress my instinctive disgust at the sight of him consuming someone's bodily fluids. "Can you tell me something about the event that makes it memorable?"

"How often do you think insane Cognizant show up on this world?"

"No idea. Not often?"

"This was the first incident I'd been involved with. Newcomers such as yourself usually keep their heads down. They know that without the Mandate, they can be killed without due process just for being here."

He downs the rest of the blood bag, no doubt to illustrate what would happen to someone with yummy blood in such circumstances. If it's a threat, it works well.

I force my voice to stay steady. "That's enough detail."

"Good." He slides down from his stool and extends his hand. "Come with me."

I look at his hand, the very one that only a second ago held a bag containing someone's blood. He gives me a look that seems to suggest the handholding isn't optional. Inwardly cringing and making plans to use a whole bottle of sanitizer later, I limply take his hand and let him lead me deeper into the apartment.

Oh, puck.

The last room we enter is his bedroom.

A vampire's bedroom, or what passes for one, given that they don't need to sleep.

My heart rate skyrockets. This place looks too much like the dream room where I do Ariel's exposure therapy. Instruments for erotic and not-so-erotic torture glitter and gleam everywhere. The bed itself has iron rings built into the headboard and the base, clearly to make it easier to chain people for nefarious purposes.

On Gomorrah, everyone thinks vampires are kinky, and this one is playing right into that stereotype.

Kain lets go of my hand and looks between me and the bed with a strange expression.

I loudly swallow.

Is he hungry... or worse?

CHAPTER EIGHTEEN

CAN'T BE HUNGRY. He just drank that whole bag, and why ruin his appetite before dinner, right? Which means—

Before I can complete this thought, Kain climbs onto the bed.

Does he think I'll follow him? Not in a million years.

He sprawls on his back, his pale eyes intent on my face. "I know it sounds crazy, but I'm a little uneasy about what's to come."

Uneasy about what? Inviting me for an exchange of bodily fluids?

He swipes at his forehead, brushing back a string of limp brown hair. "I haven't slept for decades. I can't remember the last time I dreamed at all, and now I'm about to do it with a witness."

I blink as everything clicks into place. He wants me to clear him of wrongdoing *right now*. Whew—that makes more sense. Damn sleep deprivation is making me paranoid.

"I'll be invisible as you dream," I say as soothingly as I can with all that adrenaline in my system. "There's also a good chance you'll forget the dream when you wake up."

He nods and closes his eyes. "Give me a few seconds."

I've seen this before. Vampires don't need to sleep, but when they want to, they drift right off, no mooft counting required. Before long, Kain's breathing changes, and a few minutes later, I see his eyes moving rapidly behind his eyelids in the telltale sign of REM sleep.

"Wow," I mutter, "if only it were that easy with everyone else."

Felix doesn't reply. In fact, now that I'm paying attention, I hear faint snoring on the other end of our connection. Of course, he *has* been awake all this time. Oh, well. I guess he'll miss this.

Reaching out with the hand Kain contaminated earlier, I touch his forehead and fall into his dream world.

———

I FIND myself in Kain's kitchen.

He's talking animatedly on the phone—I think it's about taxes—so I make myself invisible before he can spot me. Decades without sleep and his subconscious concocts a dream this boring? How disappointing. In any case, I can breathe a sigh of relief. He was indeed already in REM sleep, so I've skipped over the dangerous subdreams. And unlike Bernard, Kain seems to have no deep-seated nightmares to worry about—nightmares I would be in right now if they existed. Unless he *really* dislikes talking on the phone to his accountant? It wouldn't be that crazy. When it comes to death and taxes, vampires don't have to worry too much about the former.

I grope for my empty wrist. Because I'm in Kain's dream and not Pom's, Pom doesn't instantly show up here. That's probably for the best, as I think he'd prefer to miss the bit with the werewolf.

Dream manipulation time.

I manifest the date and time I want and morph the environment to an international airport at midday. I always do this as smoothly as I can manage. In this case, the kitchen already has barstools, so it becomes an airport bar. Kain doesn't question this new reality, so I slowly add noises of talking people and clanking glasses.

Still good. Kain keeps chatting on the phone.

I end the call.

He shrugs and leaves the bar as if it were the most natural thing in the world. I get bolder, adding details from his story: screams of bloody murder from the werewolf's victims, panicked humans, fellow Enforcers rushing into action. It's more art than science, giving the dreamer enough details that they can run with the dream from there, their subconscious adding in whatever is needed. As Kain begins to do this, I relax and watch the events unfold.

Foaming at the mouth, the wolf rips an old lady into pieces. Kain shoots it with a tranquilizer dart, and it lets go of the human and dashes for Terminal 8. Filth and a few other Enforcers are already waiting there, holding stun guns.

Uninterested in the bloody outcome, I ask myself a single question: Is this dream a memory? My power confirms it, just as it did in Bernard's dream. Good. If Kain were the killer, I'd be in a vulnerable real-world position, being in his dungeon bedroom and all.

Job done, I yank myself from the dream and into the waking world.

———

BEFORE KAIN WAKES UP, I use what's left of the sanitizer to finally clean my hand.

After I'm done, I softly call, "Kain. Wake up."

Fangs out, he leaps off the bed as if to battle for his life. Spotting me, he halts, recognition appearing in his eyes.

"You're officially not guilty of killing Gemma," I tell him. "This clears Firth and a bunch of other Enforcers, too."

He massages the bridge of his nose. "I was in my kitchen and the airport. That makes no sense, but at the time it was so logical and real. I somehow knew the date and time without looking at any clocks. Felt it, almost."

I nod. "Dreamers almost never ask themselves, 'How did I get here?' Those who do sometimes realize they're in a dream. It's called lucid dreaming, and it can cause problems for me, so I'm glad it's rare."

"I think I could go for centuries without dreaming again." He strides out of the bedroom, and I gladly follow.

Without stopping, he heads out of the apartment and down a spindly corridor teeming with monks. When we reach a dilapidated wooden door, he opens it. "This is your new quarters."

The place looks spartan, with just a small bed and a wooden table inside a small windowless room, but it's luxurious compared to the dungeon cell. It even has a washroom with a shower and a proper toilet.

"The stuff you wanted is there." He gestures at a pile of plastic bags behind the bed. "You have a little time while I make the arrangements for the Councilors to go to sleep."

When he leaves, I rummage through the shopping bags. Yep, everything I asked for is here, adult diapers and laxatives included. I fish out the bananas, water, and sanitizer and set it all on the table.

Vampire blood has many side effects, one of them being the suppression of hunger along with sleep. While on it, I eat based on common sense—a few hundred calories every few hours. I'm actually way behind on my quota, so I sanitize seven bananas and force myself to eat them one after another—which takes twenty minutes that feel like five hours.

Feeling like a stuffed ape, I chase the fruit with plenty of water and use the toilet while I have it handy. A side effect of eating so rarely and being constantly dehydrated is that I don't have to do this often.

The drowsiness of a food coma hits me so hard I have to slap my face to wake myself up. But I can't sleep now. Kain will be back any second. I sanitize my hands until my skin feels raw, then pull out the vial with the diluted vampire blood. Keeping it out of sight of Felix's camera, I take the tiniest sip I can manage.

Instantly, I'm wide awake. A wave of orgasmic pleasure sweeps over me, double the intensity of the last time.

Puck.

Imagining the wall is Filth's face, I slam my fist into it as hard as I can. There's no pain at all, only pressure, and the pleasure continues unabated.

Double puck.

I smash my fist into the same spot again and again, leaving bloody prints on the stone. When the skin splits on my knuckles, it mends instantly—the healing properties of vampire blood. If I break any bones, they will mend also, all without a hint of pain.

Eventually, the pleasure subsides, leaving only the equally unwelcome sexual arousal.

Wow, this time was bad. Even diluted, it's affecting me almost beyond my control. I've got to solve this case and save Mom so I can get off the vile substance, else I might end up following in Ariel's footsteps. For now, I dilute the half-empty vial with water until it's full again. Maybe an even more diluted version will work more like it used to?

Now I wish Kain would come back so I could do something useful.

Actually, there *is* something I can do. If Kit has gone to bed, which would be reasonable, I could check if she's behind all the crimes. Despite what she said about Tatum, she's still one of my main suspects.

Touching Pom, I go into a trance and meet Pom's dream form in my palace. He floats contentedly in the air, waving a furry paw at me in greeting.

"I'm going into Kit's dreams." I give myself my fiery hair. "I'd like some privacy."

If Kit didn't lie, her dreams will be X-rated, and that's not an experience I want to share with a fuzzy creature with no visible genitals.

"I'll go play Jenga," he says. A tower of wooden blocks appears on the floor. "Go do what you do."

I pat his head and hasten to the tower of sleepers.

I'm lucky for a change. Kit is here sleeping, and so is Felix—my earlier guess was right.

I touch Kit's forehead and end up smack in the middle of an orgy featuring every type of Cognizant I can think of, plus some I've never seen. Alrighty, then. It should be easy to morph this dream into the situation Kit described earlier.

I begin by giving Kit a sense that this is all happening on the date and time when Gemma was ripped apart. Then I remove a dozen or so participants and turn one of the remaining ones into Lola.

Almost there. The problem is that this Lola isn't doing what Kit described. Feeling like a total perv, I take control of Dream Lola and have her ask Kit to turn into whatever she described to me earlier, making sure to request the right number of phalluses while I'm at it.

The scene starts to look like what Kit described—and as soon as it does, I know it's a memory.

Whew. As much as I want this investigation to be over, Kit is my friend, so I'm really glad she's not the culprit.

On the way out of Kit's dream world, I contemplate talking to Felix but decide against it. Between the vampire blood and Kit's dreams, I'm too sexed up to face him.

But there's something I *can* do to take the edge off.

With a deep, delicious inhalation, I think back to the luxurious bedroom Valerian created around us using his illusionist powers. I begin the recreation with the big bed swathed in silk sheets and covered in rose petals before creating the man himself, in all his (probably fake) glory.

"Hi, beautiful," Dream Valerian murmurs. "Finally found time for me?"

"Come closer." I make my clothes disappear with a flick of my powers.

Ripping the buttons off his shirt, he strides toward me.

My overclocked libido goes into overdrive.

Dream Valerian kisses me deeper than last time, his right hand stroking my lower back as his left slides—

"What is the meaning of this?" Kain's voice sounds like thunder.

With a sigh, I pull myself away from the dream world and open my eyes to Kain's fury.

"You said your power has limits," he growls with a lisp, due to his extended fangs. "How dare you waste it on pleasuring yourself?"

What the hell? How does he know? Can he smell it on me?

Yuck. I need to bathe my brain in sanitizer.

Seeing his eyes turn into mirrors, I blurt, "I was doing my job."

His eyes fade to normal, giving me hope that I'll never learn what he intended to glamour me into doing.

"Explain," he hisses.

"Kit. I verified her alibi, and it checks out."

"I see." His fangs retreat. "I spoke to Lola the day after the murder, but it's good to confirm Kit's story. That nymph would say anything to protect her insatiable girlfriend."

He knew? Then again, Kit has never been shy about her adventures. Oh, well. I grab a water bottle and pocket my hand sanitizer. "I'm ready to connect with others and check alibis."

"Let's go to my quarters."

His quarters again? Why?

Given the earlier threat of glamour, I don't ask.

When we reach our destination, he leads me toward his dungeon/bedroom—which makes all my earlier concerns resurface.

Just before entering the dreaded room, he wheels around, so quickly I nearly smash into him.

"This is going to stay between us," he says harshly. "Understood?"

CHAPTER NINETEEN

I STARE AT HIM, my heart rate doubling.

"It's a delicate situation," he continues. "The woman hates dreamwalkers with a passion."

I blink at him, even more confused.

"Just go inside," he snaps. "Go, or I'll make you."

With Pom turning pitch black on my wrist, I enter the cursed room and freeze, unable to believe what I'm seeing.

It's Gertrude.

She's lying on Kain's bed, staring emptily at the ceiling.

"She's my primary suspect," Kain says as though she's not there. "She envied Tatum and Ryan's marriage —don't ask me why—and she fiercely and openly despised Gemma. You already know how she feels about dreamwalkers."

"But no one died by rotting to death," I say.

"Of course not. She's not stupid enough to kill that way—she'd be the only suspect."

I peer at her unmoving body. "What's wrong with her?"

"I had to glamour her," Kain says. "She has a huge problem sleeping in front of others, to put it mildly."

"She's got good reason." I step to the side and back, putting him between me and Gertrude. "Between her REM Sleep Disorder and the gangrene-giving, it would be dangerous for any witnesses."

"And yet I'll make her sleep, and you'll check to make sure she's not behind the murders." He turns to the empty-eyed woman and instructs in a honey-laced voice, "Gertrude, cuff your right ankle to the right bottom corner of the bed."

She sits up and does as ordered. Another command, and she locks her left ankle and right hand, leaving herself mostly spread-eagled. I expect Kain to do something about her left hand, but he doesn't.

"With that arm free, she can still grab one of us and make whatever she touches rot," I tell him. "You've got to lock it up."

"Do *you* want to lock it up?" he asks with a sneer. "I'm not getting anywhere near her skin."

So vampires can rot. What a gross discovery.

I look Gertrude over. With her short skirt and sleeveless top, she's showing way too much skin to approach without a hazmat suit.

"Gertrude, sleep," Kain croons.

She closes her eyes right away, her breathing evening out.

Wow, I'd give a lot for that particular power.

"Now do your thing," Kain orders.

I gingerly step closer to observe her eyelids.

"What's the holdup?" he asks.

I turn back toward him. "I have to wait until she's in REM sleep."

"Isn't REM sleep when that free arm becomes a problem?"

I sigh. "If I go in now, I'll have to deal with the subdream, which carries its own danger."

He raises an eyebrow.

"I could die in the dream world."

The eyebrow goes almost comically high.

"If I die there, I'll become homicidally insane."

The eyebrow comes back down and meets its neighbor in a frown. "Is that how things work for all dreamwalkers?"

"As far as I know."

Kain's gaze sharpens. "Could that have happened to Leal? As in, he died during dreamwalking and became—"

"Didn't Gemma get killed *after* he was already dead? Besides, are you suggesting he killed himself using those birds?"

"We do have to consider the possibility that there might've been more than one killer," he says with less enthusiasm.

"If it was Leal, the murders would've been a lot

more brutal," I say. "All of you would've known he'd gone crazy. He'd have acted like a puck."

"I see," Kain says. "Still, I say it's a good thing you've been focusing most of your attention on Gemma's murder."

"Right." I go back to watching Gertrude's eyelids.

"So what are you waiting for?"

"I just told you. The subdream—"

"Go in," he snaps. "And don't die. Waiting is riskier, trust me."

I back away from the bed as his eyes turn to mirrors. "I'll do it—"

His eyes fade to normal.

"—but there're a few more problems. If I survive the subdream section, my power will force Gertrude to snap into REM sleep. That means her loose hand will become an issue."

"I'll pull you away from her as soon as I see signs of REM sleep," he says. "You can then come back into her dreams from a distance, as I know you can do."

He knows? I was trying to keep that under wraps.

"That might work," I say grudgingly. "But there's another, bigger problem. For me to use my power, I have to touch her—and if I touch her, I'll lose my finger." I glance warily at Gertrude's exposed skin.

"Can you enter someone's dream by touching their hair?" he asks. "I've seen Gertrude zone out while one of the monks was giving her a trim, which tells me the hair should be safe to touch."

"'Should be' doesn't sound reassuring."

His eyes turn into slits. "Can you or can you not use hair to do your job?"

"No idea. In theory, I don't see why not. The body has hair all over, so I've probably done it inadvertently. But I've never tried it with the hair on someone's head, because that's a cesspool of dandruff, oil, mites, germs—"

Inside their slits, his eyes turn into mirrors again. "Bailey," he says in that special voice, "you'll touch the tips of Gertrude's hair, far from her skin. Now."

I attempt to fight the compulsion, but it overtakes me even faster than when he glamoured me before the Council meeting. My body moves forward on its own, my arm extends, and my finger lands on the strand of hair farthest away from Gertrude's face.

If my face were under my control, it would be cringing.

To my relief, my finger doesn't rot. Then again, maybe that's still to come.

"Bailey, I release you from glamour," Kain says ceremoniously. "Enter her dream now."

The only reason I don't explode into obscenities is that I'd wake Gertrude, and she'd rot me first, ask questions later.

"Stop it with the hesitation," Kain growls. "I told you I'll pull you away as soon as I see her eyelids move. Now do your job."

Fine. I hope this works, else I'm fairly sure he'll make me touch her where my finger would be in even more trouble.

Gritting my teeth so hard my jaw hurts, I will myself to enter Gertrude's dreams.

The hair is a go. I catch a whiff of ozone and experience the sensation of falling as the room darkens around me, propelling me into the familiar trance.

Now I just hope the subdream doesn't drive me insane.

CHAPTER TWENTY

I'M STANDING on a calm black ocean with magma skies above. In the distance, two creatures ride toward me astride some other kind of creatures, hooting out horrific battle cries as they come.

Something snakes from my wrist to the ground and grows into a furry unicorn.

"We'd better get out of here," I tell my new steed. "Whatever those things are, they don't sound friendly."

The unicorn snorts, and as soon as I clasp his neck, he gallops away so fast his hooves barely touch the water.

The battle cries, if that's what they are, draw closer behind us. They're terrifying. I imagine that's how pucks' teeth must sound scraping the bones of their victims. Still, for some reason, I can't shake the feeling that there's a message embedded in those ugly shrieks, just in a language I don't know.

Casting a glance over my shoulder, I take in the

monstrosities. The mounts look like warthogs crossed with spiders, and their riders remind me of naked mole rats—only huge and with tentacles.

I speed up, but one of the pairs gains on us anyway. As it pulls up next to us, the second pair shrieks directly behind me.

A tentacle lassoes my neck. Before it gets the chance to rip me away, my mount veers sideways and spears the rider with his horn.

As the thing dies, the tentacle loosens its grip on my neck.

The riderless beast roars. With an angry flutter of nostrils, my unicorn rears, and I hold on to his furry mane for dear life as he smashes a hoof into its temple, killing it instantly before kicking the head of the warthog behind us. The beast staggers, mortally wounded, but its tentacled naked mole rat rider lands on its hind legs and bares its saber-like tusks at us.

My unicorn charges.

The mole rat dodges the horn and catches my wrist with a tentacle. Like a bungee cord, the tentacle contracts, pulling the vile creature toward me. I jerk my hand, but it's useless. The thing is already on me, its tusk piercing my neck.

Blood gushes out of the wound, and I start to feel woozy.

Ignoring the pain, I headbutt my opponent in its maw, launching it back. Since it's still attached to me by its tentacle, it doesn't fly far—but it's far enough.

With a twist of his neck, my unicorn shish-kebabs the creature, dealing it a deadly blow.

———

PANTING AND BLEEDING PROFUSELY, I look around at the reddish green walls and floating impossible objects.

Of course. This is my palace, and that bloody mess was another subdream.

Yet again, I didn't have any clue that I was dreaming. Why does this happen? What will it take for me to get a clue—Unicorn Pom farting rainbows?

I zoom out of my body and heal the neck and forehead wounds.

It's official: This is the closest I've ever gotten to dream death and the subsequent insanity.

Speaking of death, I've completely forgotten about Gertrude. Since I've just put her into REM sleep, she could touch me with her free hand at any moment.

I jump back into my body and wake myself up.

CHAPTER TWENTY-ONE

MY EYES open to the sight of Gertrude's unbound hand swinging erratically.

Puck, it's now flying my way.

Before I can even think the word *dodge*, someone forcefully jerks me back. Gertrude's hand zooms right by my nose.

I sway slightly in my new location, stunned. Did that touch my nose? If so, I'll lose it—in the best case.

Kain examines my face like a plastic surgeon prepping for a rhinoplasty. "You're fine. She didn't touch you."

"Fine?" I look at my finger that touched Gertrude's hair. Though unrotted, it's still unsanitized.

"Come." Kain leads me to the kitchen sink, takes the finger I touched her hair with, and pours dish detergent on it.

"Pucker," I hiss under my breath.

I scrub my hands for several minutes to stop myself

from antagonizing a vampire, which is what I *really* want to do.

Kain hands me a roll of paper towels. I dry my hands and top it off with half a bottle of sanitizer.

"I assume you didn't get a chance to clear Gertrude," he says.

I shake my head, still too angry for words.

"Do so now. I don't want to keep her here any longer than necessary."

"There's a problem." I plop onto a barstool. "To make it fast and easy, I need to know what she did at the time of the murder. Otherwise, this might be a huge project."

"Oh, she told me that." He grabs another water bottle from the fridge and hands it to me. "She was watching a movie in her room."

"Alone?" I grudgingly take a sip of the water—no point in being dehydrated just because I'm mad at the vampire in front of me.

"Right, no witnesses." He leans against the counter. "Yet another reason I suspect her."

"Can you describe her room for me? And what movie was she watching?"

He describes her living room, then says, "The movie was *Catwoman*. I didn't realize we had that crap in our library."

"I've never seen it. What's it about?"

He waves a hand impatiently. "I haven't seen it either. It has a horrible reputation, to the point that I found it suspicious that Gertrude would watch it, of all things."

I pinch the bridge of my nose. "Well… just knowing that Catwoman's in it might be enough."

"Okay, good."

"Can you go watch Gertrude?" I say. "Let me know if she wakes up."

If he realizes I don't want him to see how I do my magic from a distance, he doesn't show it.

As soon as he's gone, I stroke Pom's fur a few times to calm myself and slide into the trance.

———

POM IS pitch black when I reappear in my dream palace. "That was some subdream, wasn't it?"

I take flight. "Let's talk on the way to the tower of sleepers. I assume you also had no idea it was a dream?"

He catches up to me in the air, his fur now a dark beet hue. "Yep, no clue."

"Even though you were a unicorn?" I make a miniature replica of the unicorn fly next to us.

"You didn't know it was a dream either." He zips forward to float in front of my face. "And you're the one with dream powers."

"But all you do is sleep and dream. Out of the two of us, you have more chances to realize that a subdream is just a dream—and once you do, you could tell me that."

"Well, I didn't know." The tips of his ears look like carrots. "Maybe next time?"

"I don't want there to be a next time." I enter the tower. "That was too close for me."

We fly in sullen silence as I locate Gertrude. As we approach, I spot the telltale miniature dark clouds flying above her head.

"Not this again," I mutter. As with Bernard, I'll have to deal with her trauma loop before I can verify her innocence.

Fine. Given the complication, I'll do a little more prep.

I locate the sleeping Felix and enter his dreams.

———

FELIX IS PLAYING a violent video game with his second roommate, a girl I jokingly call Princess Peach. They each have a pet on their laps—a cat for him and a chinchilla for her.

Felix unleashes a flurry of onscreen kicks and punches, ripping the head off Peach's character.

Interesting. With so much blood and gore, I'd expect him to faint, but he's grinning instead. Either game violence doesn't feel real to him, or it's because this is a dream. Probably the latter. In the real world, his opponent would anticipate his every move with her seer powers.

I clear my throat.

They both look at me, but only Felix's eyes have real intelligence in them.

"This is a dream," I say. "In case that wasn't obvious."

Felix jumps to his feet. "I fell asleep?"

I transport the two of us to my cloud environment. "You did."

He adjusts his "there is no spoon" t-shirt. "I'm sorry. I drank two Red Bulls and—"

"Don't worry about it." I sink into my cloud chair. "I need your help. Have you seen the movie *Catwoman*?"

He plops onto the therapy couch. "It's crap."

Pom appears next to me, and I idly fluff his fur. "I don't need your skills as a movie critic. I'm going into the dream of someone who saw this movie, and I need details."

"I think it had like a three point three out of ten on IMDb," he says, looking askance at Pom. "Halle Berry, the star of the film, was dishonored with a Razzie award for her performance."

"Okay, so it sounds like you at least know the actress who was in it." I lean forward. "What does she look like?"

He regards me thoughtfully. "A bit like you, actually."

Pom turns a curious light orange as I place him on my lap and tell Felix, "How about you picture her in your mind, so I can see for myself?"

I give him a moment before shooting him with a burst of power.

An attractive woman appears next to Pom. She's wearing the kind of leather suit that vampire addicts often wear back on Gomorrah. Must be the infamous catsuit.

Pom wrinkles his furry nose. "She doesn't look at all like Bailey."

I wistfully file away those perfect cheekbones into memory. "Yeah, she's way prettier."

"If you really need the plot, ask Ariel," Felix says, oblivious. "She loves anything to do with Batman and wouldn't have missed that movie no matter how bad it was."

"Good idea," I say. "Stay here and talk to Pom. I'll be back."

Before either of them can say anything, I return to the tower to see if Ariel is sleeping.

I'm in luck—she's here.

I touch her forehead and enter her dream.

———

AN ORC IS THROWING a giant fist at Ariel's jaw. She dodges it, pulls a huge knife from somewhere, and spears his fist in a swift motion. The orc roars and tries to kick her—but she dodges that too.

Wow. Ariel is very good at this, even adjusting for the embellishment so common in dreams. I might visit her dreams later to learn some of her fighting tricks. For now, I need to pick her brain, so I gently help her defeat the orc, and when he falls down, I step in front of her.

"Bailey." Ariel sheathes her knife. "What are you doing here?"

I smile. "And where is *here*?"

Ariel strains to answer but doesn't come up with anything.

"It's common not to question the location of a dream," I say.

She examines the dead orc. "This is a dream?"

"Orcs don't come to Earth." I make the dead body disappear. "Also, why would one attack you?"

"Right, it *is* a dream." Her perfectly smooth forehead creases. "Is it time for my therapy?"

"No, I need you for something." I guide her to my cloud office, where Felix and Pom are floating in the air over a game of checkers.

"Oh, hey, Felix. And Pomsie!" Ariel snatches my furry symbiont from the air, grinning like a five-year-old opening a present. "I missed you."

Pom turns the deep purple of happiness in her arms.

Whew. At least it's not coral pink. It would be a bit awkward, though understandable, if he got turned on by Ariel. I guess their love is platonic, at least on Pom's side. They met after I'd decided Ariel might benefit from something akin to pet therapy, and they got along so well that I eventually had to ask Pom to avoid her sessions, lest she do nothing but pet him nonstop.

"Did Ariel tell you?" Felix's unibrow dances a jig on his forehead.

"Tell her what?" Ariel clutches Pom tighter.

"*Catwoman.*" Felix looks from me to her. "Bailey wanted to know the plot of that atrocity."

"I didn't get a chance to explain." I plop into my chair. "Have you seen that movie?"

She squeezes Pom again. If he weren't a dream creature, her enthusiastic smooshing might've broken his back by now. "Felix knows I have."

"Told you." Felix grins at me. "Probably liked it, too."

"I did not." Done with squeezing, she gently scratches Pom's belly, which promptly turns blue.

"You liked *Batman and Robin.*" Felix sprawls on the therapy couch. "That isn't much better."

"*Liked* is a strong word." She gives Pom the under-the-chin scratch that cats like so much. "In my defense, it had Batman in it. And George Clooney. And—"

"Guys, I need the plot of *Catwoman* for an important job," I say. "Please."

Ariel casts a warning glare at Felix and launches into a summary of the movie.

"Thanks," I say when she's done. "Now I can leave you all to hang out here as I take care of my business, or I can let you wake up. Whichever you prefer."

"I'll stay," Felix says.

"Me too." Ariel rubs her cheek against Pom's fur.

"And me," Pom purrs.

Felix motions to the cloud and the ocean below. "How will this work?".

"When I'm done with my business, I'll wake myself up," I say. "And because I pulled you in, you'll disappear from here at that point, which means waking up."

Felix nods. "Got it. And we'll see you in person soon. Remember I told you about Ariel's cousin's best friend's daughter's Mandate ceremony? I'm definitely joining so I can look at that dreamwalker's comms for you."

"Sounds great," I say. "See you both then."

I take myself into the tower of sleepers, muttering under my breath, "Assuming I'm not dead."

Making my way to Gertrude's bed, I shimmer into invisibility and touch her forehead.

Trauma loop, here I come.

CHAPTER TWENTY-TWO

THE GERTRUDE in this dream looks younger. She's sitting on a couch with a handsome blond guy, who's sipping from a bottle of beer as she gazes longingly at his lips.

He offers her the bottle. "Want some?"

She recoils as if it were poison. "I need to be in absolute control of my faculties to suppress my power."

His grin is cocky. "All so I can touch you, right?"

She takes the bottle from his hand, puts it on the table, and kisses him. As they proceed to make out, I realize two things: this is a memory, as most trauma loops are, and the guy isn't rotting despite his contact with her. I guess gangrene-givers can turn off their powers. It makes sense. If they couldn't, how would they reproduce?

Speaking of reproduction, the guy fishes out a condom from his pocket, and they take things all the way.

I yawn, watching them. They're not very creative—definitely nothing like some of the dreams I've seen. If I ever get around to doing this with Dream Valerian, there will be a lot more acrobatics.

"You have to leave now," Gertrude says sleepily when they're done.

He gives her puppy eyes. "Can't we spoon for a few minutes?"

"Two minutes. Put a blanket between us, just in case."

He does as she says, and they cuddle through the blanket until her breathing changes. When he notices she's asleep, he carefully climbs off the couch and starts picking up his clothing. Before he can put on his pants, she sinks into REM sleep. He's none the wiser.

At this point, the dream isn't a memory but Gertrude's extrapolation of what must have happened.

Her arm swings wildly, the way it did when she nearly took out my nose. By pure chance, her hand connects with his ankle and, as if it has a mind of its own, wraps around it.

The rot is instant. In mere moments, his leg looks as if it's been infected for weeks.

He clutches his leg, screaming.

She stirs as if she's waking up, but her grip doesn't release, and the gangrene spreads and spreads until his screaming ceases and he collapses in a rotten heap.

The dream is a memory again.

Gertrude opens her eyes—and jumps off the couch,

emitting a scream of such horror and agony that my chest aches with genuine sympathy.

However awful she was to me at the trial, she doesn't deserve this.

But this is my chance to do what I came here for, so I make the guy's corpse disappear, put her back on the couch, and make her fall back asleep. I then change the room to look as Kain described, moving the couch, adjusting the clock's date and time to that of Gemma's murder, and putting *Catwoman* on pause on the TV.

Then I use my power to "wake" Gertrude here in the dream world.

Remote control in hand, she rubs her eyes in confusion, her anguish gone for now. As I hoped, she thinks she's snoozed before starting her movie. Later, when she really wakes up, she'll process the horrific incident I just witnessed, as much as such a thing can be processed.

To my relief, Gertrude falls into the new dream perfectly. She unpauses the movie and watches it, everything else forgotten. It doesn't take long before I see that watching this movie is indeed a memory.

Kain was wrong to suspect her. Her alibi checks out.

A part of me is disappointed. Given how much she seems to hate me for little reason, it would've made life easier if she were the culprit. Still, after seeing that trauma loop, I understand why she's so angry with anyone who can't help her sleep condition.

Oh, well.

Time to wake up.

———

I OPEN my eyes in Kain's sleek kitchen and head over to his bedroom, where he's supposed to be keeping an eye on Gertrude. I find him diligently engaged in that duty, standing over the bed like a sentinel.

"Hey," Felix says in my earpiece. "I just woke up."

Ignoring him, I tell Kain, "Gertrude isn't guilty. She really *was* watching a movie, like she said."

Kain curses under his breath. He looks ready to kill someone.

"What now?" I ask cautiously.

"I'll take you to deal with the next sleeper, then come back to clean up this mess." He strides out of the room.

I speed after him. "How?"

"I'll use glamour on Gertrude to make her forget what just happened," he throws over his shoulder as we exit his quarters.

"Won't she get suspicious if she's the only person not to have to undergo a dreamwalk?"

"I'll tell her she'll be the last one." He covers the corridor with long strides. "And we'll find the real killer before that."

"Assuming you do," Felix says as I strive to keep up without breaking into a jog. Thankfully, Kain slows a bit as we make the next turn.

"Where are we going?" I ask breathlessly.

"Colton's," he replies and speeds up again. "He's the only one of your suspects available tonight."

Puck it. I launch into a full-out run to catch up with him. "What do you mean?"

"Eduardo left on pack business, and Nina said she's going on some important trip to the Otherlands."

Panting, I pull up next to him. "You don't find that suspicious?"

"A little." He slows down a bit to look at me. "They know they'll have to undergo a dreamwalk tomorrow night."

"But what if they don't come back?"

He stops next to the massive wooden door. "In that case, I'll consider the case closed and the problem solved. Our main priority is stopping the murders. Justice is a distant second."

He pushes open the door and leads me to the giant's bedroom.

"Wow," Felix says. "I think that's two California king beds."

Yep, I can see where one bed ends and the other begins. I guess no one on this world makes beds for people Colton's size.

"He's not in REM sleep," I whisper to Kain. "You go deal with Gertrude, and I'll wait for my moment."

He leaves as I perch on the edge of the bed to watch Colton's closed eyes—a boring enough activity that a yawn tugs at my jaw despite the vampire blood I recently consumed.

"That dream session with Ariel and Pom was so

cool," Felix says—a welcome distraction for once. He proceeds to tell me what they did while I was dealing with Gertrude: mostly goofing around.

After a few long minutes, Kain comes back and eyes me impatiently. I point at Colton's eyelids and shrug. If I weren't afraid to wake up the giant, I'd explain that REM sleep typically happens around ninety minutes after someone first falls sleep.

Kain makes his way over to a corner and becomes very still, like an alabaster statue. Must be some weird vampire meditation.

I turn my attention back to Colton. After what feels like an hour, his eyelids finally indicate REM sleep—though if I had my way, I'd be using equipment to know for sure. If I get this wrong, I'll have to deal with the subdream again. Still, I'm pretty sure he's dreaming. His eyes, like the rest of him, are ginormous. The movement is hard to miss.

Carefully, I touch the back of the giant's hand and plummet into the dream world.

———

"ARIEL AND FELIX ARE SO FUN," Pom pants excitedly as I appear in my dream palace lobby. "You've got to bring them back some day."

"I will," I tell him as I head to the tower of sleepers. "Tell me what you guys did."

I barely listen as he repeats some of the stuff Felix

told me. I'm contemplating a theory that's been brewing in my head since we left Gertrude's room.

There's a way Kain could still be behind the murders despite his alibi. What if he used glamour to get others to do his dirty work and forget it ever happened? After all, he was able to glamour Gertrude, a fellow Council member. Then again, there's no way he's powerful enough to do it to anyone he wants. He was only able to glamour *me* thanks to my vampire blood consumption.

Hmm. Could Gertrude also be on the blood? If I suffered from her condition, I might go that route to avoid sleep as much as possible.

Either way, I'm proceeding with my current plan of action. If Kain has planted a fake alibi in someone's head, it won't check out in the dream world. In fact, I should see if I can retrieve a memory of being glamoured. I've never tried that, but it could work.

Thus determined, I locate sleeping Colton in the tower.

"Huh," Pom says. "The bed grew to fit him."

I'm not surprised. "The nook, too. That's the beauty of the dream world for you."

The good news is that no trauma loop clouds gather above Colton, so this will be a get-in, get-out situation.

I turn invisible and enter his dream.

Around us is a world lacking any technological advancements, even modest ones like the tech on Earth. Instead, I spot mud huts the size of high-rise buildings, dirt roads the width of a large speedway, enormous windmills, and plainly dressed giants walking to and fro.

Colton is trudging down the street, looking very small next to his kin. I guess it makes sense for him to be tiny. In order to live on Earth, he has to pass for a human. If he were actually human, though, he'd probably have serious pituitary gland issues.

Beginning my work, I draw in a deep fog to obscure the huts and the people. I thin the crowds on the streets and remove the huts completely, replacing them with a hilly landscape dotted with mushrooms. Finally, I set the date and time and add in the goats.

As if it were the goal all along, Colton begins serenely herding the beasts.

Yep, this is memory. Another person with an alibi.

Disappointed, I wake up.

———

WAVING FOR KAIN TO FOLLOW, I tiptoe out of Colton's bedroom and head directly for the exit.

Once we're outside the giant's quarters, I sanitize my finger. "He's not guilty. This doesn't look good for Eduardo and Nina."

Kain looks grim. "Just connect with as many Councilors as you can. Albina is nearby, so you can start with her."

I don't object, and he leads me to a regular-sized steel door, which we enter.

Albina isn't in her bed. Instead, there's a note on the pillow:

Kain, I'm very sorry, but something came up. I'll have to participate in the dream investigation tomorrow night.

Regards, Albina

"Sketchy," I say. "Is she strong enough to rip someone apart?"

"No." Kain heads out of Albina's place. "She can break matter into nothing. If she'd used her power, we would've thought the victim had disappeared without a trace. It would've been dumb of her to leave bodies behind."

We head to another subject's quarters as I ask, "Isn't it always a bad idea to leave bodies behind?"

"Unless you're Albina, it might be hard to get rid of a body in this castle. But you have a point. It's possible that the murderer is making a statement by leaving the bodies like this—in which case, it could be Albina. Somehow."

We stop next to a new wooden door, and he holds it open for me.

"Is Gertrude on vampire blood?" I ask as casually as I can.

"Indeed." He frowns. "Firth is the supplier—and the only reason I allow it is that it gives me power over her."

"Is anyone else on the Council on vampire blood?" I ask, still striving for casualness.

"Not that I know of." His fangs extend. "And Gertrude is the only person on the Council I can glamour the way I did earlier. I couldn't, for example, make Colton rip Gemma apart."

"Of course he'd say that," Felix whispers. "If I were you, I wouldn't dismiss that theory so quickly."

Ignoring Felix, I scowl at Kain. "Don't get touchy. Isn't it my job to think of all possibilities?"

"I'd rather you focus on the part of your job that's in there." He nods at the apartment.

As I step past him to enter, his fangs go away.

The sleeper in this bedroom is Isis, the Councilor who committed to healing Mom when I successfully accomplish my job.

Better be on my best behavior.

Silently, I wait until Isis goes into REM sleep before I enter the dream world. Once there, I check to make sure she shows up in the tower of sleepers and get back out, moving carefully in order not to wake her. I'll only snoop on Isis's dreams if explicitly ordered. Her power is too valuable for me to upset her. In fact, if she turns out to be the killer, I might blackmail her to save Mom instead of telling the Council about her guilt. Not that I think a healer is likely to be behind it.

The sleeper Kain takes me to next isn't familiar to me. Again, we wait for REM sleep, then I make the link and get out of the dream world.

The next Councilor I recognize. It's Hekima, the grandfatherly illusionist. He reaches another phase of REM sleep in minutes, and I pop into his dream and right back out again, as I did with the other Councilors.

The following person I kind of know as well.

Though we've never spoken personally, I've seen him in Ariel's dreams. His puckish—or more accurately, satyric—face is distinctive. It's Chester, and he's a probability manipulator—or trickster, as his kind are locally nicknamed. A probability manipulator isn't someone I'd want as an enemy, so I carefully make a connection and tiptoe out of his bedroom.

The next Councilor is a beautiful woman who takes over an hour to get to REM sleep.

The person after her only takes five minutes.

I keep making connections over and over, until we walk into the bedroom of a thin man who opens his eyes and glares at us.

"It's morning," Kain says as we scurry out of the thin guy's abode. "You'll have to continue tonight."

Yay, me. I get a little reprieve.

We head back toward my quarters.

"Was that most of them?" I ask when we get there.

"Ninety percent of the Council." He opens the door for me. "You thought you wouldn't have enough power, but what we actually ran out of is time."

I stop in the doorway. "I'm game to see if anyone is sleeping in."

He shakes his head. "I promised everyone you won't be an inconvenience. Besides, actually making a connection is less important than making them *think* you did so."

"What do you mean?" I enter the place and plop down on a chair.

He remains by the door. "My hope is that the killer

thinks you're a threat. They'll move to eliminate the threat, and that's when they'll reveal themselves to me."

I scowl at him. "So I'm bait? You're hoping they'll try to kill me so you'll know who it is?"

"Me or one of the Enforcers will protect you," he says dismissively. "And you'll get your reward."

"If I live."

He gives me a level look. "I swear your mother will be healed even if you're dead."

"Well, that's morbidly reassuring," Felix whispers.

Some of my anger dissipates. "Thank you. That means a lot."

Not bothering with a "you're welcome," Kain leaves, and I hear the lock turn in the door.

I guess I'm a prisoner. Oh, well.

The first thing I do is grab some bananas and start munching, consuming one after another while ignoring Felix's jibes.

"When you're done with that monkey business, it would be a good time for a nap," he says when I get to banana number six. "I sure could use one."

I finish the banana, clean my hands, and take out my phone to text: *You go ahead.*

"I will," he says with a yawn. "Wait, why are you texting? Do you think there're listening devices in the room?"

Can't dismiss the possibility, I text. *If Kain doesn't trust me, I wouldn't put it past him.*

"Good point. Enjoy your nap." He yawns again.

"Feel free to visit me in the dream world if you feel like it."

I make a thumbs-up gesture in front of my lapel camera.

"Talk later." I hear rustling as he puts down his headset.

I down some water and try to decide what to do next. Napping is out of the question; the vampire blood I imbibed won't let that happen. Since I haven't run out of power, I decide to finish Valerian's gig—then maybe reward myself with a visit to the dream version of my employer.

Petting Pom's fur, I enter the prerequisite trance. On the way to the tower of sleepers, I update Pom on the investigation and tell him what I'm about to do.

"You're lucky," he says when we reach Bernard's nook. "He's sleeping in today."

"I don't feel very lucky." I eye the clouds around Bernard's head. "His trauma loop consists of more than one dream, it seems."

"This one is less severe than the last," Pom says, sniffing at the clouds. "Still, I'm not going in there with you. Sorry."

I shrug and reach out to touch Bernard.

CHAPTER TWENTY-THREE

A WOMAN—BERNARD'S wife—is angrily packing a suitcase.

"Don't go." Bernard tugs on his messy beard, his hair disheveled around his tired face. "Please don't."

"I can't live this way," she says without looking at him. "That killer is more important to you than either me or your living daughter."

A killer? What a pity. Sounds like the kidnapping I witnessed ended in the worst possible way.

Bernard's hands tighten into fists, but instead of yelling at his wife—or worse—he turns on his heel and slams the door behind him so hard it nearly flies off the hinges.

He storms into his office, where I can see the scope of his obsession. The place is completely covered with newspaper clippings. On the wall is a map with pushpins, and there's even a collection of milk cartons with pictures of kids on them.

The good news for me is that this section of the trauma loop looks to be over. The bad news is that there's at least one more coming. I can feel it approaching.

A familiar pressure appears on my arm that has nothing to do with the dream. Confirming my suspicion, my cheek stings from a slap.

Just like it happened the last time, my dreamwalking trance breaks, and I open my eyes back in the waking world.

Filth stands over me with a satisfied expression on his pale, weasely face.

"Kain said you need to save your powers for the investigation," he snarls. "And here I come and catch you entertaining yourself."

I debate lying that I was doing my job but decide not to risk it. Resisting the urge to sanitize the skin he touched, I say in the nicest tone I can manage, "I'm glad you're here."

He looks at me as if I've sprouted an elephant trunk. Then a nasty smile splits his face. "Do you need something from me?" he asks in what he probably thinks is a seductive tone. It's repugnant. "Some precious liquid, perhaps?"

I fight my gag reflex. "Actually, I need information. It's related to what you're talking about."

"Oh?" He cocks an arrogant eyebrow.

I remind myself that I'm talking to a killing machine and that it wouldn't be wise to punch him in that weasely mug. "Keep in mind I'm asking for the investigation, okay?" I take a breath. "Is it true you supply Gertrude with said precious liquid?"

His fangs show up, making his face truly frightening—less weasel and more wolverine.

I surreptitiously back away. "I ask because Kain told me as much. I just want to double-check, so—"

"Kain is the only reason you're not a blood bag. Push me again, and I'll risk his wrath." His gaze drops to the vein pulsing in my neck. "I'd love to show you your place in the food chain."

I figure I can safely take this reaction as a yes. Time for some reconciliation. "I didn't mean to upset you."

He stares at me the way I plan to look at a proper Gomorran meal after all these Earth bananas.

I decide to throw him another olive branch. "Your alibi checked out, by the way. I don't know if Kain told you that."

His expression doesn't change.

Clearing my very dry throat, I say, "Is there a place where the Council keeps records of things like voting, the Mandate ceremonies, or when each member joined the Council?"

Might as well dig through some files, like a real detective.

Filth glares at me for another second, then turns on his heel and strides to the door.

I grab a bunch of bananas and follow him through the maze of corridors, keeping a few feet between us at all times, just in case.

He stops when we reach a set of doors with a fancy

design carved into them. Without a word, he opens them for me.

As soon as I step inside, he slams them shut behind me.

CHAPTER TWENTY-FOUR

RELIEVED TO BE out of his sight, I sanitize all the places where he touched me and look around, whistling appreciatively. This is the largest library of paper books I've ever seen. How many trees died to make this happen? On Gomorrah, a tree costs as much as a week of Mom's medical bills, so most people read electronically. Only the obscenely wealthy enjoy printed books.

"Anything interesting happening?" Felix asks in a gravelly voice. "I couldn't fall asleep after all."

Not much, I text him. *About to look through some records.*

The faint sound of typing emanates from the earpiece. When he's not hacking Earth banks and such, Felix makes his living working for humans as a software engineer and, ironically, as a cybersecurity consultant.

I advance deeper into the library. In the back, I spot

a person sitting in a lounge chair. He's holding a bagel in one hand and a paper book in the other.

I know him. It's Chester, the probability manipulator whose dream I entered a few hours ago—and he's not alone.

Felix stops typing. "Wow."

You can say that again. Next to Chester lies an enormous white lion ravaging something that looks suspiciously like a chunk of goat. At least I hope it's a goat and not, say, an unlucky monk.

I stop several yards away and warily eye the tableau. Neither man nor lion are paying attention to me, so I speak up. "Excuse me. I hope I'm not interrupting your breakfast."

The lion's ear twitches, but he keeps eating his grisly meal.

Chester puts down his book, revealing a satyric grin. "If it isn't the detective extraordinaire. Do you have questions for me as part of your investigation?"

I nervously peel one of the bananas. "I'm just here to review some records."

Chester's grin widens. "A coincidence, huh?"

"Doesn't he look just like the Joker from the Arkham video game franchise?" Felix whispers. "It's Ariel's favorite."

I smile at Chester and say politely, "You're a probability manipulator, right?"

"You looked into me?" He scratches the lion behind the ear as one would a cat. The beast doesn't seem to mind, perhaps because it's too busy with the meal, or perhaps because Chester's luck prevents him from getting mauled.

I swallow a piece of banana without chewing. "I created a dream link with you while you slept last night. It's only prudent for me to know more about you."

This is a lie, of course. I can't say what powers many of the Councilors I connected with have. Kain didn't bother telling me that.

"Did you hear that, Bertie?" Chester looks down at the lion. "I didn't banish you from my bed just for shits and giggles." He gives me a crooked grin. "Bert is still surly with me over that."

"He sleeps with that lion?" Felix exclaims, echoing my thoughts. "How does he still have all his limbs attached?"

"I appreciate your asking Bert not to be there." I dry-swallow another piece of banana. "I have a feeling he wouldn't like someone touching his master in the middle of the night."

Chester's grin turns sinister. "Oh, he'd love it if someone tried. If you don't count napping, killing things is Bertie's favorite pastime."

How lovely. I picture the lion engaged in said pastime and suppress a shudder. "Well, it's nice to have met you both. Research awaits."

"One second." Chester's grin evaporates. "Don't you want to know what I was doing when Gemma died?"

"You're not really a suspect." I squeeze the remains of my banana a little too hard, and it plops onto the floor, where Bert the lion gives it a disgusted glare. "Why bug you until I have to?"

"It's no trouble. I was walking Bert at the time."

The lion's ears perk up. He must recognize the word *walk* the way dogs seem to.

"Don't you think the lady doth protest too much?" Felix whispers. "If he wasn't already on your suspect list, I'd add him."

Felix might be right, but I have to tread carefully, and not just because of the lion a few feet away.

"Thanks for that," I say with a hopefully enthusiastic smile. "Now I won't need to bother you or your friend here ever again."

"Let's hope you don't," Felix whispers.

"Start your search over there." Chester points at a stack of books to his left.

"Thanks." I obligingly head where he suggests. The first book I touch happens to be about probability manipulators and the feats they can perform.

"Do you think that was an intimidation tactic?" Felix asks as I drag my finger over a section in the text that talks about a trickster's ability to increase the probability that their enemies will get cancer or suffer accidental death.

Or a way to clear himself, I text back. *Why leave bodies around when he can use more subtle means?*

"To make a statement?" Felix says, echoing Kain's earlier suggestion. "Not to mention that by the second or third accident, everyone would suspect him anyway."

True, I text. *Still, I'd need a motive before I get on his bad side.*

"Smart. Just keep in mind that if it's some kind of vendetta, it wouldn't be Chester's first. He—"

"Let's go, Bertie," I hear Chester say. "If you're a good boy, I'll take you to Africa tomorrow."

"Did he just provide himself with an excuse to run?" Felix asks.

Maybe, I text back.

I watch Chester leave the library, hand draped casually over the lion's white mane, and decide that the "trickster" label fits this particular probability manipulator extremely well.

Okay. Time to look for something useful.

I walk all around to see if the dust patterns can tell me whether anything was recently updated, or if the book jackets can give me a hint on where to start.

Nope. The room looks to have been meticulously dusted, no doubt by the monks, and the bindings on most books are identical, forcing me to have to open each tome to figure out what's inside.

I sigh and peel another banana as I look for anything resembling records.

Nothing.

I eat banana after banana and keep looking, finding nothing but useless minutiae. Is it possible they keep the day-to-day records on higher shelves? There's a ladder here, but I'd need months to go through them all.

A few hours and bananas later, when I've made

almost a full circle back to the place where Chester pointed me earlier, I spot something useful on an easy-to-reach shelf.

Voting records—score.

You seeing this? I text Felix.

His typing ceases in my earpiece. "Interesting. Can't help but notice that by starting where Chester pointed, you took the longest possible time to come across that book."

You're right, I write back. *Was he hoping I'd give up? Or is this a coincidence?*

"There are no coincidences when probability manipulators are involved. He'd be the first to tell you that."

He's probably right. Flipping to the back of the book, I eagerly check the last entry. Yep, the vote over my fate is already part of this record. I examine the names of everyone who wanted me dead.

Gertrude. No surprise there.

Eduardo the werewolf. Interesting.

Albina, the Councilor with the matter-dissolving power who dodged getting a dream link with me last night. Also interesting.

And surprise, surprise: Chester also voted to kill me.

I don't recognize a few of the other names, so I note them in my phone so I can check if they have an alibi—in part out of spite but more out of solid logic. Before the vote, the idea of using my skills for sleuthing had been mentioned. If the guilty party believed in my skill, they'd have voted to kill me to prevent me from figuring out their identity.

I text Felix my thoughts.

"I think I agree with you. But just to play devil's advocate, if the killer is cautious, they might not have voted against you."

Good point, I text back. *Still worth examining the voting records closely.*

Felix yawns. "You do that. Meanwhile, I'll give napping another shot."

I open the book to a random spot and read about a case that sounds very similar to my own. Like me, the young woman, Siti, didn't have a Mandate at the time of her crimes. Though it doesn't say what her powers were, she apparently used them to make human hospice patients feel better in their final days. According to the Council, she risked "exposing the existence of the Cognizant to the human population at large." Unfortunately for her, the outcome of her case was unlike mine: The vote did not go in her favor, and she was executed.

I recognize a lot of the names on the list of people who voted against this girl. Interestingly, Chester isn't among them. I flip pages until I find a similar type of case.

Yep, the same people voted to kill this guy as the Siti girl, but Chester did not.

I keep looking.

The voting pattern remains eerily consistent, which I guess makes sense. If one is dead set against any exposure to humans, they would be likely to remain so.

I skim the pages faster until I come across a case where the voting record is slightly different. Very interesting indeed. The defendant in this case was Princess Peach, Ariel and Felix's roommate. In her case, Chester voted for the ultimate penalty.

An even more interesting case waits on the next page. This time, Chester himself is on trial. Not much detail is given apart from "spoke about Cognizant secrets to the uninitiated." Unlike all the prior cases, where the vote was to decide execution, Chester risked nothing more than being expelled from the Council. The vote didn't go in Chester's favor; they removed him. Huh. He must've earned his way back since then. But not surprisingly, the same people who typically voted for execution in similar cases voted to expel Chester as well.

Could that be his motive? All the dead Councilors came from the list of people who voted for execution in these cases. Could Chester be getting revenge for what he perceived as an indignity? It would explain his out-of-character vote to kill me, a person who could potentially expose him.

If this is true, the next person to die will be one of the Councilors who voted to execute or expel in cases of exposure to humans.

Hey, are you napping? I text Felix.

He doesn't reply.

I go into the dream world, tell Pom he has a chance to see Felix again, and enter Felix's dream.

He's sitting on the couch, playing a video game in which creatures that look a bit like Pom fight each other with cool superpowers.

"Hey," I say. "I figured you might be asleep."

Felix looks at his video game controller, at the creatures on his screen, at me, and finally at Pom. His unibrow seesaws on his forehead. "Every single time, it's so freaking hard to believe I'm dreaming." He looks back at the screen again. "Also, why am I not doing something more interesting in my dream, like flying?"

"I'm sure you do that sometimes." I join him on the couch, and Pom flits over to sit between us. "Sorry to interrupt, but I need to talk to you about Chester."

"And I need to play the game." Pom is all but bouncing with eagerness. "What are those creatures?"

"Pokémon." Grinning, Felix hands Pom the video game controller. "Try playing as Pikachu or Jigglypuff."

A happily purple Pom starts mashing the buttons.

Felix turns to me. "So. Chester."

I tell him what I've discovered and ask, "Do you think he could be the killer?"

"Thinking about probability manipulation gives me a headache." Felix theatrically rubs his temples. "I think he could be."

"Oh?"

"Let's start with the arrow. If there was a chance Tatum could be hit with it, Chester's power would've made it a certainty. And when it comes to sneaking up on the elf, he could've used his power so the elf wouldn't have noticed his arrival until too late, or he could've made the elf fall off the cliff by accident."

I was thinking along the same lines, but it's good to hear another person confirm it.

"He could've also been behind the bird attack," Felix continues. "If there was a chance the birds would go crazy one day and peck the dreamwalker to death, Chester could've increased that probability."

"Right, but what about Gemma?" I ask. "She was ripped in half. There's no chance he could've done that, is there?"

"Maybe his lion?"

"Maybe. That thing did look like pure muscle. It has to be incredibly strong."

Felix scoots away from Pom, who's going at the game with ever-greater enthusiasm. "You should talk to Kain about this as soon as you can. But do it carefully. Part of Chester's power is being in the right place at the right time, so he might overhear."

"Then how am I—"

"Am I interrupting you again?" Kain's voice booms from the sky.

Speak of the devil. He's caught me in my trance again.

"Thanks, Felix. I've got to go." I wake myself up.

As expected, Kain is standing next to me in the library, his thin mouth more downturned than usual.

I put my hand over my rapidly beating heart. "I was working on the case, I swear."

"And?"

"We need to talk, but not here." I look around the book stacks furtively. "Can we go outside where we can't be overheard?"

Kain raises an eyebrow. "Sure."

He leads me through the stone corridors until we reach the castle entrance and emerge from the mountain to the woodsy smell of wet vegetation and the light drizzle of rain.

"Let's go talk by the moat," I say, ignoring the water droplets striking my face. Hopefully they're not too contaminated. On Earth, one never knows.

Kain nods, and we walk in silence until we almost reach our destination—at which point I realize a couple of problems with my plan.

The moat smells like a sewer, and Hekima is already standing in the middle of the bridge that goes over it.

The elderly illusionist is holding an umbrella and puffing on a pipe. I guess with all those carcinogens flowing into his lungs, he can't smell the stench wafting off the water. When he spots the two of us, he exhales a cloud of smoke and waves with his pipe.

So much for a private chat.

Kain's expression suddenly changes. "Watch out," he yells, pointing at something behind Hekima. "Run!"

Hekima spins on his heel and screams in horror.

I follow the path of Kain's finger and bite back a scream of my own.

A huge head is rising from the moat on a long

slender neck. It looks like a dinosaur, although I have no idea what kind.

Hekima starts backing away, only to slip on the wet stones, falling to his hands and knees. Mouth open for another scream, he lifts his arm defensively—just as the creature opens its tooth-filled maw and strikes, chopping off Hekima's upper torso in a single bite.

CHAPTER TWENTY-FIVE

WHAT REMAINS of Hekima spouts a fountain of blood.

I shriek.

Fangs busting out, Kain flashes toward the edge of the bridge. The beast must fear vampires, because it seizes the rest of Hekima in its jaws and disappears into the murky waters.

"What the hell?" Shaking uncontrollably, I lurch after Kain. "What was that?"

The vampire curses and glares at the water as though he's contemplating diving in.

"Are you insane?" I grab his shoulder. "Hekima is dead. Do you want to join him?"

He twists around to face me. "You're not going to tell anyone about this," he says through gritted teeth. "The rain will wash away the blood and…"

I don't know what he says next. Moving purely on adrenaline-filled autopilot, I pull out the hand sanitizer and clean my hands, as though the blood Kain speaks of is on them.

"Don't worry," I say numbly when he gives me a shake. "I won't tell anyone."

"And you realize that was another murder, right?" He stares into my eyes as though he's about to glamour me.

"It was?" I reflexively sanitize my hands again.

"Come inside." He grabs my fresh, clean hand and drags me behind him like a rag doll.

I'm not sure if he glamours me or not, but I somehow find myself back in his quarters.

"What did you want to talk to me about?" he growls. "Speak."

Shaking off the residual shock, I look around for listening devices. I don't see any, but that doesn't mean much. "Can you go to sleep again? No one can overhear us if we speak in the dream world."

He rolls his eyes but obediently stalks into his bedroom and puts himself to sleep. I slip into the dream world, ask Pom not to show himself, and find Kain. He's already deep within a dream of drinking blood from a woman I've never seen.

I make the woman disappear, convince him he's dreaming, and place us in my cloud office—in this case, to soothe my own raw nerves. Kain can fend for himself.

"Sit there." I point to where I usually sit and take the therapy couch myself. "Now, what was that thing?" I replicate the creature that ate Hekima a few feet away. "Do things like that live on Earth?"

He gives my recreation a baleful glare. "It was Nessie. She was a gift from the Council in Scotland."

I goggle at him. "As in the Loch Ness monster?"

He nods. "Humans got wind of the poor creature, so she had to be relocated."

Oh, crap—he's serious. I make Nessie disappear and create a stuffed replica of Pom's usual dream shape so I can hug him to my chest. "Why would you put something so dangerous in your moat?"

Kain shrugs wearily. "It happened before my time, back when the Council kept prisoners in the dungeon. Anyone escaping through the sewers became Nessie's lunch."

Disgusting. The cell they initially gave me as a room —if I'd used that hole-in-the-floor excuse of a toilet, I'd literally have been putting my butt on the line. I take in a deep breath and reassure myself that I never would've come near that hole to the sewer anyway, monster or no monster. Way too unsanitary.

Shoving the unpleasant image away, I ask, "Was this the first time Nessie's attacked people outside her domain?"

Kain dips his chin in a single nod. "I didn't know it was possible. Now that I think about it, I guess someone with Gemma's power could make Nessie act like that, but—"

"Is there someone else with Gemma's powers on the

Council? They could be behind Leal's death *and* this murder."

Kain sighs. "She was the only one."

"What about probability powers?" I create a replica of Chester in front of us. "I imagine there's always been some small chance Nessie would attack someone by the moat. A trickster could've boosted those odds."

"Maybe. In theory. But why?"

I tell him my suspicions about Chester.

"That doesn't track," he says. "Hekima wasn't yet on the Council when they kicked Chester out."

Puck, that's right. Hekima wasn't on the list of people who voted against Chester—or anyone else, for that matter. There goes that theory.

I hug my Pom replica harder. "So maybe it was an actual accident. Maybe Nessie got hungry after all this time without prisoners to munch on."

Kain scoffs. "The monks feed her a goat per day. I think we need to treat this as a murder, which is why I told you to keep quiet."

I don't have a good feeling about this. "What do you mean?"

"As I said, if there's another murder, your fate becomes uncertain. To put it mildly."

My heart rate triples. Since this is the dream world, I zoom out of my body to calm it the puck down.

"I bet the real reason is his reputation as the head of the Enforcers," Pom—who must've gone invisible to listen to the whole thing—whispers in my ear as soon as I'm back.

He's right. This murder happened under Kain's nose. He's bound to look bad if anyone learns about it.

Making Dream Chester disappear, I ask, "What if Hekima upset him in some way?"

"Could be," Kain says. "Why don't you check his alibi?"

"I will. Do you happen to know where he was when Tatum was shot with that arrow, by any chance? He volunteered information about his whereabouts during Gemma's murder, but—"

"Vegas. I think he was in Las Vegas." Kain stands and starts to pace the cloud. "His lion has a girlfriend among the lions at The Mirage hotel, but that's just the excuse. Chester likes to walk into casinos and use his power to win at slot machines. Usually an unsuspicious amount."

I make a mental note to check on what The Mirage's casino looks like. "As soon as Chester goes to sleep, I'll check those alibis."

"Until then, you're to stay in my quarters so I can keep an eye on you," Kain says. "We're not going to discuss any of this, in case your paranoia is right. You're also not going to eat or drink anything. We want to avoid any unfortunate accidents."

I solemnly nod and wake us up.

Opening his eyes, Kain jackknifes from the bed and heads toward his dining area without a second glance.

Fighting the urge to lie down on the fuzzy coverlet, I follow him and plop onto a barstool by the kitchen counter. He's already on his laptop and ignores me completely.

I take out my phone and look up the casino to note a few key details. Then I put my phone away and just sit there, too tired to do anything else. After a while, the last remnants of adrenaline trickle out of my system, and the strongest drowsiness I've ever experienced hits me.

I jump up and begin to pace—but I still feel on the verge of falling asleep.

This is why humans on this world use sleep deprivation as torture. It is. I'd do anything to get some shut-eye. Well, evening is only a few hours away. Maybe I could nap? If I'm lucky, it'll be dreamless. But even if it isn't, at this point I'm willing to face my worst nightmares just to make this feeling stop.

"Can I use your bed?" I ask, stifling a yawn.

Kain looks up from his laptop. "To sleep? What about your vice?"

I drop my gaze. "It's been some time since I drank. There's a chance I might be able to fall asleep—a small one, but—"

"Be my guest." He returns his attention to the screen. "I'll wake you when I need you."

What a relief. I go into the bedroom, and ignoring the BDSM paraphernalia all around me, I hurl myself into the bed.

Of course, now that I'm horizontal, sleep doesn't come—typical of how this works on vampire blood.

I give it a good attempt anyway by counting moofts.

At 5,407, Kain walks into the room. "It's time."

I wearily roll to my feet. "You think Chester is sleeping?"

"I know it. Do what you must," Kain says and heads out of the room.

Without further deliberation, I touch Pom and enter the dream world.

The looft appears in front of me, turns purple, and squeals as if he's not seen me in forever. Then again, since he's in the dream world so much, his sense of time might be warped.

"Hey, bud," I say as I head to the tower of sleepers. "How are things going?"

"I'm happy to see you." He flies circles around me. "I was worried."

My adrenaline spike must've affected him. As a parasite—I mean, symbiont—he gets all my hormones.

His ears turn red. "You thought that P-word again."

"And you read my thoughts again. If you'd read them carefully, you'd know I mentally corrected myself."

"Still," he says grumpily. "You wouldn't like it if I thought of you as a meanie-poo and then reminded myself that you're just having PMS and it's your hormones to blame."

"I don't even know where to start with that." Reaching the tower, I skim the nooks for Chester. "You realize that thanks to your symbiont nature, when I have PMS, you do as well?"

Pom's enormous eyes grow wider. "I do?"

"You're flooded with the same hormones—and get just as cranky."

He wiggles his ears. "I think you're just so irritable you *perceive* me as cranky."

Ignoring him, I fly over to Chester's bed, where a cloud gathers above his head. "Puck."

Pom sniffs the cloud. "It's bad. Like rotten eggs."

I reach for Chester's forehead. "I'm going in anyway."

CHAPTER TWENTY-SIX

"SWEETHEART?" Chester shouts from his office. "Sweetheart, the baby is crying."

No response.

He frowns and goes to the infant. Stopping next to the crib, he smiles at her, and the little girl stops wailing immediately. Either she's missed her dad, or he's using his power to increase the chances of her feeling soothed.

"I'm going to look for Mommy," he croons. "It's strange she didn't hear you. Her earsies are as sensitive as the Big Bad Wolf's."

The baby gives him a toothless grin. He reluctantly exits the nursery and starts searching the house room by room.

"Matilda?" he calls out by the master bathroom door. "You in there?"

No reply.

He tries the handle. It's locked. "Sweetheart, everything okay in there?"

Silence.

Frown returning, he tugs on the door handle. A strange click sounds, and the door unlocks—no doubt the probability of its doing so just got boosted.

He peers inside.

There's a razor blade on the tile floor and water spilling over the sides of a bathtub. Reddish water.

Pom was right. This is a bad one.

Face losing all color, Chester rushes in.

In the tub lies a gorgeous woman with flawless skin that resembles white chocolate melted over silk. Flawless skin that's marred by the no-longer-bleeding cuts on her wrists.

Frantically, he checks her pulse. "No!" He grabs her naked body and pulls it out of the tub. "No. Please no."

He points at the body with his hand and strains, using his power to its fullest potential.

It doesn't work. There must be zero chance for this woman to come back to life.

"How could this happen?" he wails.

I wish Pom were here now so I could squeeze him. A mother gone forever—it hits too close to home. Would it be so bad to run back to my dream palace to recover and come back to deal with Chester later?

I steel myself. The investigation awaits—and it's a means to save my mother, who, unlike Chester's wife, still *can* be saved.

I force my attention back to the dream at hand.

The trauma loop is now over, but some intuition forces me to let the next set of dreams play out anyway.

Chester is sitting in his living room, the baby in his arms. "I'm going to find out what happened to Mommy." He readjusts his grip on the warm milk bottle. His voice turns grim. "When I do, whoever's responsible will pay."

The rest of the dream doesn't seem to have any answers, and neither does the one after that.

Then I hit the jackpot.

Around us is the lab with cannibal doves, and Chester is there, speaking with Leal the dreamwalker.

"Our dear seer colleague, Darian, prophesied that if my wife didn't die, our child would," Chester says in a low, furious voice. "But of course you already knew that."

Leal stands up. "I didn't. I mean, we all know how much you hate Darian, but—"

Chester rises as well. "She learned that foul prophecy from a dreamwalker. How many of you scum can there be?"

"It wasn't me." Leal backs away in the direction of the bird cages. "I have no reason to lie."

"You have all the reasons." Chester's jaw flexes menacingly.

"I don't." Stopping his retreat, Leal straightens his spine. "I uncovered some interesting things in your dreams. If something were to happen to me—even by accident—everyone would learn what you did."

"You threaten me?" In his fury, Chester's face looks eerily like that of a puck.

"I'm just reminding you of the consequences of rash action," Leal says. "And driving home a simple point: I have no reason to lie to you. If your wife had asked for something I thought you'd disapprove of, I'd have come to you first. You're my fellow Councilor. She wasn't."

The dream cuts off here, and the next one isn't a memory. I let it play out in the background as I process what I've learned.

Chester had a dispute with Leal. He also had to be careful about antagonizing him. Leal had something on him, something that would've come out in case of his death. Could it be that Chester went ahead and killed him anyway? Or is my earlier theory correct, and Chester has been killing those who voted him off the Council? But then why didn't Leal make good on his threat? Why didn't his secrets about Chester get out?

Also, why did Chester kill Hekima?

In any case, this explains Chester's vote against me. It sounds as though his wife's suicide drove him to dislike seers and dreamwalkers, and I'm one of the latter.

Well, he'll hate me even more once I reveal him as the killer.

I observe his dreams flickering by until I see his lion viciously killing a man. I shift that dream into the lion walking outside the castle in a fog, Chester close behind him. I set the date and time to match Gemma's murder and wait for Chester to fill in the details.

They amble peaceably down the trail.

What the hell? This dream is a memory. Neither Chester nor his lion ripped Gemma in half.

What about shooting Tatum with the arrow?

I set the date and time to match that murder and replace the castle grounds with a casino. Chester fills in the details again, and I see him winning a small jackpot —again, a memory. If he was in Las Vegas, he couldn't have shot Tatum with an arrow in New York, probability powers or not.

"Are you satisfied now?" Chester says, looking right at me.

I stare at him openmouthed.

"You forgot to make yourself invisible." He grins. "As luck would have it, so to speak."

He's right. I indeed forgot.

"I just proved you're not guilty," I say quickly, before he decides to give me cancer or worse.

He puts a coin into a nearby slot machine and wins again. "Which is why I made sure I was in REM sleep when you needed me to be."

I use my powers to make myself look smaller and frailer. "I didn't learn anything… overly personal."

He chuckles humorlessly. "Let's cut to the chase. I know that you know that I voted to kill you." He feeds a coin into yet another slot machine and gets a river of them back. "I did that because I dislike dreamwalkers on general principle—and now you have an idea why."

I nod warily.

He grins as he pokes through a handful of coins for

the one he wants. "When my power brought us together in the library, I realized you might actually be useful. I was right, of course—you just cleared me of any wrongdoing. I think Kain suspected me somewhat, so make sure to set him straight."

"I will. Are we cool now?" *Do I have to worry about DNA mutations and things like that?* is what I want to add, but I don't in case that gives him the idea.

"If you stay out of my dreams from this moment forward, you won't need to worry about me," he says magnanimously. "Now wake up."

I do.

Locating Kain, I tell him Chester isn't guilty.

"Because of Hekima, I didn't think so either," Kain says. "So, what's next?"

"I think I should make dream connections with Eduardo and Nina to verify their alibis. After that, I can link up with the rest of the Council."

Kain nods and leads me to Nina's quarters.

The stone slab isn't blocking the way—she's expecting us.

I sweep my gaze over the area where she'd indicated she does yoga, memorizing a few key details, and follow Kain into the bedroom.

I'm in luck.

Nina's in REM sleep, so I quickly enter her dream world.

———

POM GREETS me as I speed to the tower of sleepers. "Who are you working on now?"

"Nina. And I fear she'll have a trauma loop."

"Oh?" He turns a light orange color.

I shrug. "Something about her."

When I locate Dream Nina, I breathe a sigh of relief.

"No cloud," Pom says. "I guess she's not as troubled as you thought."

"Yeah." I make sure to turn invisible. "It's your call if you want to join me or not."

"I will," he says conspiratorially and turns invisible also. "Can we talk telepathically?"

Fine, I think pointedly. *But don't get used to reading my thoughts.*

I won't, Pom says as a voice in my head. *Thank you.*

I touch the space between Nina's sharply defined dark eyebrows.

———

THE TENNIS BALL machine shoots balls at Nina at a machine-gun clip. She catches each ball using her telepathy and throws it into a basket. Another ball gun starts shooting at her from a different angle, and she diverts those projectiles just as easily.

What's she doing? Pom asks.

Training her power, I think back. *Please let me concentrate.*

I look around the tennis court for a way to turn it into Nina's apartment.

Something odd catches my attention: The windows of this building are solid black. Shrugging it off, I settle in to wait until Nina tires of practice.

She finally gathers up her things and heads for the locker room. I set the date and time to Gemma's murder and shift the location. Instead of a bathroom, Nina walks off the court into her own apartment—and as so often happens with dreamers, she doesn't blink an eye at the switcheroo.

The windows here are black as well, an odd detail I can't recall adding.

It doesn't matter, though.

Nina levitates the furniture, unrolls a mat, and flows into her first yoga pose.

Puck, I think for Pom's benefit. *This is a memory.*

So she's not guilty?

Appears that way. I'm going to wake up now. See you soon.

Before Pom can protest, I come out of the trance.

————

AFTER I UPDATE Kain on my finding, we set off to Eduardo's quarters. When we get there, the bed is empty.

Kain's fangs emerge. "He said he'd be here tonight."

"Maybe he goes to bed later?" I look around the spartan bedroom for any hints.

"We'll give him a few hours," Kain growls.

For a while after that, we walk around the castle, and I enter people's bedrooms and make connections—going down the remaining list of Councilors who voted to kill me. When we get to the last on that list, I recognize the living room we enter.

This is the dwelling of Albina, the Councilor who'd left a note apologizing for missing her dream link the last time.

I perk up. Avoiding me that time was shady. Maybe she should be higher on my list of suspects.

Kain sniffs the air, his face darkening. Fangs out in full force, he rushes into Albina's bedroom.

I sprint into the room after him, only to halt abruptly.

On my wrist, Pom turns black.

On the bed lies Albina, or so I assume. Her naked body is vampire pale, with hideous bruises on her neck. Given her disheveled appearance, it's not difficult to work out a case of erotic asphyxiation gone wrong—or worse.

Kain checks the pulse on her wrist, and I hold my breath, preparing for what he's about to say.

"Nothing." He releases her wrist. "She's dead."

CHAPTER TWENTY-SEVEN

A SURGE of adrenaline wipes away all traces of my earlier sleepiness. Kain said if more people die, I would follow—and now two have died on my watch.

Moving so fast he almost blurs, Kain rips open his wrist with his teeth and forces blood into Albina's mouth.

Nothing happens.

Actually, that's not true. Something happens, but not to Albina—to me. I stare hypnotically at the blood as Kain checks Albina's pulse again, curses, and blurs out of the room.

Stumbling out of the bedroom, I locate the kitchen and heave half-digested bananas into the sink.

Where did Kain go? What should I do? Questions swirl through my mind, but not a single answer. I grope for a glass, pour some probably contaminated tap water into it, and gulp it down.

With yet another dead body on my watch, I'm unlikely to live long enough to get sick.

On every level possible, I feel horrible. I'm shaking, my mouth and throat are on fire, and I crave sleep the way a man craves water in a desert.

The walls around me close in.

I'm having trouble breathing.

Did I just discover another dead body? Did I really witness Hekima being eaten?

Could the sleep deprivation be giving me hallucinations?

I reach for the vial of diluted vampire blood. Am I craving this? Seeing Kain's blood pour out of his body didn't gross me out as it should have. It fascinated me. Is that the first stage of addiction? Some later stage?

Then again, if I don't want to collapse and fall asleep this very second, I need to do *something*.

I can try severely limiting my dose. I pour a droplet of the watered blood into my glass and fill it again with water. Pocketing the vial, I dip my finger into the glass and flick off most of the moisture. It doesn't get more diluted than this.

I lick the finger.

The pleasure is as intense as the last time, maybe even more so. I moan and smash my forehead into the refrigerator.

I can barely feel the pain.

Pucking puck, something's trickling down my forehead.

I swipe at it and stare at the red liquid staining my

fingers. Blood. Unlike before, my wounds aren't healing. I guess my medicine was too diluted for that particular effect.

Worse still, I feel almost as sleep deprived as before.

Kain barges into the apartment with a disheveled Isis in tow.

Of course—when his blood didn't work, he went to get a healer.

Isis narrows her sleepy eyes at me and points a finger at my forehead, shooting it with golden energy.

The healing warmth feels good, but not as intensely as vampire blood.

I touch my forehead.

The wound is closed.

"Don't bother with her," Kain growls. "Your patient's in there." He drags her into the bedroom.

I follow them in just as Isis hits Albina with a beam of golden energy, which she maintains as she checks the dead woman's vitals.

The beam stops.

"I'm sorry," she says in a sleep-raspy voice. "She was beyond healing."

Kain slams a fist into the wall, burying his arm to the elbow.

Isis pulls a blanket over the body. "We should have Roger—or better yet, a human forensic expert—take a look."

Roger. That name sounds familiar. Wasn't he the one who'd made a sleeping drug for Leal?

Isis catches my gaze. "I take it you don't know who did this?"

I shake my head, and Kain gives me such a murderous glare I fully expect him to drain my blood—or worse—right here and now.

"The werewolf. Eduardo." I try to keep my voice even. "Did he have a relationship with her?" I glance at the corpse.

Jaw tight, Kain shakes his head.

"He wasn't in his room earlier," I remind him. "Maybe this is where he was."

"Take care of this," Kain barks at Isis and strides out so quickly I have to run to keep up.

By the time we get back to the werewolf's apartment, I'm wheezing for breath.

"He'd better be there," Kain growls.

We barge into the bedroom and find the large man in his bed, snoring like a geriatric dog.

Kain nods at the bed. "Do your job," he tells me in a low, hard voice.

"He's not in REM sleep," I whisper. "We've got to wait."

His voice rises in volume. "I'm running out of patience. Two more Councilors dead. If I were you, I'd make myself useful forthwith."

Puck. I guess this isn't a good time to tell him about the dreamwalker's notes where he talked about the difficulty of entering werewolf dreams.

Wait a second. How could I forget? The black windows in Nina's dream. They're—

"There," Kain says, quieter this time. "Look at his eyelids."

He's right. The werewolf has entered REM sleep—a record, considering he wasn't in bed only a few minutes ago.

Faking confidence, I sidle up to the prone figure and touch his muscled neck.

CHAPTER TWENTY-EIGHT

POM SHOWS up as soon as I enter the dream world, and I pet him to relax a little before attempting the multibody technique from Leal's diary.

Just as before, I create a second body for myself far away from where I stand, in case that helps. Next, I exit my current body and will myself to come back into both.

Nope. I end up in the original body.

I do it again, straining my willpower.

I end up in the farther body instead of the original, but not in both.

"I guess that's still something," Pom says dubiously. "You've learned a type of teleportation."

"Right, but that's not what I need."

Still, Pom has a point. This *is* a way to teleport around the dream world. Then again, isn't going to a different dream already teleportation? Or is that building reality around myself?

Leaving the metaphysics for later, I exit my body, create one in the tower of sleepers, and dismiss the original one. Reentering myself, I end up in the tower —functional teleportation.

Hey, it's something.

For good measure, I test out the multibody technique once more and fail. I guess there's no helping it. I'll need to deal with the werewolf the usual way, in one body.

I teleport to his nook, turn invisible, and touch him the same way I did in the waking world.

———

AS SOON AS I materialize inside Eduardo's dream world, I see what the problem is—and it's a big one.

Somehow, the werewolf is having two dreams at the same time, something I've never experienced and didn't think possible. The two dreams are juxtaposed on top of each other, at least from my point of view, like two movie projectors playing different movies aimed at the same screen.

In one dream—a violent nature show—Eduardo is in wolf form, ripping a gazelle to shreds and relishing the feeling of warm blood in his maw. In the other dream, Eduardo the man is doing it doggy style—or is it wolfy style?—with a woman I don't recognize.

Could she be Albina?

It's hard to tell, especially with the sex and violence crossing over into each other.

The wolf abruptly stops eating, raises his bloodied muzzle, and sniffs the air. Looking right at me with animal eyes, he howls and bounds forward. At the same moment, the naked man stops thrusting and twists to look at me.

I want to run, but the two environments make it difficult to orient myself, and pain explodes in my neck as the wolf's teeth bite down.

Before he can shut those jaws and kill me, I wake myself up.

————

BACK IN MY REAL BODY, my heart is hammering so hard I'm afraid it'll punch a hole through my ribcage. If the wolf had dug his teeth any deeper, I'd have died in the dream and would be homicidal right about now.

Speaking of homicidal, the way Kain is looking at me isn't good.

"I'm sorry." I back away. "I couldn't check his alibi."

"You what?" His fangs slide out.

"I knew this might happen. Werewolves are difficult to dreamwalk in."

Kain's eyes turn into mirrors. "Tell me the truth," he orders in a tense version of his usual honey-laced voice.

I speak robotically without meaning to. "He was dreaming two dreams at once, one for the wolf side and one for the man side. Before I could manipulate anything, he lunged at my—"

Kit bursts in. "What's going on here?"

"I release you," Kain spits at me. He turns to Kit. "I used glamour to finally get some truth out of this useless blood bag."

She frowns at me. "You're susceptible to glamour?" Glancing back at Kain, she says, "If you knew you could get her to tell the truth that way, why didn't you clear her of guilt at the hearing?"

Great question. I bet the answer is he needed me as bait to unmask the killer. Or maybe he'd hoped I'd actually solve the stupid case.

"Why are you here?" he asks Kit harshly.

"Isis woke me." Her anime-like form ripples and becomes the healer's. "She told me what happened to Albina, said Bailey mentioned a werewolf."

My attention drifts back to Eduardo. Despite seeing me in his dream, despite my waking up, and despite everyone's raised voices, the werewolf is not only still sleeping, he's dreaming like a baby.

"We should take this conversation elsewhere," I whisper, figuring that if they force me to go back into his dream—something I'd like to avoid at all costs—it's better if he stays in REM sleep.

They both glance at the sleeping werewolf and head out, with Kit assuming her usual guise on the way.

As we exit the apartment, a soul-wrenching noise blasts through the castle. It sounds as if someone's trying to replicate a bomb explosion with some infernal string instrument.

"What was that?" I exclaim when the noise stops.

My ears are still ringing.

Kit turns into a woman I've never seen. "Emergency meeting call for the Council."

"That sound could wake the dead." I sneak a glance at the werewolf's quarters.

"It's what happens when you let a siren onto the Council." Kain grabs my wrist. "Let's go."

I blink at that. "Your siren is a siren?"

"Hey, the monks used trumpets before that," Kit says, turning back into herself. "This is much better."

Without comment, Kain herds me through the corridors until I see Filth standing next to a familiar door.

"If she leaves her quarters, kill her," Kain tells him.

Filth gives me a look that seems to say, *Please leave. Pretty please with a blood cherry on top.*

"See you soon," Kit says as Kain pushes me in and slams the door behind me.

Great. The Council is going to meet, and I'm not going to be there to speak for myself.

I'm so screwed.

Washing my hands in the sink soothes me a little; sanitizing them after calms me even more. Grabbing a banana, I pace the room as I chew. When I tire of pacing, I sit on the chair and eat four more bananas in a row.

It's been at least an hour. How long does a stupid Council meeting take? I'll go crazy if I keep waiting here.

I grab hold of Pom's fur and enter the dream world.

———

"DOESN'T this make the wait even worse?" Pom asks when I apprise him of my situation. "Time feels like it passes much slower here."

"But here, I have you." I fluff the fur on top of his head. "Besides, I can also do something useful here."

I teleport to the tower and float around a bit, looking at the sleepers available to dreamwalk in. There's Felix, but I leave him alone. He deserves some sleep after that sleep deprivation marathon I put him through. I look for Nina but don't find her, which is too bad. I want to discuss something important with her. It makes sense she's not here, though; she's at the Council meeting.

Interestingly, though, some other Councilors *are* sleeping—skipping the meeting to do so. This includes Eduardo the werewolf, the deep sleeper himself.

"Is that good for you or bad for you?" Pom asks when I point this out.

"Good, I guess. Most of the sleepers voted to kill me, so if there's another vote taking place right now, their absence will help my cause."

Pom gives the sleeping werewolf a pouty glare. "Do you plan to enter his dreams again?"

"No pucking way." I fly past the werewolf's room without a second thought. "I'll just work on Bernard again."

I approach the Mario/Wario doppelgänger.

Yep. He's still got clouds indicative of a trauma loop

—and I already saw his child get kidnapped and his wife leaving. How much worse can it get?

Bracing myself, I touch his forehead.

———

BERNARD IS SITTING on the edge of his seat in a courtroom. His wife and daughter are in a separate section, and he gives them a longing look they don't return. He turns to glare at the defendant, a wiry, balding middle-aged man with shifty eyes. As if he feels Bernard's death stare, the man turns around and winks at him nastily, then looks back at the judge, who's holding a paper in her hands.

"The bastard did it," Bernard mutters under his breath. "He did it, and he's mocking me."

The judge begins to speak, commanding Bernard's full attention. He looks like he's holding his breath.

"...find the defendant not guilty," the judge states.

Bernard leaps to his feet. "That's bullshit! The—"

The dream cuts off before he can be held in contempt of court.

Wow. I feel another trauma loop coming on. This is probably a record number. Most people have one, maybe two. Did Valerian know how tough this job would be? Is that why he paid me extra? Or maybe he simply needs the final results that badly—results I've yet to produce.

Speaking of Valerian, I feel a sudden urge to take a break from Bernard's doom and gloom and revisit my uber-attractive employer in my dream bedroom. I can think of many ways his simulacra could make the time pass. He could feed me plump, juicy grapes, massage my feet with his strong, warm hands, use that sensual mouth for—

"Bailey," Kit's voice booms. "Wake up."

There goes *that* idea.

I come out of my trance, the taste of sweet grapes fading from my tongue.

CHAPTER TWENTY-NINE

"YOU'RE ONE COOL CUCUMBER," Kit says when I open my eyes. "I don't know if I'd be able to sleep under such circumstances."

"I wasn't sleeping, per se." I sit up. "How screwed am I?"

She perches on the edge of the bed and puts down the stack of papers she's holding. "The good news is they won't kill you outright. I had to use all my oratory skills to pull that off, but Kain helped."

"He did?" I move from the bed into a chair opposite her. That doesn't sound like the vampire I know.

She turns into Kain. "He's not as bad as he seems. He's just in a shitty position. Since he's the head of the Enforcers, everyone blames him for not preventing the murders. Clearly, he's decided to shift some of that pressure onto you."

As I thought. "Makes me feel so much better. What a saint."

Kit shifts back into herself. "The head of the Enforcers before Kain left very big shoes to fill."

I take in a deep breath. "What's the bad news?"

"You've got three more days to find the killer," Kit says. "And, if anyone else dies, that's it for you."

"Pucking great." I leap out of the chair and start pacing the room. I'm failing. Failing badly. If I don't get my act together, Mom stands no chance.

"I swear I did my best," Kit says. "But when Kain told everyone about Hekima and Albina's death, Gertrude made it sound like they voted to spare you in the hope that you could solve this thing. She said we needed to revote. Then Kain chimed in to give you another chance. I told them you can't prevent someone as powerful as one of us from murdering, but they didn't care." She shimmers, transforming herself into Eduardo. "You're lucky a few negative ninnies like their beauty sleep so much. As unbelievable as it sounds, the vote could've gone worse. One of the options was to kill you now."

I grimace, stopping in front of her. "Why don't I feel lucky?"

"If you want, I can help you escape." She turns into me. "There's going to be a Mandate ceremony soon, and we can disguise you to sneak out along with the guests. I can pretend to be you for a while, give you a head start."

Tempting. Very tempting—and very nice of her to offer.

Regretfully, I shake my head. "I need Isis to heal my

mom. Besides, Kain has my DNA. I don't want to have to look over my shoulder for the rest of my days." It's the same reasons I had to turn down Valerian's offer in the beginning.

Like it or not, I have to see this through.

Kit turns into Isis. "You're also lucky no one's killed *her* yet."

She's right. That wouldn't be good at all. "Speaking of luck," I say, pushing away the upsetting possibility, "did Chester vote for or against me just now? He had an alibi, but I still wonder if he could be behind it all."

"He voted to give you another chance," she replies in Chester's voice while still wearing Isis's face. "Chester can be a pain, but I don't think he's the culprit."

"Fine," I say tiredly. With the adrenaline leaving my system, the sleep deprivation is hitting me again, hard. I sink back into the chair. "Now what?"

Kit assumes her preferred anime blonde guise and hands me the stack of papers. "Kain made everyone write down what they were doing during the murders. They all swore to go to sleep in a bit, and Kain will check everyone's compliance shortly. The idea is that you'll dreamwalk in the rest of the Council as soon as possible."

"Not a bad idea." I glance at the papers. "I haven't finished connecting with everyone, though."

"That's where I come in. I'll walk you into the right people's bedrooms." She waggles her eyebrows lasciviously.

Ugh. Leave it to Kit to make the necessities of my power feel dirty.

"There's another problem," I say. "Some of the people I suspect didn't attend your meeting."

"Kain thought of that also. All but Eduardo"—she points at a highlighted section on the top paper—"were in the company of fellow Council members at the time of the murders, so you can clear multiple people for the price of one alibi."

"I already know what Eduardo was doing, or at least what he said he was doing."

"Kain mentioned your difficulties with his werewolf nature." Her forehead creases in a concerned frown. "What will you do?"

"I figure I'll start with the others and leave him for last. The more people I clear, the worse he looks, right?"

"Makes sense. Well, if you're ready, how about we—"

There's a knock on the door.

"Yes?" Kit asks in my voice.

"It's Nina," says a familiar voice.

"Come in," Kit says, fully transforming into me.

Nina walks in. Her gaze flits between Kit and me. "With all this waking up in the middle of the night, I guess I should be grateful I'm not seeing triple."

"Thank you for your vote," Kit says, still as me. "You're one of the good ones."

Nina heaves an exasperated sigh. "Can whichever one of you is Kit give us privacy?"

I look at Kit, and Kit looks at me.

"I can do this all day," I say.

Kit pouts.

"What I have to say wouldn't interest you that much, anyway," Nina says reassuringly.

Kit's pout gets poutier.

Nina raises her hand. "I solemnly swear we're not going to Netflix and chill without you."

"Fine." Kit trudges toward the door. "Be like that."

"If you leave looking like me, Firth might try to kill you," I say to Kit's back.

Her nails grow to the size of talons. "In that case, I'm definitely not changing. Might be fun to see him try."

Outside the door, I hear Filth say something nasty. Before I can figure out if he's calling me a B- or a C-word, a thud stops his rant in its tracks. In the silence come heavy footsteps.

Nina rolls her eyes. "I wonder if she turned into Colton or some orc."

"Anything's possible with her." I tilt my head, studying Nina. "I think I know why you came."

She sits on the edge of the bed. "Kain said you cleared me already, which means you've been into my dreams."

"I did and I have." I draw in a breath. "And I saw the black windows."

"So you did. Do you mind?" She points at one of my water bottles.

"Not at all."

Before I can get up and give her a bottle, she uses telekinesis to make it fly into her hand. Swiftly, she drains it and then sits, chewing on her pierced lip.

"You came to me," I remind her as the silence wears on.

She floats the water bottle back. "Sorry. This isn't easy."

I smile reassuringly. "Just start somewhere, see how it goes."

She fiddles with her nose ring. "I'm Leal's dead man's switch."

"You're what?"

She takes a deep breath. "I allowed Leal to make it so that if he dies, I'd know damaging information about his killer."

I gape at her. "You know who killed him?"

"That's just the thing." She plays with a stud above her lip before touching the one above her chin. "Until I know for sure who did it, the information won't reveal itself to me."

"I don't understand."

"I thought you knew about black windows," she says. "You're a dreamwalker like him."

"I kind of do," I say cautiously. At least I do now, having read his notes. "They're a way to hide a dream."

She nods. "A dream that can be someone's memory. Or my own."

"So the black windows I saw in your—"

"One contains something I desperately wanted to forget. Whatever it was, forgetting it was the payment for letting Leal use my subconscious as a safe." She wraps her arms around her slim frame.

"And the other windows?"

"Each will be about something someone on the Council didn't want anyone else to know," she says. "Those windows are programmed to show me a dream about someone that I believe caused Leal harm."

I sit up straighter. "What if *you* had killed him?"

"My own memory would come back to me." She visibly shudders.

"A memory of what?" I ask, frowning.

"I don't know," she says softly. "That's the whole point. After Leal did his thing, I forgot what it was. All I remember is that I don't want to remember whatever it was."

Huh. So I was right when I thought she might have a trauma loop. After Leal created her black window, she forgot whatever it was—not the healthiest way to deal with problems. Then again, if the memory was truly impossible to live with, repressing it might've been her only good option.

Nina extends her hand, and I feel myself levitate. Before I can blink, my back is brushing the ceiling.

"Hey!" I flail my arms and legs—to no avail. "What are you doing?"

She stares at me unblinkingly. "I want to make sure you really hear what I say next."

I stop flailing and give her my full attention.

"If you go into my dream and make me recall

whatever Leal locked away, I will kill you when I wake up," she says evenly.

Whew. I was worried she'd demand something impossible. Relieved, I bob my head. "Got it. That really got through, I swear. For good measure, I'll stay out of your dreams, period."

She lowers me to my feet, and I sink into the chair, knees shaking.

"You may want to enter my dreams," she says as if nothing has happened. "It's worth taking a look at the other windows. They might contain clues as to who the killer is."

I lay my palm over Pom's black fur to calm my racing heartbeat. "Do you know which window is which? I wouldn't want to accidentally—"

"I know the one to avoid."

Pom's fur goes from black to light orange.

"How would I even—"

"Leal would fly into the windows from time to time," she says. "I remember seeing dreams when he'd do it, but I would forget them when I woke up."

Interesting. I'm learning something about dreamwalker craft after all. "He'd just fly into them?"

"That's what it looked like to me, but it might be more involved than that. He said he risked losing his power for the day each time. A few times it even happened, and we'd have to resume our dream collaboration the next day."

Oh, puck. That could be seriously problematic. "In my current position, losing my power for a day would be tantamount to suicide. You were there for that vote. You know that."

She shrugs. "Perhaps consider the black windows your last resort?"

I nod slowly. She's right; I don't have to try some crazy, unproven technique. Yet. "Let's see if I can find the killer without them. Speaking of, I should probably start soon."

She stands up. "I'll get Kit for you."

"Thanks." I give her what I hope is a warm smile. "And if you could go to sleep afterward, so I have the option to check out those windows, I'd appreciate it."

"Remember what I said about my own black window." She glances at the spot on the ceiling where she'd pinned me, then at the table I would've crashed into if she'd dropped me.

I gulp. "Don't worry. I remember."

"Great."

She leaves, and I resume pacing.

When Kit doesn't immediately return, I decide to go into the dream world to see if some of the sleepers I haven't cleared are ready for me.

I ignore Felix and the still-sleeping werewolf and locate one of the Councilors from the list of those who voted to kill me. According to the papers Kit brought, this guy was having cocktails with a few other Council members. Since I've already seen the room, I go into his dream to check if he was really there.

He was indeed. In one fell swoop, I clear him and everyone else sharing cocktails.

When I wake up, it's to the sight of a large male orangutan eating a banana.

"Kit?" I say to the ape. "Please tell me that's you."

The orangutan morphs into Kit and tosses the half-eaten banana into the trash. "I wanted to see if it would taste better when I'm in that form." She grimaces. "It didn't."

She leads me to the bedroom of an older guy. I wait an hour for him to reach REM sleep before swiftly ascertaining he's not the murderer. I clear the next Councilor the same way, and the next five as well.

With each not guilty verdict, I grow more and more worried. What will the Council do when I tell them I couldn't figure out who the murderer is?

Nothing good.

"What time is it?" I ask Kit. "How many people are left?"

She looks at her watch. "It's eight in the morning. Vickie, the siren, is our last suspect."

The last suspect. What will I do if she's not guilty? I guess that will be the time to risk either my sanity with the werewolf or my power for the day with Nina.

Vickie is in REM sleep when we arrive, as expected. REM periods become more prolonged toward morning. I touch the siren's forehead and end up in the dream world. Most of the Councilors are gone from the tower of sleepers, but Nina, my possible plan B, is still sleeping. So is the werewolf, who's plan C, where c stands for crazy.

I check the siren. She really had been playing the piano, as she told Kain.

I exit the dream world, and Kit and I leave the siren's apartment—only to bump straight into Kain.

"Update," he demands.

Kit keeps moving. "I'll be in my room, getting my beauty sleep."

"Can you give me five minutes?" I ask Kain.

He grudgingly agrees. I turn away from him and use Pom to go back into the dream world.

Pom greets me, and I tell him what happened on the way to the tower of sleepers.

"So by process of elimination," he says, "it's the werewolf."

I nod mournfully. "Which blows. They'll make me go into his dream to check, and he'll make me go insane."

"It's all moot now." Pom points behind me, and I whirl around. "He woke up."

He's right. The werewolf isn't in his nook anymore.

I exhale the breath I was holding. "It's just a stay of execution. They can ask him to go to sleep again."

Pom's fur darkens. "Maybe whatever you find inside Nina's black windows will be so damning you won't need to dreamwalk in him in the first place."

"Maybe," I say and seek out Nina.

She's still asleep.

Oh, well.

Here goes plan B.

CHAPTER THIRTY

THIS TIME, Nina's dreaming about eating sushi. She doesn't use chopsticks like the customers nearby. Instead, pieces of raw fish dip themselves into soy sauce and fly into her mouth.

The windows in the restaurant are black, just like the windows from her other dreams.

"Remember me?" I slide into the booth across from her, pick up a piece of raw salmon, and plop it onto my tongue. If someone were to put a gun to my head in the waking world to make me repeat that action, I'd probably refuse. Death by gun is certain but less painful than having your brain eaten by the parasites that live in raw fish on Earth.

Nina looks around. "This is a dream?"

"I imagine the Mandate would prevent you from using your powers in a human restaurant," I say.

"You're right." She looks at the windows. "I think I remember what you've come here to do."

"Yep." I follow her gaze. "Now which is the one to avoid?"

"That one." She points at the black window nearest the restaurant entrance.

"Got it." I eat a piece of fatty tuna. "So I just fly in?"

"That's what Leal did."

I stand up, already bobbing a few inches off the ground. "Before I go, I was wondering… Why didn't you tell me about the black windows earlier?"

"I needed you to know I wasn't guilty. After all, my black window is a motive for me to kill Leal."

I lift my eyebrows.

"I would've killed him if he'd tried to use whatever I forgot against me," she explains with the calmness of someone discussing the weather. "Same if he'd tried to make me remember whatever I forgot."

Note to self: Definitely don't piss off Nina.

"Makes sense," I say. "But why do you think Leal set up a dead man's switch in the first place? Why use your dreams?"

A piece of squid sails into her mouth, and she looks thoughtful as she chews. "For all we know, he might have another fail-safe besides me. Or many. When I asked the same question, he said computers could be hacked and that lots of hackers would be eager for that job. But dreamwalkers are rare, and dreamwalkers who know about black windows are rarer still."

She's got me there. I nod wisely.

"You know what? Try that window." She points at the black glass to my left.

"Why?" I float higher.

"I don't know." She studies the window intently. "I'm hoping that on some level I know which ones have something to do with the murders."

That's good enough for me. "Let's go for that one, then." I confidently torpedo into the black window she just chose.

———

I HALF EXPECT the onyx glass to shatter around me, slicing my skin, but instead I end up plunging into a freezing black lake. Struggling to swim, I will myself to become lighter than water.

It doesn't work.

I will the water to become saltier and thus heavier, but that doesn't work either—nor does willing myself a life vest.

My ragged breathing speeds up. What the hell? I try exiting my body so I can strategize, but I'm stuck inside myself as much as I'm stuck in this lake.

Fine. I'll just swim.

Stroke after stroke, I edge closer to the nearest shore, testing my powers as I go. Changing water to clouds doesn't work. Teleportation doesn't, either. I call out to Pom but get no answer. So odd.

Unlike the times I'm in a subdream, I know that I'm in the dream world now. It's just that my powers don't work. I guess I'll have to do the obvious—just keep swimming.

I focus on swimming, only swimming. And swimming. And swimming. My breathing grows labored, yet the shore is still far away. After what feels like an hour, every muscle is aching, even some I didn't know I had.

The shore is still a mile away, and I feel like giving up.

But I can't sink. Sinking will either kill me—and make me go insane—or it might be the way one "fails to enter" a black window, which carries the penalty of losing power for the day.

Gasping for air, I let the motions of my arms and legs become my whole world. With every excruciating stroke, I tell myself that my muscles aren't really burning, that it's not real air I'm greedily gulping. Everything around me is as real as a mirage.

The moment my hand touches the dirt of the shore, the lake—and my exhaustion—disappears.

————

I FIND myself in a dream where Gemma is alive and standing in a well-lit gym. One of the windows is black. Perhaps my way back?

In front of her, a donkey-sized wolf is running on a treadmill nearby. Must be a werewolf. He or she is going cheetah fast, working the machine so hard it creaks under the strain.

"Don't stop," Gemma orders. "I want to see what your kind's really capable of."

Foaming at the mouth, the werewolf keeps running until the machine starts to smoke and stops on its own.

"Good boy," Gemma says. "Now let's see if you can use the elliptical."

Moving as if under glamour, the werewolf attempts to mount a machine clearly not designed for an animal with paws. Gemma watches his struggles with amusement.

This is weird. Why did Leal store this dream as blackmail? Also, is this an actual memory he stole from Gemma or just a figment of his imagination? My usual sense of "memory or not" isn't working, but that could be because the dream is stored in Nina's dream space, not Gemma's.

The wolf looks to be in pain as he futilely tries to climb onto the elliptical, over and over.

Then it hits me.

Gemma's power was controlling animals, regular animals, yet here in this dream she's able to control werewolves in animal form, too. This must be something only the most powerful of her kind are able to do; I had no idea it was even possible.

Maybe Eduardo, as alpha of the pack, found out and disapproved. Having been subjected to glamour, I can say without a shadow of doubt that if I were a werewolf, I'd very much disapprove. Puck, maybe this is his friend she's putting through hell, or even Eduardo himself.

In other words, this could be a motive for Eduardo to kill Gemma—a solid motive, at that.

I watch Gemma put the poor wolf through a half-dozen more cruel ordeals before I end up back in the sushi place.

Nina blinks at me with an amazed expression.

"You saw that?" I ask.

"I think I saw through your eyes. It's so strange to know that I'll forget it as soon as I wake up. It's so clear in my mind now."

I steal another piece of salmon from her plate. "Do you think Eduardo would've killed Gemma over what I just saw?"

She traces circles on her napkin with a fingernail. "If someone on the Council had that sort of power over *me,* I'm not sure I'd let them live."

That note not to mess with this woman? I mentally underline it as well.

"I'm going to check another black window," I say. "Which one do you want me to try next?"

"How about that one?" She gestures across the bar. "I have a feeling that will also be about Eduardo, though no idea how I know."

I gulp down a glass of water and launch myself into the window she chose. This time, I pay closer attention to what happens during the process.

As soon as the tip of my head touches the glass, I'm plunging into the cold water, only this lake is much larger, so I have to swim at least a mile farther. Only curiosity and iron will prevent me from drowning.

When my hand touches the shore, a new dream starts.

————

I FIND myself in a bedroom with a black window. Tatum is in this dream, making the room smell yummy in the disturbingly sexual way typical of her kind. And she is very much alive. Entwined with Eduardo in his human form, she's going at it with the enthusiasm of a teenage male bunny, but all the skills of a courtesan.

It's a shame someone this good at something is no longer alive. I bet she could've written a book that would make the Kama Sutra seem dry.

When they're done with all the gymnastics, Eduardo wraps himself around her sweat-covered body. Licking her delicate earlobe, he murmurs, "I love you. Leave the wimp… please."

Tatum stretches in his arms like a cat. "You don't *really* love me, my pet. You're just under my spell."

He lets her go, his eyes turning wolfish. "I'm not under anyone's spell. I just want you—and I get what I want."

"Of course," she purrs. "Big bad alpha is *always* in control."

The room smells yummier than ever, and Eduardo's pupils dilate. Soon, other parts of his anatomy fill up with new vigor.

Wow.

The next session is more impressive than the last, and more such sessions follow. After Tatum uses her powers to make him go crazy with lust five more times, the dream stops.

———

NINA IS BLUSHING when I get back to the sushi place, and I can't really blame her.

"Well, that just happened," I say lightly.

"I know." She sips her plum wine. "Tatum was also controlling Eduardo with her powers—a grave offense."

"When he said she should leave the wimp, he meant her husband, Ryan the elf, right?"

"Without a doubt," she says. "Eduardo sometimes called him that when they disagreed."

Finally, a promising lead. "So what happened? Did Ryan find out about the affair, get pissed, and plant an arrow in Tatum? Or did the werewolf learn how to use a bow like an elf?"

"I imagine the latter," she says. "He could easily have pushed Ryan off the cliff. In his wolf form, he could've gotten close enough before Ryan realized what was happening."

"But I don't understand why he'd kill them both. I mean, I can see why he'd kill the husband of the woman he desired, but—"

"He probably killed her to regain control. There was pressure within the pack for him to take a mate, and that has to be another werewolf. He could've killed the elf to cover his tracks. Or he could just as easily have done it in a jealous rage—and that kind of thing doesn't follow logic," she adds with a shrug.

"I don't know," I say. "It feels too premeditated for a

jealous rage. But let's say Eduardo's the killer. Why would he kill Leal too?"

Nina floats a piece of shrimp into her mouth. "That's hard to say. Maybe because he knew Leal would know his motives for killing the others. Or maybe Leal knew something else."

I consider that. "You know, Leal *was* going out of his way to get into the dreams of werewolves."

Her gaze sharpens. "There you go. Maybe he succeeded, and one of the windows is going to hold Eduardo's secret."

I look at said windows. "Which one do you think it is?"

"No idea," she says. "My intuition isn't making any more suggestions."

"Puck. I guess I can try one at random."

"Let's just hope you don't learn a secret that someone will later want to kill you over."

"Great, thanks," I mutter. Taking a breath, I eeny-meeny-miny-moe myself a window. "Here goes nothing."

I fly at the black surface before I can change my mind.

———

THIS TIME, it would be more accurate to call the lake a sea. It's so big I can't even see the shore. Having no other choice, I swim.

And swim.

And swim.

When my muscles tire to the point of failure, I finally glimpse the shore in the far distance. The sight gives me a boost of strength to swim some more. But an hour later, I can swim no longer. The shore is five hundred yards away, but it might as well be across an ocean.

I grit my teeth and keep moving my leaden limbs.

A muscle in my leg cramps, and I begin to sink.

Puck. I've got to at least hold my breath.

Nope. That's an impossibility with breathing this ragged.

Burning like acid, water flows into my sinuses, and pain explodes in my lungs.

A few agonizing seconds later, I drown.

CHAPTER THIRTY-ONE

I'M IN THE HALLWAY, my back to Kain and my heart drumming with terror.

I just died in my dream. Does that mean I'm homicidally insane?

Examining myself for murderous desires, I don't find any—no more than usual, at least.

Whew. I must've merely lost my powers.

Touching Pom, I attempt to enter the dream world.

Nothing happens.

So that's that. No more dreamwalking until tomorrow. With a sinking feeling, I face Kain.

"Who's the killer?" he barks.

I brace myself. "I checked almost everyone. They're all clear."

His fangs pop out. "I didn't ask you who *isn't* the killer. I asked who *is*."

"I think it's Eduardo." I wish I sounded more certain.

"You figured out how to enter his dreams?"

I shake my head. "He woke up before I could."

Kain's eyebrows snap together. "Then…?"

"I have reason to believe he was having an affair with Tatum. He was jealous of Ryan and didn't like Leal for stealing some secret."

Kain's upper lip curls, exposing more of the fangs. "You could say that about most of the Council. How did you arrive at *him*?"

"By process of elimination."

"That's not much of a proof." But the fangs slowly retreat.

Emboldened, I suggest, "Why don't we go talk to him anyway? The least he can do is not fight me when I enter his dreams again."

"Fine." He grabs my shoulder and drags me to the werewolf's apartment.

At the doorway, he sniffs the air and rushes in, leaving the door ajar. In the bedroom, Eduardo is still sleeping—or looks like he's sleeping. Kain must've sniffed out something else, because he checks Eduardo's pulse.

"Dead." He spins around, his face a mask of fury. "Your alleged murderer was murdered."

I back away.

His eyes turn into mirrors. "Do not move."

The glamour roots me in place, despite every instinct screaming for me to run.

Kain rips open his own wrist and forces blood into Eduardo's mouth. Just as with Albina, nothing happens, apart from my mouth watering in a disturbing way.

Kain curses and flashes out of the room, leaving me alone with the corpse.

I still can't move. My nose starts to itch and I can't even scratch it, which feels like a creative form of torture.

Soon, Kain comes back with Isis. As before, she shoots the victim with her power, but he doesn't stir. They bustle out, paying no attention to me.

A while passes.

My legs cramp, and the itch on my nose gives birth to a daughter itch under my left boob. On some level, I'm grateful for the discomfort, because it keeps my mind off the fact that I'm standing next to a dead guy. And the fact that I'm going to be dead myself soon for so spectacularly failing at my job.

Kain comes back with a new group of people. Gertrude is with him, and the siren as well, plus a person I've never seen: a pale, ginger-haired dude with glasses so thick they make his eyes look tiny. He's carrying a suitcase.

"Roger," Kain says to the new guy. "Tell us why he died."

Roger hovers over Eduardo's body with a magnifying glass. Zooming in on the crook of his elbow, he says, "There's a puncture wound. Strange. I didn't think he was a drug user."

"I don't think he was," Gertrude says.

"He used steroids to get even bigger than he already

was," Kain says disapprovingly. "Maybe that went wrong?"

Roger shrugs and sets about systematically searching the room. Kneeling to peer under the bed, he grunts approvingly and stands, clutching a syringe. When he holds it up to the light, there are a few ounces of liquid inside.

"Let's have a look-see." He opens his suitcase and takes out some high-tech gizmo that looks as though it came from Gomorrah. Placing a droplet of the liquid into the instrument, he waits.

Beep.

He pushes his glasses farther up his nose and squints at a tiny screen on the side of the device. "Interesting. I know this formula. I made this substance myself for Leal, your dearly departed dreamwalker. He was using it to try to put his birds into REM sleep for a few hours, at which point they would die. I'd been trying to improve the formula before he stopped needing it anymore. You know, on account of being dead."

Right. Leal's notes did mention someone named Roger working on the sleep drug—the one I couldn't locate in his lab. And now I know why: because the killer took it and used it for one of the murders.

No wonder Eduardo had been in REM sleep and wouldn't wake up.

Gertrude points at me accusingly. "It was her. She murdered poor Eduardo."

If the glamour weren't stopping me from speaking,

I'd ask her why I would want to kill the werewolf—especially since he was my only suspect.

As if she heard my question, she continues. "I bet she found this drug in Leal's lab and used it on Eduardo because she had trouble entering his dreams without it."

I know I didn't do it, but I guess it's vaguely feasible. Keeping him in REM sleep for so long would give me the most opportunity to dreamwalk in him. But why would I be so dumb as to give a lethal drug to a member of the Council?

"It doesn't matter if she did it." Kain's fangs are so prominent his speech slurs. "Besides, she couldn't have killed the others."

Gertrude puts her hands on her hips. "Still, if she—"

"What do you want?" Kain barks. "If she killed Eduardo, she'd be executed—but we're going to execute her anyway, for allowing another murder. Do you want to kill her twice?"

Gertrude scowls. "I just don't want her to weasel out of her rightful punishment like she did before."

"Oh, she won't," Kain says coldly. He points his finger millimeters from my itching nose. "She's done."

CHAPTER THIRTY-TWO

I AM? If it weren't for the damn glamour, I'd have lots to say on this matter.

What's truly insane is that the glamour is even preventing my body from freaking out. My breathing is normal and my heartbeat is steady. The only sign of my turmoil is Pom's fur. It's darker than a black hole.

"Should I call the Council meeting?" the siren asks in a heavenly voice.

"Give me a second." Kain's eyes turn into mirrors as he glances my way. "Walk behind me."

I zombie-walk after him across half the castle to a familiar dungeon.

Of course. I should've guessed I'd end up here to await my execution.

The place still smells like fermented sewage, but thanks to the glamour, my gag reflex isn't bothering me right now.

Kain makes a sharp right into the cell that was my

original quarters. With the bed, table, and chair now gone, it looks even drearier—an impressive feat.

He catches my gaze. "I release you."

Instantly, my heart begins hammering against my ribcage like a starved woodpecker.

"You will wait here." He moves toward the door.

"Morning," Felix says in my ear, drowsy but loud. "Did I miss anything?"

Puck. What horrible timing. I turn my back, fish out my phone as quickly as I can, and type out: *Hush. Let's talk in a sec—*

A steely hand grabs my shoulder, spinning me around. "None of that." Kain grabs the phone and crushes it in his grip.

"Bailey?" Felix squawks. "What's going on?"

Kain makes pincers with his fingers and snatches the earpiece from my ear with a strike worthy of a cobra.

It's as I feared. With his vampire hearing, he detected Felix's voice. I wonder if he's been hearing it all along but just didn't bother to do something about it. I hope he at least doesn't know who's on the other end of the conversation—I don't want Felix to get in trouble.

"Consider her dead," Kain growls into the earpiece. "And if I learn who you are, you will be as well."

Okay, so he doesn't know. One piece of good news in this avalanche of manure.

Tossing the device on the floor, Kain grinds it into powder with his foot. Then he rips the camera Felix was seeing through from my shirt and gives it the same treatment.

"You should've solved the case," he tells me grimly and strides toward the cell entrance.

My gaze falls on the sliding bolt on my side of the door. As soon as he's outside, I lunge and snap it into place.

"That's not going to help," Kain sneers from the other side of the bars. "I can rip that door off the hinges. Or I could just let you sit in this cell until you starve."

On that cheerful note, he padlocks the door on his side and leaves.

My breathing is so fast I'm inhaling too much of the foul dungeon air. Bile rising, I frantically locate the horrific hole in the floor meant to be a toilet and lose the bananas from my stomach into it.

Perfect. Now I'll starve that much sooner.

Muttering obscenities under my breath, I stand up and begin to pace. I feel like a caged animal. The seconds tick by, each one longer than the next. It feels like an hour passes as I pace back and forth, trying to avoid the sewage hole. After the third time I nearly fall into it, I plop down on the floor and hug my knees to my body.

Puck. Puck. Puck. How could I have screwed up so badly? The goal was to save Mom. Now I'll be executed, and without me, she's as good as dead too. If I'd finished Valerian's job, I could beg him to pay her bills, extending her life a while longer, but I don't have my phone or my powers so I can't even do that much.

My throat constricts, my eyes burning as a sob bubbles up in my chest. Another sob quickly follows—those bastards travel in packs—and no matter how hard I try, I can't stop the tears from sliding down my cheeks. I cry for myself and for my mom, for all the dreams I'll never walk in and the conversations the two of us will never get to have. *For the apologies I'll never get to make.* I've never wished I could turn back the clock so intensely, have never wanted to rewrite history this much. But I only have that power in the dream world; out here, I'm as useless as a human, utterly at the mercy of the Council and their whims.

Eventually, my tears dry up and I just sit, beyond miserable. If I had my powers, I could at least escape into the dream world. But no such luck, at least not until tomorrow—assuming there is a tomorrow.

Of course, there *is* another form of escape, a way I could make myself feel better. The vial of vampire blood is still in my pocket. Even as diluted as it is, it would make me feel good. Very good.

But no. I'm showing signs of addiction—there's no doubt about that anymore. Then again, I'm awaiting my execution, so does it matter?

I take out the vial. It's so tempting. It would make me forget everything, if only for a little while. And when I'm dead, I won't have to deal with the consequences of addiction.

No, screw that. I'm not dying an addict. Besides,

using this stuff might've contributed to how I ended up in this hellhole. I can't help the feeling that if I'd just let myself get a good night of sleep, with my mind fresh, I would've figured out who the murderer is.

Grimly resolved, I push up to my feet and step over to the hole in the floor. Unscrewing the vial, I make sure Nessie isn't staring at me from the murky water and ceremoniously pour out the liquid.

"Never again," I vow out loud.

To my surprise, I feel a little better—enough to resume pacing for a while instead of crying. Eventually, I tire and sit again, my eyes dry and gritty as I count the bars on the cell door.

A yawn tugs at my mouth. The effects of the vampire blood are wearing off. And for the first time in four months, I have no reason to fight the exhaustion, to hold off on the sleep I've been craving for so, so long.

Well, I guess there's one reason.

Something tells me I'll face my own trauma loop.

I yawn again. The weight of the world presses on my eyelids with a titanic foot. Without the vampire blood, fighting a four-month sleep debt is like holding my breath beyond a couple of minutes. Failure is guaranteed.

Fine. So be it.

I get as comfortable as I can on the stone floor, close my eyes, and instantly fall asleep.

CHAPTER THIRTY-THREE

I'M in the apartment I've been sharing with Mom on Gomorrah. She's looking at me, her pretty brown eyes sad as always. I know for a fact she's had at least a week of poor sleep, yet she's as beautiful as ever. Whatever pleasant facial features I have, I undoubtedly inherited from her. In fact, out of the two of us, she's the one who looks like Halle Berry.

"Not this again," she says, sounding tired.

"Your symptoms are worsening." My voice rises an octave; I can't help it. "I heard you screaming at night."

Her face turns ashen. "Did you walk into my bedroom?"

I glare at her. "No. More importantly, I didn't break my promise. I didn't invade your precious dreams."

She exhales in relief. "I just had a nightmare, that's all."

"About what?" I cross my arms in front of my chest.

"Can't remember. Can we talk about something else now?"

"Was it something to do with my father?" I watch for her reaction.

Some emotion flashes in Mom's eyes, but so fleetingly I can't be sure I really saw it, let alone figure out what it was. "How many times do I have to tell you?" she snaps. "I don't remember him, nor is it a topic I like to talk about."

"If you don't remember, how do you know you don't want to talk about it?"

She shrugs and looks away.

"Fine. You haven't been eating much, either. And haven't left the house in forever. In fact, this is the first time this week I've seen you in real life." I pointedly glance at the last-generation VR goggles on the end table.

Her jaw juts out mulishly. "Maybe it's because no one pesters me in VR. I'm the parent and you're the child, remember?"

I reach deep for my patience. "Look, Mom. I see your symptoms all the time. If you would just let me into—"

"No!" She beelines for the door, throwing over her shoulder, "Don't ever suggest that again."

"If your symptoms keep worsening, I might not have a choice," I yell at her back. "If your life's on the line, I'll break my stupid oath!"

She freezes and turns to look at me, her expression so full of betrayal I regret my words instantly.

"You wouldn't," she says hollowly, backing up toward the door. "Please say you wouldn't."

"Fine." She's been making me swear not to dreamwalk in her since I was a kid—and I've kept my promise, despite the overwhelming temptation. "But you have to see *someone*. A conventional shrink, perhaps? Maybe make a friend and talk to them? Or—"

"You don't understand! I've tried everything."

"Not *everything*."

With a growl, she turns on her heel and storms out, slamming the door behind her.

"Well, good!" I shout to the closed door. "At least you'll get some fresh air."

———

I'M in the emergency room. Mom's unconscious body is hooked up to an array of machines that do everything for her, from breathing to eating. Her brain activity is completely flat.

"She got hit by a car," the elf social worker says, as if from a distance. "We're figuring out what to do…"

I tune out the rest of it, my guilt and grief so overwhelming I can barely stand straight, let alone think. *She went out because of my nagging. She went out angry and didn't see that pucking car coming at her.*

"…don't have a lot of experience with this," the elf's voice reaches me again. "Self-driving car algorithms prevent pretty much all accidents. The last time—"

"Who gives a puck?" I bite out. "You think it makes

me feel better that my mom is a one-in-a-million victim?"

The social worker backs away from me, mumbling platitudes—and I realize why she was telling me this.

Money.

Gomorrah has free universal healthcare, but on occasion, the free hospitals can't handle something, so they defer to paid establishments, ones usually patronized only by the rich. *Like this place.* And given the extreme rarity of what happened to Mom, there's no insurance that would cover it, just like there's no insurance for getting hit by a meteorite.

"I'll pay whatever's necessary to continue her care," I say to the elf. "Let me know what I need to sign."

She looks relieved. "I'll have a doctor speak with you shortly."

The wait for the doctor is the longest twenty minutes of my life.

When he finally arrives, I feel a slight sense of relief. He's a gnome, a rarity in the medical profession. Gnomes have a reputation of being the best in any scientific field, but they rarely choose medicine. Here, apparently, is the rare gnome who did—although it figures that the best of the best would be working in this *paid* facility.

"I'm Dr. Xipil," the round-cheeked gnome says in a voice distorted by his breathing mask. "When your mother first got here, I thought we'd lose her. After five nanosurgeries and a vampire blood transfusion, we were able to heal most of the bodily trauma. Her brain, however, is a different story."

He peppers me with a torrent of medical jargon that boils down to this: Mom is in a coma, and her brain isn't running her body's functions as it should.

"There isn't much more we can do," he says. "It's possible that a healer might help, but given the expense of—"

I hold up a hand. "Assume money isn't an obstacle."

"Then you should try hiring a healer. In the meantime, you need to keep her on the machines." He frowns. "Bear in mind, most hospitals would unplug her at this point, but here we can keep her hooked up until—"

———

I WAKE up drenched in cold sweat. Blinking my tear-swollen eyes open, I realize I'm still in the stinky cell.

I was right to fear falling asleep. Without being in control in the dream world, I can't avoid the memories I've been trying to suppress—my own trauma loop. Though I've been telling myself that I've been taking vampire blood to have more waking moments in which to make money, avoiding these dreams was a big part of my motivation.

Well, I've faced them now.

If I were one of my clients, I would feel less intensely about what happened. But I don't. Maybe I need another dreamwalker's assistance in order to enjoy the healing effects of dreaming.

Still, at the very least, I'm no longer terrified of going to sleep. In fact, I can't wait to sleep more. The drowsiness is like a heavy blanket cocooning me, dulling the impact of the painful memories.

I yawn, struggling to keep my eyes open. I don't want to fall asleep again before I do what I recommend to my clients: examine my emotions with an open mind.

Guilt, of course, is the main one. I know Mom's accident wasn't *really* my fault. It was good advice to tell her to leave the apartment. Living as a shut-in, staying in VR for days on end, wasn't healthy. But I *was* the reason she'd stormed out onto the street. It wasn't just the driving algorithm that had failed; Mom must not have seen that car, either. That part's my fault—and I'll always carry that knowledge with me.

Underneath the guilt is anger. At her, at myself, at the pucking algorithm that didn't stop the car in time. At the Council, for interfering with the Bernard job and tasking me with this impossible mystery, then punishing me for failing to solve it. And deeper still is the hollow ache that I've carried with me for as long as I can remember… a longing for a father, for some family other than my moody, taciturn mom. A part of me has always hoped that one day, she'll relent and tell me about our family, about where we came from and why she's been unwilling to talk about them all these years. Now that hope is gone, extinguished as surely as my life is about to be. I'll never learn about my past—or kiss a guy in real life.

I'm going to die a virgin.

I picture Valerian and his sensual lips, his ocean-blue eyes, the way his body looks in that bespoke suit… Puck, we should've done it at least in the dream world.

Speaking of—how much time has passed? Based on how sore my body is from lying on the stone floor, I must've snoozed for at least a few hours. Could my powers be back?

I touch Pom and try to go into the dream world that way.

Nope.

Despite the disappointment banding my chest, I yawn so loudly it fills the small room. Maybe the introspection can wait until I get more sleep—or better yet, until I'm in the afterlife.

Even the thought of the pending execution doesn't suppress my next yawn.

Fine. Why fight it?

I close my eyes again and instantly fall asleep.

CHAPTER THIRTY-FOUR

ISIS and I are riding in a limo, and I'm giddy with excitement.

"Again, props to you," Isis says. "I can't believe Eduardo was behind it all—and you're the only one who figured it out."

Something about what she says feels wrong, but I let it go because what really matters is that we're on the way to finally heal Mom. I look out at the city as Isis showers me with compliments. If Manhattan could pass for a small outskirt of Gomorrah, that's not the case for Brooklyn.

We get stuck in traffic twice, but eventually, the limo reaches JFK airport and drops us off among the hordes of people rushing to their flights. We navigate our way to a secret door guarded by wards; no human could ever go this way. Opening it, we slip into an underground labyrinth of corridors leading to the hub —an enormous circular room with reflective floors, a fairly typical setup as far as these things go. The circumference of the hub is peppered with gates, each colorful plasma warp point leading to a different Otherland. Hubs like this give the Cognizant access to countless universes, each as different from each other as Earth is from Gomorrah.

"My world is this way." I point at the turquoise gate opposite us.

"I've been to Gomorrah," Isis says. "Who hasn't?"

"Let me guess." I head for the gate. "Earth Club?"

"Hey, everyone goes there," she says defensively.

Sure, everybody from *this* backward place. There are much better clubs for us natives.

Catching up with me, Isis sashays into the gate first. I follow, as usual finding it fascinating how the front of me disappears into the shimmer of the gate as I walk into it.

We cross the gate's threshold, and we're not underground anymore, nor are we on Earth.

We're on top of a proper-sized skyscraper on Gomorrah.

I inhale the familiar ozone-scented air and smile. Isis looks at me like I'm crazy. I shrug and head for the elevator. As usual, the time here doesn't match New York on Earth. It was daytime there, yet here it's night, a time when the differences between the two worlds are the most telling.

I look up. There's no moon on Gomorrah, and I'm glad. That thing always looks ready to crash into Earth in some horrible cataclysm. Instead, we have a majestic nebula. The yellows and reds of its interstellar dust and gases form long trails that look like fire falling from the sky.

"I wonder if ancient Cognizant blabbed to humans about this sky," Isis says, falling into step next to me. "It looks exactly like fire and brimstone about to rain down on us."

"Who knows," I say, glancing down at the city sprawled below us.

The world of Gomorrah has only one city, a mega-metropolis that shares its name. It's larger than the entirety of the North American continent. The tallest building on Earth would look like a one-story suburban house here. The scale is staggering, even for those of us who grew up here. On a cloudy day, there's no skyline at all, as the tops of most buildings disappear into the clouds.

We take the elevator down to ground level and exit through the lobby onto the street. Immediately, I spot an orc, an elf, and a dwarf staggering drunkenly from some bar.

"Ahhh." I exhale. "Home sweet home."

Isis grins. "No place like it."

"I still haven't gotten acclimated to the homogenous human crowds in New York," I say.

She nods at a life-sized hologram of a supermodel beamed toward us by the nearest storefront. "Do you miss that also?"

"That's propaganda I could do without," I say and lead the way to a parking lot on the corner.

"Finally, normal-looking cars," I say as we approach. "The cars on Earth remind me of horse-drawn buggies."

"Yeah, these look like sleek spaceships." Isis looks around. "Hey, I smell food."

She's right. And this isn't just food—it's safe food. There's no such thing as foodborne illness here. I sniff the air, salivating at the thought of eating something that's not a banana, and the mouthwatering aroma of manna fills my nostrils.

I point at a vehicle Earth humans would probably describe as a flying saucer. "It's the Gomorrah version of a food truck. You've got to try it."

I get us each two packets of manna and rip into mine on the spot, moaning in pleasure as the flavor explodes over my starved taste buds.

After the first bite, Isis digs in with equal gusto. "If it were possible to have an orgasm from eating, this would do it," she says with her mouth full. "How many calories are in this thing?"

I hand her the second packet. "Don't worry. You can't gain weight from manna."

After I've had my fill, I remember our very important mission and get us a car. As we ride to the hospital, Isis gapes at our surroundings like the tourist she is.

"Everything looks like a set from *Ghost in the Shell*," she says, "or *Blade Runner*."

I grin. "Don't you think the orcs and elves break the cyberpunk vibe?"

She laughs, and we chatter the rest of the way about Felix's favorite topic, the cross-Otherland "borrowing" of creative ideas, including movies, video games, and books. Isis finds it as amusing as I do that there's Pac-Man and Mary Poppins on both Gomorrah and Earth —only in the Gomorran version, Mary Poppins is a vampire.

When the car stops at the hospital, we hurry into the intensive care unit.

"Miss Spade," calls a voice so high it borders on ultrasonic. "I need to talk to you."

I will myself to slow down and smile at the billing administrator—or Horseshoe Bat as I call her, in part because she seems batty and in part because her face reminds me of the Earth creature.

"I'll pay whatever I owe," I tell her preemptively.

"Good." She looks disappointed not to have to give me a lecture. "If you could step into my office—"

"Look, lady, my time is valuable," Isis says. "Get out of our way or I'll heal all your patients, and there go your profits."

"You're a healer?" Horseshoe Bat bats her eyelashes at Isis. "Maybe we—"

"Out of the way," Isis growls.

Horseshoe Bat retreats.

I locate Dr. Xipil in the unit and apprise him of what Isis is here to do. He grabs a few colleagues, and we meet in Mom's room.

Mom looks the same. Machines maintain all her basic bodily functions, and her brain activity is flat.

Dr. Xipil shifts his weight uneasily. "Do you want us to unplug her first?"

"Too risky," Isis says. "Let me do my thing first."

He glances at her hands and shuffles back a step or two. "Go ahead."

Isis shoots Mom with an arc of golden energy.

I hold my breath.

Mom's brain activity goes from flat to frantic.

My breath whooshes out. It's all I can do to not rush over to her as she gasps and flails, clearly bothered by the breathing apparatus.

Maintaining her focus, Isis speaks over her shoulder. "Now you take your crap out. Quick."

The medical staff scurry to comply as Isis keeps a steady stream of healing energy directed at Mom.

When the last machine is disconnected, Mom's eyes blink open, and she gives me a tender smile.

"Mom," I say, my voice choked. "How are you doing?"

"I feel great," she says, looking around. "Where am I?"

"You're at the hospital," I say, wiping a tear with my sleeve. I tug more fabric discreetly into my palm so I can make another pass at my nose. "There's been an accident and—"

That's when I notice it.

Pom.

Or, more precisely, the lack of Pom on my wrist.

Hold on. Pom is never missing from my wrist. Not unless I'm dreaming.

The world around me freezes.

Of course. This isn't actually happening. It's a fantasy. It's what might've happened if Eduardo had turned out to be the killer, as I thought.

Unable to stand the disappointment, I shut out Mom's beatific face and will myself to my dream palace.

CHAPTER THIRTY-FIVE

POM APPEARS AT MY ELBOW. "Hey! How're things going?"

Usually I wouldn't worry the little guy, but since his fate is tied to mine, I give him the bad news—and as I speak, he turns ever-darker shades of black.

"It's so unfair," he says when I finish. "You did your best for them."

My hair goes fiery without my conscious direction. "Don't get me started."

Pom's huge, lavender eyes turn overly bright, his fur lightening to gray—a rare color signifying deep sadness. "I don't want them to hurt you. Can you take me to their dreams? Maybe if I beg, they'll change their minds."

My chest tightens. My looft is clearly more worried about me than himself. I fluff his fur. "I don't think that would work, but you just gave me an idea. Before they execute me, I'll tell them about you, mention that you're a protected species on Gomorrah. Maybe they can attach you to someone or something else. They've got goats, for example, or maybe they could—"

"I've been meaning to tell you something." His ears turn a deep beet color. "I was still early in my development when I attached to you at the zoo. Once I got to know you, I let myself grow something like your circulatory and nervous systems—and now they're irreversibly interlinked with yours."

He can't mean—

"I can't be removed without killing us both," he confirms, reading my face. "I didn't tell you because I didn't want you to call me a parasite again. Or a tumor."

"A tumor? Come on, what kind of a monster do you think I am?" I give him a hug, my eyes watering. "Sweetie, I never would've wanted to take you off my wrist in either case. We're symbionts for life. I'm just sorry I screwed up so badly, because now that life is going to be very short."

"It's not your fault," he says. His ears fade to gray again. "It's the stupid Council."

I sigh in silent agreement and take to the air, floating among the impossible shapes decorating my palace's lobby.

Pom loops around me. "I wonder who the killer actually is. That's ultimately who's to blame."

I flick the tip of one of his ears. "That's a great question. Everyone on the Council seems to be *not* guilty."

His ears turn light orange. "Could it be someone not on the Council?"

I stare at him. It's unlikely, but... "Maybe, Pom, maybe. Access to the castle is restricted, but people do get in. For instance, Felix and Ariel will be at a Mandate ceremony."

The rest of Pom turns light orange. "Could someone have hidden in the castle after such an event? Maybe that's who's killing the victims."

Huh. It's possible. I sink both hands into his fur as my mind flips through the alternatives. "What about the monks? One of them could've done it. They're the closest to something like a butler—and in Earth mysteries, it's always the butler who's done it."

Pom wriggles out of my hold and circles around me. "I thought the monks didn't have any powers."

"They don't. That's why no one suspects them. Killing the most powerful Cognizant isn't easy."

"Then who else could it have been?"

I have no idea. I rub my forehead. "Someone good at sneaking?"

With no answers to give him, I can't face the hope and trust in his eyes. Floating over to a prism mirror, I stare blankly at my iridescent reflection. It has to be someone from outside the castle, someone from outside the Council's domain entirely. As busy as they've kept me, I've had no time to notice who might be—

The mirror reflects a dream manifestation of a lightbulb above my head as the idea hits me.

There *is* someone who's able to get in and out of the castle on a whim. He did it the very first day I was there.

"Valerian!" I exclaim, whirling around. "Valerian uses his illusionist powers to make himself invisible."

Pom's lavender eyes widen, his pupils transforming into red hearts. "But don't you want him?"

I'm not going to dignify that with a response. "Think about it. His power is uniquely useful against powerful Cognizant."

"How so?"

"An illusionist can make you see anything." I change our surroundings to illustrate my point, creating a room where the ceiling is the floor and the floor is the ceiling, with pucks scampering across the walls. "An illusionist can use his powers to make others do the dirty work for him, so Valerian could've made Ryan see an enemy where his wife stood, causing him to shoot her with his own arrow." I change our surroundings to the scene of Tatum's death, the arrow protruding cruelly from her chest before conjuring up a translucent Valerian, who sends an arc of his mojo at the elf.

Then I show Pom what happens from Ryan's point of view: Tatum becomes Eduardo and begins screaming at the elf, telling Ryan what he's done with his wife, calling him a cuckold and worse. Eventually, Ryan snaps and, raising his bow, shoots the "werewolf" in the chest.

Except, of course, it wasn't the werewolf. It was Tatum.

"Huh," Pom says. "Go on."

I dispel the crime scene and make a cliff appear. "Valerian could also have made it so that Ryan walked off the cliff on his own—no push needed. Or he could've made himself invisible and simply pushed." I make that scenario play out in front of Pom. "Or maybe both. Maybe Ryan realized he'd shot his own wife instead of an illusion, so he committed suicide."

"It tracks." Pom's ears wiggle. "But what about the others?"

I recreate the bird attack crime scene. "Valerian could've made Gemma think Leal was her enemy, and then had her summon the birds to kill him. For that matter, he could've made the birds see something tasty where Leal was standing, thus causing that attack." I create Leal and turn him into a bowl of grain.

Pom turns black. "Illusionists have too much power."

"Yeah. Yeah, they do." I recreate Gemma's torn body. "Here again, Valerian could've made someone strong—probably Eduardo—see an enemy attacking, so Eduardo ripped the 'enemy' in half. Or he could've shown Eduardo the illusion of Gemma provoking him, until he snapped and killed her. He could've even used his powers to drive that werewolf insane at JFK, to make sure the Enforcers were away."

Pom bobs his head, his eyes bigger than usual.

I'm on a roll now. It's coming together so clearly.

"Finally, Valerian could've shown Eduardo something that drove him to choke Albina to death." I create a bedroom with Albina lying in bed, then swap her for Ryan the elf. "Alternatively, the choking might've been part of sex play, but Valerian could've made Eduardo think that Albina was asking him to squeeze harder. He could've used illusion to hide any sign she was choking."

Pom's ears droop. He looks sick. "What about Eduardo? Could you make someone give themselves an injection using illusions?"

"Sure," I say. "Valerian could've made himself invisible, then waltzed in and swapped the syringe with steroids for the one with the REM drug." I recreate the scene. A translucent Valerian watches as Eduardo accidentally kills himself. "For all we know, Valerian was still there, invisible to us when we found the body."

Pom's fur trembles.

I turn the translucent Valerian more opaque and study his perfect features. Can someone with such a gorgeous face be a killer?

What am I thinking? Of course he can. Besides, who says Valerian even looks this way? He might look like a leper with missing teeth and—

"You think they'll stay the execution when you tell them all this?" Pom asks.

I make Valerian disappear. "Well… this theory has a major flaw: I have no clue *why* he would kill all these Councilors. Motive is a pretty important part of crime investigations. Without that, plus some kind of proof, the Council won't listen to me. At the end of the day, this is just a wild theory."

"I still think you should talk to someone," Pom says. "Maybe Kit will think of a motive. How about we go into the tower and see if someone from the Council is sleeping?"

I shake my head glumly. "I'd need my powers to enter other people's dreams."

"You haven't recovered yet? I thought that's how you create stuff like this." He waves a paw around us.

"Just changing my surroundings doesn't mean I have my powers back. Even humans can learn to do something like this, à la lucid dreaming. To really know if I've recovered, I need to try to enter someone's dream."

"Let's do that, then." He torpedoes toward the tower of sleepers, and I hurry to catch up.

"Felix and Ariel aren't here," he says when we get to the nooks.

I take a quick glance at where a few of the Councilors would be if they were sleeping, but they aren't there. "Maybe it's daytime in New York."

"Then why is Bernard sleeping?" Pom points at the mustachioed man's room.

"He's been keeping odd hours." I make my way over to the clouds representing more dreams in the poor guy's trauma loop. "I guess I could use him to see if my powers are back. That'll give us a clue as to how long it's been in the waking world."

Pom gives me a baffled look. "You're going to finish Valerian's job? Even though we think he's the killer?"

"I don't have to finish the job. I could guide Bernard through the rest of his trauma loop but not do what Valerian actually hired me for. Then again, I think I *should* finish it."

Pom's ears twitch quizzically.

"If I finish, when Felix goes to sleep, I could ask him to send word to Valerian that the job is complete, so he remits the funds as promised. Killer or not, Valerian's got lots of money."

Pom turns an indeterminate mix of colors. "I guess."

I approach the sleeping Bernard. "I'll deal with his remaining dreams in the trauma loop first, then decide."

"Good luck," Pom says, bouncing up and down.

I give him a wave, make myself invisible, and touch Bernard's scarred forehead.

CHAPTER THIRTY-SIX

I'M IN. My powers are back—and I almost wish they weren't.

A dirty, beaten-up man is chained to a radiator in an abandoned warehouse.

I recognize him instantly. It's the wiry, balding middle-aged defendant from Bernard's courtroom dream, the one pronounced not guilty of murdering Bernard's boy. When his smell reaches me, I gag. What the hell? He stinks so bad my only option is to disable my olfactory sense. He also looks much thinner than at the trial, his shifty eyes filled with insanity and desperation.

His face stony, Bernard approaches, wood saw in hand.

"I'm sorry," the chained guy croaks. "Please let me out. I didn't mean to kill him. Things got out of control. I was abused when I was—"

"You want out? Here." Bernard drops the saw and kicks it within the prisoner's reach.

The guy frantically saws at the chain but only destroys the tool in the process. He hurls the toothless saw back at Bernard with a guttural cry—and misses.

"You can't cut metal with a wood saw," Bernard says coldly. "You know what you really need to do. You're just not ready yet."

Oh, no. I kind of knew where this was going, but still. Mega yuck.

A few days pass in a blink, and Bernard returns with a new saw identical to the last. This time, the insanity in the prisoner's eyes is even clearer. He doesn't even plead with Bernard, just sits there, gaze glued to the saw in his tormentor's hands. Without a word, Bernard drops the saw to the floor and kicks it over. The guy grabs it and reluctantly places the sharp edge above his wrist.

I shift my gaze to Bernard's face, and when the nauseating sounds begin, I disable my hearing. From Bernard's expression, you'd think it was *his* wrist being sawed in half. He's muttering something, and though I'm not great at reading lips, I think he's saying, "I'm a monster. I've become worse than the very evil I was trying to—"

Suddenly, his eyes widen to the size of plates.

I follow his gaze.

His right arm a gory mess, the prisoner leaps at Bernard with an animalistic snarl, shouting something.

I reenable my hearing.

The guttural roar is something I'd expect from a wounded bear, not a man.

Clutching the saw in his remaining hand, the man slices at Bernard's face. The teeth of the saw bite into his forehead, and Bernard screams in pain.

I shudder. So this is how he got that scar.

Bernard shoves his attacker away. The malnourished man tips backward but instantly begins crawling back toward Bernard, growling like a demon.

Hand trembling, Bernard reaches into his pocket and pulls out a gun.

Bang.

The growling stops, but the guy still crawls forward.

Bang.

The crawling stops as well.

Bernard keeps shooting until his gun is empty. Then he falls onto his hands and knees and vomits.

The dream shifts at this point. Bernard is staring at the empty walls of his apartment.

I swallow down the bitter tang of the previous dream. Okay, so his trauma loop is over. That's a good thing. Now that it's handled, I could in theory perform my job.

This dream is a memory, though, and I'm curious to let it play out.

The phone rings, and he lets voicemail pick up.

It's the ex-wife. "Your daughter's birthday is today. She misses you. Call her."

A shiver ripples through Bernard. "Why?" he

whispers raggedly. "Why would she want to talk to a monster?"

The next dream is also a memory but takes place years later. Bernard watches his daughter from afar, his eyes filled with regret.

The next dream is later still. Bernard is sitting in a large conference hall surrounded by other humans. I recognize the keynote speaker.

It's Valerian.

In this memory, Valerian looks exactly as he appeared to me. Does that mean this is what he really looks like?

"By the end of next year, Bale Inc. will take virtual reality to the next level," the gorgeous illusionist says passionately, channeling Tony Robbins. "Further down the line, the world you see around you"—he clicks his remote control, and a space view of Earth appears on the screen behind him—"will be one of the many possible places people can inhabit. My hope is that most will thrive in these limitless illusory worlds that we will create for them, worlds undistinguishable from vanilla reality. It will be the biggest…"

I stop listening because something dawns on me.

What Valerian is trying to do. And why.

He wants to bring illusory worlds to billions of Earth humans. More than that, he wants his name—his and his company's—to be the name everyone associates with these worlds. He wants his name to be synonymous with illusions.

It's a mind-boggling ambition.

There's a relationship between Cognizant powers and the human belief in said powers. That's how Lilith, a vampire who declared herself a goddess of blood on a world she subjugated, became nearly unstoppable. By making his company synonymous with illusions, Valerian might become the most powerful illusionist on Earth, if not throughout the Cogniverse, all without declaring himself a god—something that would get him executed by the local Cognizant.

This must be why he hires me for shady jobs such as what I might be about to do: He needs to keep his nose clean as far as the Earth Councils are concerned.

Bernard's dream shifts to a time some nine months later. He's sitting in a meeting room with a bunch of people. Valerian is there too, looking at Bernard expectantly with those hypnotic blue eyes.

"The VR motion sickness is the most urgent issue to resolve before we go live," Valerian says. "Has your team made any progress on that?"

Bernard glances at his notepad. "We've been slaving at it for months, but we don't have much. We don't even know if the problem is caused by sensory conflict or postural instability. You're against removing body visualization…"

I ignore the rest of Bernard's speech. It's time to decide if I want to finish the job Valerian hired me for. Given this dream, it would take almost no effort to do so, as the dream happens to be about the very issue in question. Valerian is working on producing VR products that don't make people nauseated, a major hurdle facing the industry at the moment, so he's hired me to secretly provide Bernard with an inspiration—a solution to come "in a dream." The task is trivial, of course, since Gomorrah is light years ahead of Earth when it comes to all technology, but especially anything to do with virtual reality.

Fine. Given how easy this is, I'm just going to do it.

I leave my body and jump into Valerian's, then stride up to the drawing board. "What if we tried this?" I proceed to present a comprehensive solution, from hardware to software tricks.

Bernard's eyes light up greedily as I draw an algorithm that's particularly ahead of its time. I can't help but grin; the most difficult part of this job was actually memorizing all this.

When I'm done, I exit Valerian's body and wake Bernard with a jolt of my power. If I allow him to dream more, he could forget what he's just learned.

Pom is waiting eagerly in Bernard's nook in the tower of sleepers.

"That's it," I tell him when I reappear. "I've gone *Inception* on his ass."

Pom claps his tiny paws together. "So he'll make a technological discovery when he wakes up?"

"And he'll be positive he came up with it on his own. Valerian, of course, will profit." I leave the nook behind me to fly alongside Pom. "I wonder how often my kind has been responsible for big discoveries that are really just information from another world? Maybe this is how Earth's Dmitri Mendeleev came up with the periodic table in his dream. Niels Bohr is also said to have come up with the structure of the atom in his dream, and even Albert Einstein—"

I stop short because I notice something that can't be.

A sleeper who shouldn't be sleeping, yet is.

I look at Pom. "You see him too, right?" I point at the nook in question.

Pom turns a hodgepodge of colors. "I see. But isn't that—"

"Exactly." I whoosh toward the room.

"But how?" He flies after me.

"I think he was doing his best to stay awake until I'm executed, but he must've accidentally fallen asleep." I loom over the sleeper, still having trouble believing my eyes.

"Do you think it means—"

"Oh yeah." My voice crackles with excitement. "This must be the murderer."

CHAPTER THIRTY-SEVEN

WE BOTH EXAMINE the deceptively kind, grandfatherly face in front of us—a face belonging to someone who's supposedly dead.

A face belonging to Dr. Hekima.

"But he died," Pom says, bewildered. "Nessie ate him."

I shake my head. "Hekima's an illusionist. He made me and Kain believe we'd seen his death in a way that conveniently left no body to be examined."

Pom's pupils morph into red hearts again. "So Valerian isn't the killer after all?"

I grin at him. "No, but the way Hekima pulled off the crimes is probably the way I said Valerian would've. I almost figured it out—I just suspected the wrong illusionist."

Pom's ears flap back and forth. "But why did he kill all those people?"

That's what I have to go in and find out. I point at the clouds swirling over Hekima's head. "I bet his trauma loop has something to do with it."

Dragging in a steadying breath, I touch the illusionist's wrinkled forehead with unsteady fingers and jump into his dream.

———

"PLEASE, SITI," a younger version of Hekima says. "What you're doing isn't safe."

He's talking to a teen who looks just like him, frizzy hair, kind face, and all. Her name sounds vaguely familiar to me.

"I'm easing people's pain, Daddy," Siti says. "If you weren't under the stupid Mandate, you'd do the same thing. You know you would."

Hekima sighs. "I'm not saying what you're doing isn't kind. It is. It's just that using your powers that way is forbidden by—"

Puck, now I recall where I heard her name. It was when I was researching the voting patterns. The case about the young woman who eased the pain of human hospice patients in their final days—her name was Siti.

"I make them think they're somewhere beautiful," Siti says, confirming my suspicions, "and sometimes I surround them with their loved ones. Is that so wrong?"

It all clicks into place. Siti was caught. There was a

Council trial, and Eduardo, Tatum, Ryan, Gemma, Leal, Albina, and a bunch of others voted for the ultimate penalty—and the Council executed the poor girl.

When Hekima learned what had happened, he gained prominence in the Cognizant community by running the Orientation program Felix mentioned—all so that one day he'd be chosen to serve on the Council and be positioned to take his revenge.

And he's not done yet. There are still people on the Council who voted to execute his daughter. With me out of the picture and everyone else thinking him dead, he's free to finish what he started, one Councilor at a time.

Realizing I missed a shift from one dream to another, I start paying closer attention.

Hekima is standing over an unmarked grave, tears streaming down his face.

"I'm sorry, Siti," he says thickly. "I should've forced you to stop. I should've dragged you to another world before you got caught. I should've—"

He stops talking and looks right at me.

Puck. What's wrong with me? I forgot to make myself invisible again—and at the worst time ever.

I belatedly disappear, but it's too late. Hekima saw me, I can tell by his expression. Looking at the spot where I stood, he smashes his fist into his own nose—and that must cause him to wake up.

I end up back in the tower of sleepers, Hekima gone from the bed.

"He knows that I know," I tell Pom grimly.

He turns black and grabs my wrist with his little paws. "Wake up and do something."

So I wake myself—and end up back on the dirty floor of my stinky dungeon cell.

CHAPTER THIRTY-EIGHT

THEN AGAIN, all is not the same as when I first got locked in here. Having slept, I feel amazing. I must've gotten at least a few additional hours of rest. Leaping to my feet, I whip out my sanitizer and wipe down every part of me that touched the floor.

Wow, my mind is sharp as a diamond. No wonder I couldn't solve the case earlier. After months of sleep deprivation, I was a shadow of myself. I resist the urge to smack my forehead. Why did it take me so long to kick vampire blood? Given my work with insomniacs, I know better than anyone that lack of sleep can lead to impaired thinking, memory problems, and eventually even death.

Here's how bad my memory had become: I'd forgotten about my lockpicks. I still have them in my pocket from when I broke into Bernard's apartment. My hand slaps my pocket—yep, still there. I dash over to the rusty padlock on the door of my cell.

Oh yeah, I can handle this. Hopefully.

The lock puts up a small fight but eventually yields. I slide open the bolt on my side and open the cell door. Now what?

If I'd done this before I realized Hekima was the murderer, I would've had to escape from a heavily guarded castle and elude Enforcer vampires for the rest of my life—a venture with almost zero chance of success. But now, armed with my new discovery, I only need to locate someone from the Council and tell them what I know.

Assuming Hekima doesn't stop me.

And assuming they believe me.

Still, better chance now than before.

I take a dozen hurried steps down the corridor before Filth rounds the corner, beady eyes locking onto me.

Puck. The last thing I need.

"I figured out who's been killing the Councilors," I say quickly. "It's Hekima. He—"

"Don't care." Filth smiles nastily, and his eyes turn into mirrors as his voice shifts to glamour mode. "Freeze, stupid blood bag."

CHAPTER THIRTY-NINE

I WRIGGLE my toes inside my shoes. I was right—they're wriggling away. His glamour didn't work. The vampire blood has left my system and my resistance to glamour is back—or Filth simply isn't as powerful as Kain when it comes to penetrating my defenses.

I pretend like I *am* frozen, though, and frantically ponder my next move.

Filth takes a syringe out of his pocket. "I've been designated as your executioner. The Council wants me to provide you with a choice between euthanasia"—he waves the syringe in the air—"or starvation." He nods at the room behind me.

Inside my chest, my heart is jackrabbiting, but I do my best to keep my face placid, as if frozen by glamour.

"I'll simplify it for you, though." He turns the syringe needle downward and presses the plunger until all the poison is on the floor. "I'll drink you dry, then toss your body out for Nessie to munch on. As far as the Council is concerned, you opted for starvation and then proved dumb enough to try to escape via the sewers."

He's thought this through. Anyone who doesn't know me well might even believe him—never mind that I'd sooner starve a hundred times before I'd jump into that excuse for a toilet... even if there weren't a monster lurking in the sewers.

Filth stalks toward me.

I furtively position the lockpicks to stick out of my fist and wait for my moment. This is a vampire, and no martial arts training can overcome the fact that even a skinny, weaselly specimen like him is ten times stronger than I am, and impossibly fast. The element of surprise is my only hope—and a faint one, if I'm honest with myself.

"I *could* command you not to feel anything," he says when he's within striking distance, "but I won't. This will hurt."

He's right. It will hurt.

Him.

Without warning, I smash my fist into his face. With a disgustingly squishy sound, the lockpicks enter his right eye.

He staggers back, roaring in pain. I fight the urge to heave, and kick him in the groin. He roars again and strikes me with the back of his hand. My head jerks sideways, and stars explode in my vision.

He throws a punch at my jaw. I somehow dodge it, moving purely on autopilot. By now, I've recovered enough to hit him, only he moves preternaturally fast and I miss. Before I can block, his elbow crashes into my midsection. My solar plexus explodes in pain, and I bend over, wheezing.

He grabs me by my shirt and effortlessly tosses me into the air. As I fly through the hallway, I spot a ray of hope down the corridor.

Thud. I crash into the iron bars with my back, and the two molecules of oxygen left in my lungs escape with a *whoosh*. The pain tries to drag me into unconsciousness, but I fight it with my whole being. I need to stall in case that ray of hope wasn't a hallucination of my rattled brain.

Gulping in greedy breaths, I look up at Filth pleadingly and raise my hand as if I need to say something.

He doesn't look like he wants to talk. His eye hasn't healed. Some vamps have better recuperation abilities than others, and his is clearly on the lower end of the spectrum.

Fangs sliding out, he hisses, "I'll make this slow."

CHAPTER FORTY

I SPIT out blood and croak, "I told Kit. She knows—she knows about Hekima. About seeing him in the dream world. You won't get away with this."

There's a flash of movement at the end of the corridor.

Yep. There's no doubt now.

I sneak a peek through Filth's legs.

Creeping toward us are Ariel and Felix. He's dressed in a tux, and she's wearing a dress that shows off every curve. In her hand is a butterfly knife. I don't even want to think about where she hid it when they went through castle security.

They must be here for the Mandate ceremony Felix mentioned.

I can't get my hopes up, though. Without his robot suit or some powerful weapon, Felix is basically human. Ariel is another matter. She's an uber and they're strong—but not quite vampire strong. And Ariel has issues with vampires.

Filth grips my throat and lifts me off the ground with one hand. "I believe your Kit bullshit as much as I believe in Hekima's miraculous resurrection." With a swift chomp, he sinks his fangs into my neck, startling a pained cry from me.

It hurts even more because it's the grossest thing to ever happen to me.

He begins to suck—and that's when Ariel rips him away by the shoulder while stabbing him in the torso.

My tailbone hits the floor, hard. Gritting my teeth against a wave of nauseating pain, I scoot away from the combatants, clasping my bleeding neck. Vampire saliva is known to act as a coagulant, but I've never been bitten and have no idea how long it'll take for my neck to stop bleeding. Also, gross.

Ignoring the stab wound, Filth throws a punch at Ariel's face. She dodges, rips the knife out, and stabs him an inch lower.

Felix kneels next to me. "Are you okay?"

"Help me up," I rasp, extending my free hand toward him. My throat's in agony, and not just from the wound on the side. Filth all but crushed my trachea while lifting me off the ground.

Felix grips my hand and helps me to my feet while Ariel and Filth fight, moving so fast it's hard to follow them.

Swaying in place, I pull my hand away from the

wound in my neck. The bleeding seems to have stopped. Seeing that I'm not in imminent danger of dying, Felix jumps in to help Ariel, but Filth knocks him out with a punch to the temple. As Felix collapses, Ariel uses the distraction to slice a bone-deep gash in Filth's bicep. The vampire grunts in pain as blood sprays them both.

If Felix weren't already knocked out, he'd faint from the gore. I'm less sensitive to these things, and even I feel woozy. Or maybe I'm just woozy from the blood loss. Either way, it's my turn to help Ariel—and I want it to count. Ignoring the pain in my bruised throat, I sprint back to my jail cell, grab the heavy padlock I defeated earlier, and rush back.

Filth smashes an elbow into Ariel's solar plexus, same as he did with me. But Ariel must've done an obscene number of crunches and built abs of steel, because she keeps fighting as if nothing's happened.

I wait for a moment when Filth's back is to me, then lunge forward and slam the padlock into the back of his head.

What would've stunned or knocked out a human only seems to distract the vampire. He throws a punch at my face. I duck. He still manages to block Ariel's next hit.

I jump back and hurl the padlock at his head with all my might. He twists out of the way—and that's what puts his throat within reach of Ariel's blade.

Whoosh.

Blood gushes from the gaping neck wound.

Puck, I might've underestimated Ariel's strength. She's nearly beheaded Filth with one slice.

Some sort of gurgling sound escapes Filth's mouth, but Ariel takes no chances. She chops at his throat again and again, until the head and body separate completely —a wound no vampire in history has been able to heal.

Filth's torso collapses to the ground, and his head rolls over to Felix. At that moment, Felix's eyes flutter open. As soon as he sees the bloody mess next to him, he faints again.

Ariel stares at her bloody knife with eerie fascination. She looks—oh crap, she looks on the verge of licking the blade.

This is it. Her vampire blood addiction is being put to a real test.

I hold my breath. It's better if she does this on her own. She's at the stage where what she needs most is to believe in her ability to resist temptation.

I, too, was recently on my way to addiction, but I feel zero urge to imbibe any of the crimson liquid around us. Then again, I should find the situation a lot more gross than I actually do. Is that a bad sign? Still, I've got a feeling that if I avoid vamp blood for a while, it will eventually seem as yucky as other bodily fluids.

Ariel's jaw firms. I guess she's made her choice.

She lifts the knife.

My fingernails bite into the palms of my hands. *Don't lick it!*

She tosses the knife into the jail cell. It clanks on the

floor as she ceremoniously spits on Filth's body and turns away.

Grinning, I clap her on the shoulder. "See? You *can* resist the temptation in the real world."

She grins back, then kicks Filth's head back toward his body and walks over to kneel next to Felix. Her lips quirk in a rueful smile as she lifts his limp arm and lets it drop. "Out cold. I guess a severed head is where he draws the line."

Something flickers in my peripheral vision, but when I look down the hall, I see nothing. When Ariel follows my gaze, however, she stiffens, her smile disappearing.

"Leave now!" she yells at the empty hallway. "If you don't, you'll join your underling here." She jerks her chin toward Filth's remains.

Underling? Is she talking to Kain? Then I realize what's happening—and my remaining blood turns to ice.

"That's not Kain!" I shout. "It's Hekima. He's using illusions on you."

She doesn't seem to hear me. Leaping to her feet, she rushes an invisible foe, throws a punch at nothing, and dodges an invisible strike. Jaw clenched tight, she follows her illusory enemy until she's a few feet from where I'm still standing, gaping at her.

She looks at my feet and screams. "No!"

Puck. I can guess what Hekima is showing her: Kain is here, and he's just killed me. I'll bet Hekima's making me look like Kain, a trick he used to commit those other murders as well.

As if to prove my theory correct, Ariel balls her hands and advances on me, her beautiful face twisted with hate. "You're dead."

CHAPTER FORTY-ONE

PUCK, puck, puck. I don't think I can bring myself to hit Ariel or hurt her in any way—not that my qualms are anything but academic. After seeing what she did to Filth, I know I don't stand a chance of hurting her. She'll be the one doing the hurting, and it won't even take that long.

My heart gallops at two hundred miles per hour. This is called a fight or flight response for a reason—and the time to fight is over.

Turning on my heel, I bolt for the jail cell.

Ariel's footsteps echo behind me. Panting like a dog after a day in a desert, I leap inside the cell and slam the door in her face, sliding the bolt into the locked position.

"You think this will stop me?" She slams her palms against the bars.

I jump back. "I certainly hope so."

She grabs a bar in each hand and strains to pull

them apart, her lean muscles flexing beneath her skimpy dress.

No way. She can't—

But the heavy-duty bars are bending. She's stronger than any uber I've heard of.

I'm so dead.

Or not. I scoop her knife from the floor and frantically squirt a bunch of hand sanitizer onto the hilt. *No blood, can't have all this blood.* Once it's clean, I turn to face the door, where she's diligently working on the bars.

Would she give up if I stabbed her? Maybe I could do it in the arm or some other nonlethal place?

The bars are almost wide enough for her to fit her head through. I look around frantically for some alternate solution. Looking down, I finally see it—a horrible, horrible option, something I'd normally say is a fate worse than death. Except here, faced head on with my mortality, I realize this fate may be just a little bit better. I guess my will to live overrides my squeamishness.

Maybe.

I dash to the hole leading to the sewer.

My first mistake is looking down. When I see the murky, foul-smelling liquid down there, I decide maybe Ariel can kill me after all. If I have to be killed, it might be nicer for a friend to do it.

Except it's not just my life that's on the line. Pom will die as well—and so will Mom, if I don't convince the Council that Hekima's the murderer.

Shaking all over, I sanitize the blade of the butterfly knife, fold it, and slip it into my pocket. And yes, I realize how crazy I am to do this, given what I'm about to dive into. Gulping in a breath of fetid air, I plug my ears with my index fingers and my nose with my pinkies, like a kid learning to dive for the first time, and sneak one last peek at the cell bars to see if maybe Hekima has given up.

Nope. Ariel is sticking her head into the opening she's just made. It's now or never.

Squeezing my eyes shut, I jump feet first into the sewer abyss.

CHAPTER FORTY-TWO

AS I FALL, obscenities in all the languages I speak repeat on a loop in my head.

Sploosh.

The gooey substance closes over my head, and I don't feel anything resembling a floor under my feet. The sewer must be really deep. *Don't think about flesh-eating bacteria and the open wound in my neck. Or brain-eating amoebas. Or the people-eating monster that's made these sewers a home. Or where the monster goes to the bathroom. Or—*

Survival instinct wrenches my hands away from my face, and I begin to flail. My head emerges, and I suck in a breath. The stench is unbearable, as if someone had formulated the worst odor that could exist in nature. What the hell is this stuff?

I'd rather not know. That way lies insanity.

Everything around me is dark, but there's a faint light in the far distance. I swim toward it. No one jumps into the sewer behind me. That's good. I guess Hekima can't maintain the illusion without joining Ariel, and he isn't willing to follow me here. He doesn't want his earlier lie of being eaten by Nessie to become reality.

Speaking of the monster, I haven't been eaten by her either. Not yet, anyway.

I keep on swimming.

The horrific liquid is thick and viscous, and I'd rather not think about why that is. At least that makes floating here easier than in the lakes from the black windows in Nina's dreams. Now that I'm out of immediate mortal danger, the grossness of what I'm doing is overwhelming. Is it possible to die from disgust? Desperate, I remind myself that even when I'm clean, there are more microbes in and on me than cells with my own DNA.

Nope, that doesn't help at all. Better not think, period.

I focus on the movement of my arms. Upstroke. Downstroke. Upstroke. Downstroke. The light is nearer. It's daylight outside the castle's mountain.

My foot bumps against something mushy, and I'm able to stand and rest. *Best not to think about what I'm standing on.*

In the direction I came from, the muck ripples. Has Ariel finally jumped in? Hekima? I pull out the knife, unfolding it frantically—not that it'll help much. Defending myself with this knife will be like trying to put out a forest fire with a water gun.

The ripples intensify, and a head emerges from the mucky water.

My stomach drops to my feet.

There's no mistaking the long neck and the maw full of dagger-like teeth.

It's Nessie, and she's here to eat me.

CHAPTER FORTY-THREE

I SQUEEZE the knife so hard my knuckles whiten.

"Go away!" I shout at the creature.

She doesn't even blink. Her head rises from the muck atop a neck like an anaconda.

"I'm not a pucking goat," I shout, waving the knife. "Last warning."

Nessie strikes. Her maw opens as her head flashes toward me. It takes all my martial arts training to stay still and wait for my moment. When the teeth are ready to close around me, I strike.

My blade sinks into her squishy tongue. Yes!

Nessie jerks her head back, ripping the knife from my hand. I dive for the sewer exit and swim for all I'm worth.

Behind me, Nessie roars.

My arms windmill with insane speed, and the light draws nearer. I might be beating a world record of some kind—assuming some sadist keeps track of sewer swim times.

The beast roars again. She's gaining on me. I impossibly speed up, the proximity of the exit urging me on.

When I finally burst into the light, my eyes take a second to adjust. I'm in the moat in front of the castle, just outside the mountain. The shore is nearby, filled with monks carrying a goat.

Just my luck—Nessie has come across me at lunch time. The good news is that if I hurry, she might eat the goat instead of me.

Fresh air gives my muscles a much-needed boost, and I close the distance in seconds. The stunned monks help me stumble out of the water.

"Nessie," I pant. "I think she—"

Before I can finish, two monks seize the poor goat and heave it into the moat.

A familiar head appears above the water. Nessie opens her maw again. There's no sign of the knife I left there, or a wound of any kind. I guess it makes sense that she has some super-healing ability. She's an incredibly long-lived creature; the legends about her go way back.

A blink later, the goat is gone. So is Nessie.

Whew.

I fish my hand sanitizer out of my soaked pocket and use it all up on my face and hands. "I need to see someone on the Council."

The tallest of the monks eyes me like I'm crazy. "You can't. They're in a meeting and—"

"Does this sound like a normal request?" I growl. "They're going to want to know what just happened, why I just emerged from the sewer with Nessie on my tail, trying to tell them the truth about who's kill—"

He holds up a hand. "I'll take you there."

With a wary glance at me, he heads for the castle. I follow, doing my best to shake off the worst of the slime clinging to me before we reach the familiar door into the coliseum where the Council meets.

"They'll be upset if you just barge in," the monk says, wrinkling his nose. "And not just because of your smell."

I shrug, and trying not to breathe too deeply, I step into the Council chambers.

CHAPTER FORTY-FOUR

KAIN IS STANDING in the center of the amphitheater, the place usually reserved for whoever's in trouble.

"I suggest we vote," Nina is saying. "Those in—"

"I know who the murderer is," I announce loudly.

All heads turn toward me.

Kain sniffs the air and looks half perplexed, half horrified. I open my mouth to say more when someone pushes me out of the way. I stagger and look around.

No one's visible.

My pulse spikes into the stratosphere.

Hekima. He's here.

CHAPTER FORTY-FIVE

INSTANTLY, my surroundings change.

I'm still in an amphitheater, only one a thousand times larger than where the Council meets. It looks like the Colosseum in Rome, only brand new. Confirming the Rome connection, screaming people appear in the seats. They look like extras in a movie about gladiators.

The emperor rises. It's Hekima, dressed in a purple toga, with a gold laurel wreath perched on top of his frizzy gray curls.

He's looking down at me, his dark eyes filled with genuine sadness. "You remind me of Siti," he says in a warm, grandfatherly tone. "I wish I could let you live, but you know too much. It's me or you—basically self-defense."

My upper lip curls. "Whatever you need to tell yourself. If Siti were alive, she'd be ashamed of you."

He looks as if I've punched him. Stiffening, he sinks onto his imperial seat, and an expression of concentration appears on his face. He must be showing illusions to the members of the Council.

The crowd cheers as though a rock star just walked onstage. I look down. My filthy clothing is gone, replaced with a hybrid of armor and a bikini—apparently Hekima's dirty fantasy of what a gladiatrix would wear.

I scowl up at him. "I know this costume is an illusion, but it makes no sense as battle gear." I slide my hand over my exposed cleavage. "It's basically daring someone to stab me in the heart."

As if in reply, the doors leading to the stage burst open and a puck saunters out.

It's an illusion. I know that. There can be no pucks on Earth. Hekima is making me see that hairy body, the horns and the hoofed feet. In the real world, this is someone from the Council, or maybe no one at all. Yet the sights, sounds, and even smells are exactly as if I were at the real Colosseum facing a goat-reeking puck. Not that I have much room to talk—though now that I'm in Hekima's illusion, I can't smell my own funk.

The monster opens its mouth, flashing a grill a shark would envy and bathing me in the stench of decomposing meat.

The crowd goes wild.

Is pain one of the senses illusionists can control? Will it feel real when those teeth tear at my flesh?

The puck lunges at me and tries to punch me in the mouth. I dodge and strike at his sternum. I miss—yet I don't see how I could have. Either I'm fighting someone smaller than a puck, or there's no one around me at all.

The puck smashes a fist into my face.

Ouch.

That hurt, and my lip feels genuinely split. Either there's a real person fighting me, or Hekima's powers are megastrong.

I dodge another swing, then another. My face stings, but not proportionally to how much it would hurt if a real puck hit me—they're incredibly powerful. Since I see no reason Hekima would hold back on illusory pain, I conclude that my opponent is real and isn't super-strong. I guess that's good. Still, I need to finish this battle before my opponent inevitably uses his or her Council-level powers.

The puck sweeps my feet. I jump over his hoof and throw a punch at his throat. My hand connects with flesh that feels more like a jawbone than neck. The puck staggers and falls down.

Yeah, right. No way a puck would be bested by such a hit.

The crowd goes wild.

The doors fly open again, and a monster more terrifying than a puck ambles out.

It's a drekavac, a creature that kills by causing unspeakable pain.

I stagger back. Just looking at the thing is painful. It's a nightmarish, insectoid wraith with too many tentacles and teeth.

Then something dawns on me.

If Hekima wants this encounter to seem realistic, he'll use someone with the power to kill with a single touch.

Blood drains from my face.

There's a Councilor perfectly suited for this, one whose touch causes gangrene.

Gertrude.

CHAPTER FORTY-SIX

"I CAN'T FIGHT GERTRUDE!" I scream, in case Hekima cares.

He doesn't.

I back away and do my best to strategize. Even if I land a punch, I'll lose.

The drekavac charges and whips at me with a tentacle.

I dodge.

Shrieking, the monster sends another tentacle my way.

I leap to the side but barely miss getting touched.

There has to be something more effective I can do, some way to penetrate this illusion.

Another tentacle strike, another dodge.

A chat with Pom suddenly pops into my mind. He once claimed that if he were awake, he could show me what Valerian really looks like, based on the assumption that an illusionist wouldn't think to target my symbiont.

Two tentacles go for me at once, and I perform a backflip to get away. The crowd cheers.

The problem is that Pom must be awake to see through my eyes, and he sleeps all the time. Unless—

Pom, I mentally shout as I dodge yet another tentacle strike. *Pom, wake up!*

Nothing happens. A tentacle lashes at my legs, and I jump over it.

Pom! Pom! Pom!

"What's with the shouting?" Pom says groggily in my head.

I'm inside an illusion, I mentally shout. *Need you to see through it, or we both die!*

"Should've led with that." He sounds much more awake. "How's this?"

The world flashes with every color of the rainbow, and I barely dodge the next tentacle strike. When the swirl settles, I do my best to make sense of the visual confusion. The Colosseum isn't gone, but it looks a bit ghostly.

Then I realize it's actually overlaid with reality, a reality that looks odd. The edges of objects are fuzzy, and something strange is going on with colors. For instance, I see an orc fighting Colton the giant, but instead of the orc being green, both fighters are monochrome.

Puck, that's not an orc. It's Kit. Hekima is having her fight for her life, and Pom doesn't like it. Neither do I. I bet all that black is Pom's feelings seeping into my perception.

Whoosh. A ghostly tentacle flies at my face, only now I see that the tentacle isn't a tentacle at all. It is, as I suspected, Gertrude's arm. Fingers outstretched, she's trying to touch my cheek in the real world.

I sidestep and grab her arm near the elbow, where her sleeve protects my hand from her skin. I'm not sure what she's seeing in her own version of Hekima's illusion, but it must be something terrible because her face contorts with fear.

This won't help matters.

I twist her arm behind her back and pull hard. She drops to her knees, crying out in pain. I grab hold of one of my slimy shoes and club Gertrude with the makeshift weapon. There's no way I'm risking a touch again, even if it's only her hair.

She claws at me with her free hand, so I smack her again and again. My arm muscles burn, but I accomplish my goal.

Gertrude collapses.

This is when I notice who else is lying unconscious nearby.

Felix.

He must've recovered from his blood-induced fainting spell, only to fall under Hekima's influence. He must've been the "puck" I fought. No wonder his punches didn't hurt much—and no wonder I was able to win. He's a little sensitive about it, but Felix's powers aren't useful in hand-to-hand combat.

I rush over and check his vitals. He'll probably have a headache, but he'll be fine—and his headache isn't going to be half as bad as Gertrude's. I glance back to see how Kit is doing and see her morph from an orc into a giant much bigger than Colton. She raises a massive fist in an arc so wide, she knocks a couple of nearby Councilors off their feet. *Pow!* She smashes that fist into Colton's temple.

He roars in pain. Poor dude. I bet his headache's going to be even worse than Gertrude's.

Someone needs to stop this madness. The real Hekima is on the other side of the room with a wall of Councilors between him and anyone wishing to cause him harm. Everyone in his line of defense shows grim determination; they must each be experiencing illusions in which they're protecting someone or something they care about. There goes my hope of knocking *him* out.

I recognize some of the defenders—Isis and Chester—and note that not a single one of them is among those Hekima still wants to get revenge on.

I soon see why.

Nina, standing a stone's throw from me, raises her hands with a look of concentration. The stone benches where the Councilors usually sit rip out of the ground, break apart, and begin zooming all over the room.

I dodge one, then another—but not all the Councilors are so fortunate. Unlike me, they can't see what's real. At least four get hit in the head. I can't help but notice they're all on Hekima's kill list.

Two benches fly in Hekima's direction, giving me hope that his revenge may backfire. But no. A bench that seemed to be flying at Chester lands an inch away from him. How lucky for Chester—and Hekima, by extension. The other bench lands in front of the wall of Councilors, hitting Vickie on the head.

Isis shoots an arc of golden energy at the siren, healing her instantly.

Is Hekima being nice to the siren because she's not on his list? Nah, that's giving him too much credit. The real reason becomes apparent a moment later. Gulping in a large breath of air, Vickie shrieks at a nearby Councilor on the list, and two seconds later, only the man's skeleton remains.

Puck. What do I do? I can't get to Hekima, and if Nina keeps flinging those benches around, I might get knocked out too.

I sweep my gaze over the room for ideas and spot Ariel fighting Kain. There's too much hatred on their faces for two people who don't know each other— Hekima's illusions in action again.

Ariel smashes a fist into Kain's ear. He strikes back. She blocks with her forearm, but the force of his hit is so powerful that the back of her hand recoils and splits her lip.

Crap. Fighting Kain isn't as easy as taking down Filth—and I don't know if Ariel even realizes she's battling a vampire.

Another bench piece crashes down next to my feet, courtesy of Nina. Now *that* could work. I scan the floor for the biggest chunk of stone I can lift and find one that weighs about thirty pounds. Straining, I raise the rock above my head and charge at Kain.

Oblivious to my existence, Kain lands a punch in Ariel's midsection. Ariel crumples in pain.

Before Kain can go for the kill, I slam the stone into his head.

The vampire sways, a stunned look on his face. Ariel recovers enough to stumble toward him, and I shove the stone into her hands. With a startled expression, she grabs on. I can't guess what it must feel like to have a bloody rock materialize in your grasp, but Ariel's a trooper. She doesn't waste time pondering her good fortune.

Easily lifting the stone, she smashes it into Kain's face.

Kain staggers back.

Ariel hits him again.

Kain stumbles to the floor.

Ariel jumps on his chest and slams the rock down on his forehead, again and again.

"Enough!" I yell at her, but she doesn't seem to hear me. She bashes and bashes what remains of Kain's head, way past the point of his demise. Clearly, whatever illusion Hekima is giving her has generated a murderous rage.

I feel a surge of pity for the vampire—for all our differences, he was just trying to do his job—but I remind myself that Kain's death is on Hekima's conscience. Same goes for the Councilors Hekima wanted revenge on.

They're dead now too.

But Hekima himself? He's staring at me.

Puck.

I frantically look for a smaller rock, but he points his hand at Nina.

"Wait!" I yell.

Too late.

An invisible telekinetic force hurls me into the air.

CHAPTER FORTY-SEVEN

I FLAIL as I sail through the air.

This isn't the dream world. This flight will end in a painful crash at best, a bashed-in head à la Kain at worst. Heart pounding, I rummage through my pockets for something to throw at Hekima.

Nina boomerangs me a new direction, breaking my concentration. Does she think I'm a drone or something?

My patting hands discover an object in the last pocket I check. Is that what I think it is? Clearly, sleep deprivation made my memory worse than I thought. Here's yet another tool from the Bernard job I've completely forgotten about.

I pull out the sleep grenade as Nina makes me circle the room even faster.

If I use the grenade, everyone here will fall asleep. That includes Nina, which means I'll crash-land. If I don't use the grenade, she's bound to tire of playing with her drone and crash me into something. Not a big difference. At least this way, I stand a chance.

So be it.

Holding my breath, I activate the grenade and toss it.

Gas fills the room, and I feel myself plummet. I keep holding my breath until I land atop Chester's sleeping body.

Ouch. That hurt, but I'll definitely live. But there's one problem: I can't hold my breath any longer.

Lungs screaming for air, I inhale—and join everyone in sleep.

CHAPTER FORTY-EIGHT

I'M STANDING under a shower that sprays tomato juice instead of water, soaking the pink tutu I'm wearing. A purple llama stands just outside the stream, chewing the shower curtain.

"Can you pass me the body wash?" the llama says in a Scottish accent, after the curtain is kaput.

I obligingly reach for the bottle, only to notice something missing from my wrist.

Pom isn't where he should be.

Of course. I'm dreaming. For the millionth time, I wonder why such absurdities as the tutu and the llama don't clue me in.

Recalling what happened right before I fell asleep, I change my outfit and head for my dream palace.

I'm lucky Chester fell where he did. Was that his luck or mine? It's possible that his probability power guided my fall so as to save him from Hekima's trap.

Hopefully that means I can figure out how to do exactly that.

Pom materializes in front of me. "Did it help when I let you see what I see?"

I pull him close and fluff his fur. "Yep, but no time to talk. I think I have a plan."

"Good luck." His ears turn black. "If you don't mind, I'll stay out of it—I have a feeling it's going to be scary."

"Suit yourself."

I teleport to the tower of sleepers. A few Councilors are already here, but not Hekima. He must not have reached REM sleep yet.

Since Kit *is* here, I enter her dream. Surprise, surprise, she's dreaming of an orgy.

I interrupt the proceedings. "Hey, Kit, this is a wet dream. We need to talk."

When she looks at me, I remove the naked people and the bedroom from around us and replace them with a recreation of the Council meeting chamber—or at least the way the place looked before Hekima's massacre.

"Have a seat," I tell her, and fill her in on everything that's happened.

By the time I finish, her eyes are almost as wide as Pom's. "I can't believe it was Hekima. But that does explain what happened to me. I saw Colton admit that *he* was the murderer, and then he attacked me."

"I bet Colton thought you admitted the same thing."

"So many dead." She shakes her head mournfully.

"About that. Filth and Kain's deaths—"

"—are Hekima's fault." She turns into Hekima and imitates cutting a throat. "I'll make sure the rest of the Council understand that you, Felix, and Ariel aren't guilty of anything, nor is anyone who killed a colleague due to Hekima's trickery. Don't worry."

Great. And it's almost true. No one needs to know the particulars of Filth's demise. He had it coming, but Ariel could still get into trouble unless Hekima takes the blame.

"Thank you," I say.

Kit reverts to her usual guise. "What now?"

"I'm going to bring more Councilors here and ask you to bring them up to speed."

Leaving her, I go back to the tower of sleepers and enter Nina's dream. She's flying over a field of daisies. I take to the air and loft up next to her.

Her eyes boggle.

"You're in a dream," I say.

She floats down to earth and bends to literally smell the flowers. "Seems so real."

"I know."

She rubs her forehead. "Did I really—"

"Let's hold off on the explanation for a moment." I take us to the dream version of the Council meeting room. "Kit, please tell Nina what happened. I'll get the others."

Without waiting for a reply, I return to the tower of sleepers and get Chester, followed by Colton, Isis, the siren, and a few other Councilors.

Eventually, I spot Hekima in one of the nooks.

My sleep grenade has finally worked on him.

I return to the Council meeting place.

"Do you have a plan?" Isis asks when I appear.

"I do. But before we go into that, I want to make sure we're all good." I look at each Councilor one by one. "Is my execution canceled?"

Isis raises her chin. "The majority of the Council is here, and we've voted for amnesty in your case. Furthermore, I'm still going to heal your mother."

My heart leaps. "Today?"

"If we survive Hekima," she says with an eye roll. "Are you ready to talk about your plan in regard to that little problem?"

I take a deep breath and face the Councilors. "The plan is simple. You all try to wake up. Meanwhile, I'll go into Hekima's dream to make sure he keeps dreaming and therefore can't thwart you. Once you're in the waking world, knock him out."

"I'll do it," Kit says eagerly.

"I'm closer to him," Chester says.

"Doesn't matter who," I say. "Just wake up."

"How?" Nina asks.

"Will yourself to wake up. If that doesn't work, use a little bit of pain."

Chester disappears right away, but most others stand there with expressions of concentration. Then Kit punches herself, and that wakes her up. Colton does the same and also disappears. Nina looks like she's having trouble, so I give her a jolt to assist her.

When the last Councilor is gone, I take myself to

Hekima's room in the tower of sleepers. It would be extremely unfortunate if he happened to wake up before someone could knock him out.

Making it a point to turn myself invisible, I touch him on the forehead.

———

HEKIMA IS SITTING on a couch reading a book. A confused expression appears on his face. He lowers the book to his lap and raises it again, and even I see the text is different on the second go. His confusion deepens.

Crap. What he's just done is one of the many techniques lucid dreamers use to determine whether they're in a dream or not, a bit like what I do with Pom on my wrist. Text often becomes blurry and changeable in dreams. If Hekima ascertains this isn't real, he could wake himself up.

I gently shoot him with my power to keep him in the dream state. It's not a surefire method; if he punches himself the way he did in the graveyard, he could still wake up.

As if hearing my thoughts, Hekima stands up and raises his fist to do exactly what I don't want him to do.

I make his couch grow two plush arms like a giant teddy bear, and the arms grab him by the wrists, preventing him from hurting himself.

He looks right at me. "Ah, Bailey. I'm definitely dreaming."

To my shock, I become visible.

What the hell? Is this what had happened the last time I'd been in his dream? Maybe I hadn't forgotten to make myself invisible after all. Maybe he'd done the same thing to me then.

Hekima gives me a level look. "I'm an experienced lucid dreamer. I may not be able to enter other people's dreams, but I'm not so easy to fool."

He looks at the teddy bear bindings, and they turn to dust.

Puck.

Before he can punch himself, I teleport to him and grasp his wrists myself. No matter how good he is at lucid dreaming, he can't wish *me* away.

"You can't wake up even if you hit yourself," I say, hoping he can't read the lie on my face. "I have you sedated."

His lips curve in his grandfatherly smile. "I grew up side by side with your kind on Soma. I know all the tricks."

"Soma?" I ask, partly to stall for time but also because I'm genuinely intrigued. I've never heard of this place before, and it sounds like I should have, if it's where a bunch of "my kind" live.

Hekima cocks his head. "You're not from Soma? Then perhaps this will work."

An arc of pulsing red energy streams from his fingers into my head.

Pucking puck.

He's trying to use his illusion powers inside a dream —and it does work.

Well, sort of.

I'm back in the gladiatorial arena, but I'm also still holding his wrists. This odd state of being isn't like Pom letting me see through his eyes, but more like the werewolf's dream, where I'm being torn between two places at the same time.

The biggest orc I've ever seen ambles into the arena, and the crowd goes wild.

Hekima tries to twist out of my hold.

Puck. To fight the orc, I'll need to let go of Hekima's wrists. But what would happen if I didn't fight the orc? I'm dealing with an illusion, but inside a dream. For all intents and purposes, there's no difference between those two, so if the orc kills me in a dream, I might die, and the consequence would be murderous insanity. If this is similar to the werewolf situation, though, maybe the solution is the same as it was there.

Leal's so-called multibody technique.

The orc is almost upon me. I don't have time to dwell on the fact that the multibody thing failed the last time I tried it. I'm just going to have to trust in the mind-boosting power of sleep.

I zoom out of my body and create a second Bailey in the path of the orc, this one with fiery hair. Straining my bodiless self to the point of fainting, I will myself to enter both bodies.

Bam. The orc smashes his fist into my stomach—the stomach of the me with fiery hair.

It worked!

Fiery Me crumples in pain, but the me still holding Hekima's wrists feels nothing but the illusionist's struggles. Fiery Me hits the orc with everything I have, and the orc flies through the arena and crash-lands in a crater.

The crowd pees their pants in excitement.

Hekima tries to headbutt me. I make my head the consistency of a plush pillow to make sure he doesn't feel any pain.

At the same time, Fiery Me teleports to the weakened orc and waits for the crowd to quiet. As soon as it does, the flaming hair rises from my head and torches my opponent to a crisp.

Some in the crowd have heart attacks.

Hekima bares his teeth. "You're powerful. Even some of the dreamwalkers on Soma couldn't do the multibody technique."

Soma again—and the place sounds more interesting by the moment. Both of me reply in unison, "Tell me more. What is Soma? Where is it?" At Hekima's incredulous stare, both of me add quickly, "I'll do my best to get the Council to go easy on you if you tell me the truth."

Kit or Chester must be about to knock him out by now, but I almost wish they weren't. My question isn't a stalling tactic. If Soma is where dreamwalkers live, I want to learn all about it. With Mom refusing to speak about our roots, I've always wondered if—

Hekima's face twists. "We never should've left Soma. Siti would still be alive. On Soma, we—"

A shriek of unspeakable pain erupts from him as his dream bursts like a soap bubble, and I find myself back in the tower of sleepers.

Puck. Just when he was getting to the good part, someone knocked him out. Oh, well. Hopefully I'll be able to question him when he recovers. They didn't execute *me* right away, so there should be time.

I give myself a jolt and wake up.

CHAPTER FORTY-NINE

I FEEL AMAZING—AND not just because of more sleep. My pain and injuries are gone without a trace. I open my eyes and see why. Isis is moving calmly around the Council meeting room, healing everyone with her powers.

Rising to my feet, I look for Hekima—and instantly avert my gaze, wishing I could rub sanitizer on my eyeballs.

So much for my plan to question him.

Hekima is no more. At least I assume those are *his* remains in a pile approximately where he last stood. Someone has done something unspeakable to the grandfatherly illusionist.

His skin—all of it—is missing.

Kit grins at me. "He won't be bothering anyone ever again."

I swallow down a surge of nausea. "What happened? You were supposed to knock him out."

Kit shimmers briefly, and I catch the outline of a drekavac. "A promise is a promise."

Oh, right. She'd said she would kill Tatum's killer as a drekavac. This raw meat is the result. I don't know what it says about Kit that she was able to do this—or me, that I'm more upset about losing out on a chance to learn about Soma than the unspeakable torment Hekima must've experienced in his final moments. Then again, he did murder all those Councilors and was going to kill me and my friends, not to mention some members of the Council who had nothing to do with his daughter's unfortunate fate.

"Speaking of promises," I say, pushing aside all thoughts of Hekima and Soma for the moment. "I need to talk to Isis."

It's time the Council gave me my reward and healed my mom.

Kit follows me, and we wind our way through the confusion of Councilors, catching up with Isis as she heals her last patient.

"Can we go to Gomorrah now, as agreed?" I ask.

She wrinkles her nose. "One condition: You need to take a serious shower. Or maybe ten."

Kit sniffs the air. "Oh, yeah. I'm on board with ten. And I should have some clothes in your size."

"Deal," I say, doing my best not to inhale my own stench. As much as I want to get Mom out of the coma right away, I doubt she'd want to wake up to the perfume of the sewers.

The three of us go to Kit's quarters, where she grabs

a box of garbage bags, an entire rack of clothes, and two big bottles of soap and shampoo. We take it all back to my quarters.

"I'll be back in an hour." Isis looks me over. "Or do you think you need two?"

"Two should do it."

They leave, and I bustle into the bathroom with the soap, shampoo, and garbage bags.

The first thing I do is take out Leal's comms from my pocket. I hope it's a waterproof model—or if not, that Felix can get the info from it anyway. Cleaning the thing, I put it into a bag.

My stinky clothes go into another bag. That bag goes into another bag and so on until I run out of bags. Then I turn on scorching water and begin lathering and rinsing. Even after I run out of products, I stay under the spray, hoping to wash off any remaining cooties. Eventually, I get pruney enough to improve the stools of an army of cannibals. Reluctantly turning off the shower, I dry off, use my last remaining hand sanitizer on my body, and dress in Kit's clothes.

Pocketing the bag with the comms gizmo, I inhale the air.

No stench.

But hmm... Now that I'm paying attention, I do detect a faint pine scent.

Wait a minute—

Someone clears his throat.

"Valerian?" I look around the empty room with wild eyes. "I just smelled you."

"You did?" He materializes two feet away, as gorgeous as the last time I saw him. "I'm losing my touch."

Pom, I mentally shout. *Pom, wake up!*

What is it? Pom's voice is groggy. *Can I not get uninterrupted sleep anymore?*

Quickly, what does this guy look like?

Pom sounds thoroughly bored. *Tall and muscular. Wide in the shoulders. Dark hair, blue eyes. Chin dimple, well-defined cheekbones.*

Don't describe him—show him to me, I mentally growl.

Why? You're seeing what I'm seeing.

I feel the tension leave my forehead. *I am? There's no illusion? He really looks like a pucking sex god?*

A beat of silence, then: *I don't know what a pucking sex god looks like.*

A silly grin threatens to stretch my lips. *Right. You can go back to sleep now. Thank you.*

How about you only wake me up in emergencies going forward? Pom grumbles.

Whatever, I reply as Valerian arches a black eyebrow in amusement.

Puck, I've again been staring at him in silence, like an idiot.

Pulling myself together, I scowl up at him. "How long have you been hiding there?"

His sexy lips quirk. "Are you asking if I saw you like this?" He casts an illusion, conjuring up a more attractive version of me—who looks exceptionally naked thanks to the sanitizer glistening like oil on her perfect skin.

"Or this?" he continues as I stare at him openmouthed. This time, the modelesque Bailey is engaged in what looks like the *Playboy* version of showering. I doubt my movements were remotely that sensuous, and I doubt even more that I paid that much attention to my boobs.

Still, my cheeks—and other places—feel hotter than the surface of the sun. "You watched me in the shower?"

A mischievous grin appears on his face, reinforcing the feeling that I've met him before. Except I haven't. He's the kind of man I'd remember forever. "I came here to thank you." He dispels the shower illusion. "Bernard made the breakthrough I needed. The money has been transferred to your account on Gomorrah."

Right. The money. He's got me so off balance I almost forgot about that.

"Good," I manage to say. "But that doesn't excuse your invading my personal space."

His grin turns wicked. "You're right. It's rude of me. You showed me yours; the least I can do is show you mine."

Another Valerian appears to the side of us, gloriously naked and covered in some liquid.

Oh. My. Estrogen.

Sex god doesn't even begin to cover it. My blood rushes to all sorts of private places, and I feel a bizarrely unsanitary urge to lick every one of those toned muscles.

The fully clothed Valerian winks as his naked doppelgänger steps into the shower and lathers himself with soap.

Can you faint from arousal? Or have a heart attack?

He makes his showering self disappear. "Are we even now?"

I just stand there, doing my best not to fan myself.

He steps closer, ocean-blue eyes gleaming. "You know, I still feel like we know each other from somewhere."

I dampen my suddenly dry lips. "Same."

"I wonder if there's a way to jog our memories?" He leans toward me, and the room around us transforms into a familiar lush bedroom with a king-sized bed covered in silk sheets and rose petals.

My lungs cease functioning, and my body feels like I'm in the middle of a heat wave. For some reason, the thought of those sensual lips on mine doesn't—

The door to the room bangs open, making my heart spring into my throat.

"Ready?" Isis asks as if Valerian isn't here—and I bet for her, he isn't.

"Yeah," I reply breathlessly. "Let's go."

"Rain check," Valerian whispers in his heated molasses voice. When I look back, he's gone.

I blow out a shaky breath. Mom better appreciate the sacrifices I'm making to heal her.

Isis leads me to the parking lot, where a limo is

already waiting for us. I spot Ariel and Felix walking to another car and call out to them.

"Can you give me a second?" I ask Isis.

"Sure."

She climbs into the limo and closes the door as I hurry over to my friends. Their nice clothes are ruined, but their bodies seem fine—at least Ariel's. Felix is more covered up, so it's harder to tell.

"How are you guys?"

Ariel makes a check mark in the air. "Killed not one but two vampires, yet didn't drink any blood."

I beam at her. "I think you're officially cured."

Felix shuffles from foot to foot. "Kit said Hekima made me fight you. I'm so sorry I hit you."

"Well, I knocked you out." I grin and pantomime a punch. "I think that makes us even."

The limo with Isis honks.

"I've got to go." I take out the bag with the comms device and hand it to Felix. "This is the gizmo we spoke about. I'd be grateful if you could pull anything you can from it, especially if it has to do with a place called Soma."

Felix's unibrow comes to life. "Is that a whole Otherland or a town?"

"No idea. I just know it has something to do with dreamwalkers. I'd like to learn more."

He pockets the bag. "I'll work on this ASAP."

"Thanks. I'll see you guys later." Suppressing all thoughts of germs, I give each of them a hug.

It's amazing what a little swim in the sewers does to one's squeamishness.

————

THE RIDE to JFK happens almost as it did in my dream, but when we get to Gomorrah, I don't waste time on snacks. I get us a car right away, so anxious to get to the hospital I almost forget to breathe.

No one brings up the billing as I locate Dr. Xipil and introduce Isis. As he did in my dream, the gnome doctor gathers a few colleagues in Mom's room. My heart squeezes as I look at her. Her brain activity is flat, and the pucking machines make her look so frail.

"Do we unplug the patient?" Dr. Xipil asks Isis.

"No," she says, "not until I'm done."

"Makes sense." He stares intently at her hands.

Again—or rather, for the first time in real life—Isis shoots my mom with an arc of golden energy as I watch with bated breath.

With an eerie sensation of déjà vu, Mom's brain activity goes from flat to frantic, and my heartbeat spikes alongside it. I can already picture all the things I'm going to say to her, how I'm going to apologize for the fight we had, for all the times that—

"Remove the machines," Isis orders. "Now."

The medical staff does as she says, while Isis keeps the healing energy pouring into my mom. If someone were monitoring my heartbeat, the needle would be jumping up and down like a seismograph during an earthquake.

The machines get disconnected, but unlike in my dream, Mom's eyelids stay shut. Isis stops the flow of healing energy and touches Mom's forehead.

"There's nothing more to heal," she says, "but something seems to be wrong. Is she sleeping?"

I try not to panic as Dr. Xipil looks at the brain scan. "It doesn't look like regular coma activity," he says. "It *is* reminiscent of sleep, but something seems off. I've never seen anything like this."

Oh, that doesn't sound good at all. I clench my hands, the nails digging into my palms as Isis says, "How about we wake her up?"

The doctor gently shakes my mom's shoulder.

Nothing happens.

He shakes her less gently—still nothing.

Isis rolls her eyes and slaps my mom on the cheek. The others gasp, and one man moves to stop her. Dr. Xipil shakes his head in warning.

Mom doesn't wake up.

I feel like I'm on the verge of a meltdown.

Isis grabs a cup of water from a nearby doctor's assistant and splashes Mom in the face.

Still nothing.

"Maybe we wait for her to wake up naturally?" Dr. Xipil suggests.

Isis shrugs, so we all wait.

And wait.

And wait.

Each second that passes increases my anxiety. Unable to stand still, I pace around the room, nearly tripping over the doctor's feet twice. "I'll be back in a few," he says after it happens for the third time, and disappears for the next hour.

When he finally reappears, Isis grips me by the shoulder. "I need to go. There's not much more I can do. Sleeping is more your area of expertise."

I inhale sharply. "But—"

She turns on her heel and exits.

Dr. Xipil regards me speculatively. "What did she mean about your expertise?"

I push back a frizzy curl with an unsteady hand. "I'm a dreamwalker. If Mom is really sleeping, theoretically I can go into her dreams."

His eyes narrow. "So do it. Maybe you can wake her up from within."

"I..." I cast a glance at Mom's prone figure. Worry for her is like a worm eating me on the inside, but I can't ignore the heavy weight of my promise. "I can't," I say bleakly. "She doesn't want me in her dreams. Let's just give her a chance to wake up."

Dr. Xipil looks exasperated. "You stay here and wait then. Get me when she awakens."

I can tell he wanted to say *if* she awakens.

He and the rest of the staff disappear to go about their business, and I take a seat on a low-slung couch near the bed, silently begging Mom to wake up. But she just keeps sleeping. An hour goes by, then another and another. Eventually, exhaustion overcomes me—my four-month sleep debt is still weighing on me—so I ask a nurse to keep an eye on Mom in my stead and close my eyes for a few minutes. I doubt I'll actually fall asleep; I just need to rest for a little bit...

I wake up to Dr. Xipil's voice and jackknife to my feet.

"Any progress?" I ask, frantically rubbing the sleep from my eyes. "How long have I—"

"Thirty-six hours asleep—ten for you—and not a single REM cycle," he says. "I tried giving her stimulants, but it didn't help. This might be a type of coma I've never heard of, one that can only happen when a healer is involved. Your powers may be the thing to try next."

My breath catches in my throat. They're going to make me do it. "Dr. Xipil, I don't know if... I mean—"

"I'm sure your mother didn't anticipate this situation when she said she doesn't want you dreamwalking in her."

My hands begin to tremble. Why is this so hard? I look at Mom's serene face. "I don't know. I just don't know."

"If you don't wake her up now, we'll have to put the feeding tube back in."

I swallow, staring at Mom, already seeing her with all those tubes poking out of her. Would she rather have that, really? If it were me, I'd want my daughter to do everything in her power to wake me. Maybe Dr. Xipil is right. There's no way Mom could've anticipated this dilemma. It's one thing to keep me out of her dreams when she's dealing with depressive episodes; it's another matter entirely when her life—or at least, her consciousness—is on the line.

I square my shoulders. Screw my promises. I'll beg Mom's forgiveness when she wakes. "I'll do it," I tell the doctor. "But since she's not in REM sleep, you need to prepare to subdue me if I start acting weird. You remember that case about a dreamwalker killing people?"

Nodding solemnly, he leaves and comes back a few minutes later with a syringe and several burly security guys. They form a semicircle around me, hard faces reflecting equal parts curiosity and concern. I ignore them, mentally steeling myself to survive yet another subdream.

There's never been a worthier reason to risk my sanity.

Stepping over to Mom's bed, I place my hand on her cool, still forehead.

"See you soon," I say softly, and taking a deep breath, I jump into her dreams.

SNEAK PEEKS

Thank you for reading! I hope you loved Bailey's story! Her adventures continue in *Dream Hunter (The Bailey Spade Series: Book 2)*.

What was missing from my life? A crazy cult that worships the ancient god of nightmares, that's what.

When I break my most sacred vow and invade my mom's dreams, things get complicated, fast. With Valerian's help, I'm on a quest to boost my powers and learn to forgive myself —all while saving my home world from complete annihilation at the hands of deranged cultists.

In other words, a regular Wednesday.

Visit my website at www.dimazales.com to get your copy today!

Do you want to be notified of my new releases? Sign up for my email list at www.dimazales.com!

Love audiobooks? This series, and all of my other books, are available in audio.

Want to read my other books? You can check out:

- *The Sasha Urban Series* - the fantastical urban fantasy series set in the same universe as Bailey Spade, where Felix and Ariel first appear
- *Mind Dimensions* - the action-packed urban fantasy adventures of Darren, who can stop time and read minds
- *Upgrade* - the thrilling sci-fi tale of Mike Cohen, whose new technology will transform our brains *and* the world
- *The Last Humans* - the futuristic sci-fi/dystopian story of Theo, who lives in a world where nothing is as it seems
- *The Sorcery Code* - the epic fantasy adventures of sorcerer Blaise and his creation, the beautiful and powerful Gala

And now, please turn the page for a sneak peek at Chapter 1 of *Dream Hunter* and an excerpt from *The Girl Who Sees (Sasha Urban Series: Book 1).*

SNEAK PEEK AT DREAM HUNTER

I stand on the surface of a calm black ocean, with fiery, angry-looking skies above my head. Six humanoid figures are sprinting toward me, their strange feet making them look like they're tiptoeing on the water. Their right index fingers sport sword-like claws, and they lack noses and eyes. In general, their heads are pretty lacking—no hair, no ears, just baby-smooth skin and a huge mouth in the middle of where the face would be. And if that weren't creepy enough, the horror nearest me starts screeching like a cat in heat.

To my shock, I realize it's saying something.

"You!" the creature is shrieking. "You're not dead?"

I gape at it. "Why would I be? What are you? How do you know me?"

The creature slices at me with its sword-claw, and I duck to avoid losing my head.

"Stay still!" the monstrosity screeches. "If I slay you now, Master will be pleased."

Yeah, right. An appendage-like growth extends from my wrist, turning into a furry sword in time to parry the next sword-claw strike. "What master?" I demand as I lunge and slash.

My opponent's cleaved in half before it can answer.

A second creature reaches me, swinging its sword-claw. "Master hates you!" it screeches when I parry. "Your existence is a blight."

I counterattack with my furry blade, burying it in my opponent's chest. "Me, a blight?" I yank out the blade. "Talk about the pot calling the kettle black."

The time for talking about their master must be over. The next two attackers come at me with even greater violence. Their claws hack and slash without any strategy, making them easy prey for my furry blade.

The next two are more cautious. They circle me silently, looking for an opening.

I feint, then lop one's head right off. The next opponent ducks beneath my blade by crouching on the water. As I loom over it, it strikes out with its claw, stabbing me in the thigh.

I jump back, crying out in pain. The affected muscle burns agonizingly.

The monster goes for the kill, but I parry. With a screeching yell, it lunges again—and its claw pierces my shoulder.

Ignoring the dizzying wave of agony, I swing my blade and slice its head clean off.

———

I'm in a huge palatial lobby with reddish green walls and yellowish blue marble floors, the richly appetizing scent of manna filling my nostrils as impossibly shaped objects float in front of my eyes.

My dream palace. I made it.

Blood is still oozing from my thigh and shoulder. Pucking puck. That subdream was worse than others. If there'd been one more monster in there, I'd be foaming at the mouth and trying to kill everyone in the waking world. It's a good thing I asked Mom's doctor to prepare for that eventuality. If I'd emerged from my dreamwalking trance in a homicidal mood, he could've subdued me with the help of the burly security guys he brought in—or knocked me out with whatever's in his syringe.

Well, the good thing is, none of that is necessary now, since I'm safely in the dream world. I exit my body, heal it, give myself a fiery hair makeover, and jump back into myself.

Pom shows up next to one of the impossible shapes. He's a looft, a symbiotic creature permanently attached to my wrist who's also my companion here in the dream world. The size of a large bird, with gargantuan lavender-colored eyes, triangular pointy ears, and fluffy fur that changes colors to match his emotions, he usually belongs in the dictionary next to the word "cute."

Currently, though, he's solid black and his ears are droopy. "I accidentally read your mind again," he confesses guiltily. "You're here to wake up Lidia, aren't you?"

Reminded of my important mission, I take flight, heading for the tower of sleepers. "That's right. Mom was stuck in non-REM sleep—hence the subdream we just experienced."

He zooms around me, shuddering. "Scary."

"For sure. But hey, you were a sword this time." I demonstrate by recreating the weapon I just used. "Did you have any clue that was actually a dream?"

He turns an even darker black. "No. I was just living in the moment, not questioning being that sword—as weird as that sounds."

"Same here. No clue I was dreaming."

Pom circles around my head. "The creatures spoke this time."

So they did. How weird. I think back to all the other subdreams I've experienced and the bizarre, terrifying creatures I've met in them. "Maybe they've always tried to speak," I say. "But this time, they had mouths that let them be understood."

Pom's fur takes on a light orange hue. "Where do subdreams come from?"

I slow my flight. He's raised a question I've pondered a lot, without ever coming up with a satisfactory answer. "I don't know. I've nicknamed them subdreams because I think they tap deeper into the subconscious than regular dreams do."

"Whose subconscious, yours or the dreamer's?"

"Great question." I conjure up the creatures from the subdream I experienced when I invaded Bernard's non-REM sleep—the ones that look like oversized bacteria and viruses. "Theoretically, these could be my fears of contamination made flesh."

Pom peers at them as I recreate the creatures I encountered in Gertrude's subdream—tentacled giant naked mole rats riding warthog-spider hybrids. "Nothing about these riders fits that pattern," I say, studying them, "so they might be something Gertrude dreamed up."

Pom floats in front of my face. "So you think it was your mom who created the monsters we just defeated?"

"Could be. Though I don't like the implications."

He blinks at me.

"The monsters said their master hated me," I explain. "If Mom created them, she'd be their master, right?" Reaching the glass-walled tower of sleepers, I locate the nook where Mom's form resides now that I've forced her into REM sleep. "I know we had that fight before her accident," I continue as I fly toward it, "but I hope she doesn't *really* feel that my existence is a blight—whatever that means."

Pom flies next to me. "You feel bad about that fight, don't you?"

"Of course. I made Mom think I might invade her dreams, something she made me promise never to do. *That's* why she got so upset and stormed out. Her accident wouldn't have happened if it weren't for my big mouth."

Pom turns gray, a color rare for him. "You didn't know what would happen."

"True." I take a breath to suppress the heavy swell of emotions thinking about Mom's accident always generates. "In any case, it doesn't matter now. I *am* breaking my promise."

"To save her life."

"Yes." Outside, in the waking world, Mom is in a strange coma-like sleep, one that neither Isis, a powerful healer, nor Dr. Xipil, a rare gnome doctor, could get her out of. The only thing left to try was for me to go into her dreams and wake her from within.

Hopefully she'll understand and forgive me.

Entering her nook, I land next to the bed. To my surprise, there's no trauma loop cloud above her head —something I always suspected I'd find if I dreamwalked in her. Before the accident, she'd displayed all the symptoms I've seen in my most troubled clients.

"I'm sure she'll forgive you," Pom says sagely, landing behind me. "What's more important is that you forgive yourself. From my experience, that's harder."

I turn to see if he's kidding, but he's still that depressing gray color. "What experience are you talking about? What did you ever need to forgive yourself for?"

His cute face twists into a miserable expression, and

his ears droop. "I permanently attached myself to you without asking your permission."

So he had. I certainly hadn't expected to end up with a symbiont when I petted a mooft—a cow-like creature loofts normally live on—at a Gomorran zoo. But now I can't imagine my life without him.

"Sweetie." I snatch him up, bringing him up to my eye level. "I already told you, I wouldn't want to take you off even if I could."

The tips of his ears turn a light shade of purple. "You told me that when you thought you'd be executed. Now that you know you'll live, do you still mean it?"

"We're symbionts for life," I say solemnly. "Don't you ever forget it."

The rest of Pom turns purple, and he grins. "We make a good pair of symbionts, don't we?"

"I don't know what I'd do without you." I kiss his furry forehead and set him down. "Now how about I do what I came here to do?"

We both look over at Mom. Her beautiful features appear so peaceful in her slumber.

"Do you want some privacy?" Pom asks.

"Please." It's been four months since Mom entered her coma. The chances that I'll cry when we finally speak are pretty high, and seeing that might upset Pom.

He obligingly disappears.

I place my hand on Mom's forehead. "I'm sorry," I whisper. "If I could save you without breaking my promise, I would."

Steeling myself, I dive into her dream.

———

Visit www.dimazales.com to learn more!

SNEAK PEEK AT THE GIRL WHO SEES
(SASHA URBAN SERIES: BOOK 1)

I'm an illusionist, not a psychic.

Going on TV is supposed to advance my career, but things go wrong.

Like vampires and zombies kind of wrong.

My name is Sasha Urban, and this is how I learned what I am.

———

"By day, Sasha works for the infamous Nero Gorin at his hedge fund," Kacie says, reciting the intro I've prepared. The words reach me as if I'm in an underground bunker. "By night, she performs at the sumptuous, Zagat-rated—"

The sips of Sea Breeze churn painfully in my

stomach. It's going to be my turn to speak in a couple of seconds.

The crowd looks at me menacingly.

The cliché of picturing them in their undies just makes me want to gag, so I picture them sleeping—which doesn't work either.

Without Ariel's medication, I might've run out screaming.

Scanning the audience again, I admit what should've been unsurprising: Mom didn't come. When I sent her the invitation, I knew this was likely, but on some level, I must've still been holding out for her to show up. I only had one invite to give out, and I now wish I'd given it to someone else. Mom has never approved of my passion for "silly tricks," as she puts it, probably because she's worried that my income could fall drastically if I pursued magic as a career. And since she benefits from that income—

"Sasha?" Kacie repeats, her smile extending almost to her ears. "Welcome to my show, dear."

I swallow and choke out, "Thanks for having me, Kacie." If I hadn't practiced it a million times, I would've messed up even this basic greeting. "I hope I can add a little mystery to everyone's day."

"I'm certainly intrigued." Kacie looks from me to the camera and back. "I understand you're going to predict the future today. Is that right, Sasha?"

Damn Darian. Why did he put me in this situation? Before he asked me not to end the show with a disclaimer, I had my act and speech perfectly planned out. Now I have to tread carefully and pick only the "safe" lines from the patter I've rehearsed so many times.

Kacie is looking at me expectantly, so I nod and plunge ahead, steadying my voice as I say, "My day job at the hedge fund requires me to predict how the market and individual investments might behave. I do so by absorbing a lot of financial and political data and using it to make my forecasts. As it turns out, I'm very good at this."

Though magicians often lie in their patter, every word I just said is the truth. As much as I hate my job, I do excel at the forecasting aspect of it. I'm so successful at it, in fact, that my boss Nero puts up with my crap.

Having said that, the only reason I bring up my job at all is because every book on magic performance instructs you to make your material personal. Comedians use the same trick. And since nothing is more personal to me than my current purgatory, into the patter it went.

"Well then." Kacie turns to the camera. "Sounds like a demonstration is in order."

"Definitely," I say, and hoping nobody notices the tremor in my hands, I casually roll up my sleeves—a move every magician worth her salt does before performing to rule out suspicion of the go-to "something up your sleeve" explanation.

Swallowing to moisten my dry throat, I say to Kacie, "Two days ago, you and I spoke on the phone, and I asked you to think of a playing card. Did you choose one?"

I hold my breath, my heart thrashing in my chest. What she says next will determine how amazing my first trick will seem to millions of people.

"Certainly," she replies. "I have a card in mind."

I exhale in relief, most of my nervousness melting away. She didn't accidentally rat me out—which means I messed with her memory as intended. What I actually told her on the phone was, "Think of a card in the deck that represents you, or one that feels personal to you."

There's a world of difference between "think of a random card" and "think of a card that represents you." One is a free choice; another is a directed choice.

From my experience, most women will think of the Queen of Hearts when confronted with my carefully worded instruction. This psychological ploy works doubly well for extroverts like Kacie, especially ones who use as much red lipstick as she does.

"It's very important that the viewers understand that you had an absolutely free choice," I tell her. I really enjoy saying that line, given how evilly false it is. "Please also confirm to everyone that I offered you a chance to change your mind if you so desired."

The second part is true. I did tell her she could change the card, but I said it offhandedly, as an afterthought, not giving her a chance to really think it through. It was a risk, of course, but people almost never change their minds after they have a card picked, especially if they are stuck on the idea that the original card "represents them."

"That's exactly what she said." Kacie is on the verge of clapping her carefully manicured hands together in excitement. It's amazing how magic can turn this polished woman into a little girl again.

Deciding that fortune favors the bold, I say, "This is your last chance to change your mind. If you want, you can do so now."

Kacie shakes her head, clearly in a rush to know what happens next.

Great.

She's sticking with her choice.

"For the first time, please name your card out loud." I make a sweeping, go-ahead gesture with my right hand and prepare to not look disappointed if I have to resort to plan B.

"The Queen of Hearts," Kacie announces triumphantly.

I swallow a grin. Showing my excitement might hint at my method, just as revealing disappointment would.

Slowly, I turn my outstretched arm toward Kacie. "Remember, you could've changed your mind at any time."

She gasps, her spidery eyelashes fluttering in rapid blinks.

"Is that real?" Her voice is full of awe. She obviously forgot the selection process and believes she genuinely had free choice of any card.

"I got this a few months ago," I say, keeping my arm steady to make sure it remains within everyone's sight.

Someone in the audience whispers one of my favorite phrases: "There's no way."

The camera zooms in on my forearm.

The big screen behind us shows my pale skin and the intricate tattoo adorning it.

The Queen of Hearts.

"Would you like to touch it?" I slide all the way to the edge of the couch and thrust the tattoo at Kacie. "Make sure it's not just drawn on there."

Kacie's cool fingers massage the tattoo, and she slowly shakes her head, whispering in amazement under her breath.

I now allow myself a huge grin. Every time an effect succeeds like this and I see the awe on people's faces, I get a huge rush.

This is why I'm pursuing this career of honest deception despite my fear of public speaking.

Risking a glance at the crowd, I notice that they're even more impressed than Kacie—as they should be. As far as they know, I told Kacie to "think of any card."

"And of course, this is the only tattoo I have on my body." I turn my ink-free left arm toward the camera and lift my hair up to display the back of my neck. I debate showing my tramp-stamp-free lower back, but since that requires getting up on still-unsteady legs, I decide not to risk it and quip, "At least the only tattoo in a place I could show on national television."

The joke bursts the pent-up tension from the revelation, and everyone laughs.

I beam at them.

I'll remember this moment forever.

The act has gone perfectly.

Of course, there's a slight problem. The people who have seen me perform at the restaurant—like Darian—might catch on to the fact that I always reveal the Queen of Hearts.

I meet his inscrutable green gaze in the VIP section of the first row and wink. Is he any closer to figuring out the method behind the effect, having seen it twice?

Hopefully, he thinks I'm a careful manipulator who can make people think anything I desire—which I guess isn't *that* far from the truth. The question that should be eating at Darian now is: "What if Kacie *didn't* name the Queen of Hearts?"

The answer to that question is very simple: I'd go to plan B. I have a deck of cards in my right pocket—something I never leave home without. If Kacie named the wrong card, I'd try not to look disappointed and would use my already-extended right hand to retrieve the deck from my pocket. I'd ask Kacie to name a number between one and fifty-two, and I'd count to that number from the top of the deck to "magically" reveal her card—an effect that feels like a prediction, and for other magicians might seem like a bigger miracle than the tattoo version. No one—besides Darian—would be the wiser.

Enthusiastic clapping brings my attention back to the audience.

"Thank you." I bow slightly, ignoring the sweat trickling down my spine. "That was just a small appetizer before the main event."

Kacie, the crowd, and even Darian (who knows the method of what's about to come) are hanging on to my every word. Maybe it's presumptuous, but I can picture the people at home scooting closer to their TV screens.

After all, they just saw me predict, via a tattoo no less, a free thought that occurred in a human mind, yet I call it an appetizer.

My pulse is still too fast, and I become aware of an odd sensation—like I'm filling up with warm energy. Is this the Valium kicking in? I hope it's not the cocktail mixing with the medicine.

Pushing the worry aside, I focus on my performance.

"A few weeks ago," I say evenly, "I mailed an important letter to Kacie." I actually mailed it to her assistant, but she doesn't correct me, so I proceed. "Kacie, do you have that letter now?"

Kacie triumphantly picks up a large sealed envelope.

"This envelope was at the studio at all times, was it not?" I ask and lock eyes with Darian.

A horrific idea just popped into my head.

What if he doesn't want me to deny being a psychic so he can play the cursed video and make me look like a fraud?

Debunking a fake psychic might make for good TV.

Shoving that awful thought away, I refocus on Kacie as she says, "Yes, and it's sealed. There's no sneaky business here."

I could kiss her. Now I don't have to emphasize how untampered the envelope was and how impossible it was for me to access.

"Great. Thank you," I say. "Now, before we get to the envelope, can you please put up the front page of *The New York Times* on that big screen behind me?"

The familiar page appears on the screen, with the biggest story of the day prominently featured. The headline reads: *MAJOR EARTHQUAKE HITS MEXICO; DOZENS KILLED.* Under the article is an image of a tall building lying on its side, with people digging in the rubble.

This is my moment, but I can't help a huge pang of guilt. What I'm about to do is going to seem that much more dramatic because of this terrible tragedy. Of course, I had no control over today's headlines, and this sort of outcome is always a risk with this illusion. One mentalist accidentally predicted Elvis's death like this, and to this day, he's stalked by conspiracy theorists.

Swallowing the guilt, I say in my most authoritative tone, "Kacie, please open the envelope and show everyone what's inside."

"I'm not sure I want to open this," Kacie whispers, but her fingers are already ripping at the paper in front of her.

She reaches into the envelope gingerly, as though it has anthrax inside. Pulling out the big sheet of paper, she looks at it, and blood leaves her cheeks.

I want to kiss her yet again. Her reaction is fueling the audience's anticipation.

Finally, the entertainer inside Kacie takes over, and she turns the paper toward the camera with a flourish.

On the paper, there's a hand-drawn recreation of the newspaper still on the screen behind us. In the neatest script I could manage, I wrote *MAJOR EARTHQUAKE HITS MEXICO; DOZENS KILLED*. Using my shoddy artistic abilities, I also drew a big building on its side and a couple of matchstick people next to some splotches of ink that represent the rubble.

One of the studio's graphics people puts my prediction letter side by side with *The New York Times*, and the visual is very powerful.

I prepared a spiel about the difficulty of predicting earthquakes, but I don't go into it. There's no need. The audience is in the rare state of silent shock, and I don't want to ruin it with words. This is the coolest reaction a magician can hope for—frightened awe.

Alternatively, the audience might be sucking in a breath to start booing me off the stage.

Darian breaks the spell by beginning a slow clap, like in a teen movie.

The roar of the applause that follows is the best thing I've ever heard. I jackknife to my feet and take a bow.

"Bravo," Kacie says, her voice still uneven. Into the

camera, she says, "We have to take a quick commercial break and will be back in a moment."

The commercial music turns on, and I'm glad. If I freak out now, at least it won't be broadcast live.

The audience slows their clapping, and I notice a few people in the crowd who didn't react at all. One is a sickly looking older gentleman in the third row, and the rest are pale men in aviator sunglasses and black suits who remind me of security guards. They're all the way at the back of the studio.

I look at Darian. He's stopped clapping and is staring at the unhealthy-looking senior citizen. Something about the man must upset him because Darian's face darkens. Bringing his finger to his ear, he mouths something, and one of the men in black repeats the gesture.

Is he talking to the studio security, and if so, why?

Concealing my puzzlement, I glance at Kacie. She's fanning herself with the envelope, clearly still recovering from my prediction.

I remain on my feet, waiting for the applause to cease. As honored as I am by the ovation, I hope it ends soon because my knees feel weak, and the odd, warm-energy sensation is back, but much stronger this time. It's like I'm being flooded with it, and my pulse accelerates further, my breathing quickening uncontrollably.

What's happening?

Is this the panic attack I've been trying to stave off?

My nails dig into my palms. If I didn't keep them so short for dealing with cards, I'd be bleeding.

Another tsunami of oddly pleasant energy rushes into my body, making my extremities tingle.

My toes curl inside my high heels. Did I just orgasm in front of a hundred people?

The pleasure lasts only a moment, and as intensity builds, the sensation morphs into pain.

The bright studio lights turn into suns, and my vision blurs. I squeeze my eyes shut, my muscles locking up as I begin to shake uncontrollably.

Am I having a seizure? A stroke?

The intensity of the experience is now beyond pain. I'm going into shock, like the day I got my tongue pierced, only infinitely worse. It's as though my whole body has turned into a nerve ending that someone zapped with a billion volts of electricity.

If I weren't feeling the ground under my feet, I'd be convinced I'm levitating, with lightning striking me, Highlander style.

I bear the sensation for only a few short moments before something short-circuits in my brain and I collapse, my consciousness winking out.

———

Visit www.dimazales.com to learn more!

ABOUT THE AUTHOR

Dima Zales is a *New York Times* and *USA Today* bestselling author of science fiction and fantasy. Prior to becoming a writer, he worked in the software development industry in New York as both a programmer and an executive. From high-frequency trading software for big banks to mobile apps for popular magazines, Dima has done it all. In 2013, he left the software industry in order to concentrate on his writing career and moved to Palm Coast, Florida, where he currently resides.

Please visit www.dimazales.com to learn more.

Printed in Great Britain
by Amazon